Friends Forever

Friends Forever

Ann Bowes

Fryup Press

First published in 2007
by
Fryup Press, Bracken Hill, Glaisdale
Whitby, North Yorkshire.
YO21 2QZ
Ann@danbymoors.fsnet.co.uk

ISBN   978-0-9545951-4-2

Cover photographs Allan & Ann Bowes
Cover design by Ann Bowes

A CIP catalogue record for this title is available from
The British Library

Printed by
York Publishing Services
York

Dedicated to Allan
for his patience, understanding and support

Acknowledgements

Helen and Mick, for generously giving their support,
advice and time.

David at YPS, for his never-ending patience, guidance
and good humour.

Friends Forever

Chapter 1

When Louise awoke the early light was streaming into her room. She scrambled out of bed and crossed to the window. She loved the view from her bedroom. It wasn't always as bright and clear as it was this morning. More often than not, the towering mountains were shrouded in mist and low cloud. Today they looked beautiful. By looking round to the left, she could just see the morning sunlight shimmering on the waters of Lake Derwent, a spectacular sight. She sighed wistfully, realizing that this was her last morning. She hoped she was making the right decision.

After a quick shower she felt almost human, which was surprising considering how late they'd got to bed. She presented quite a picture, her trim figure dressed in jeans and summer top, with her unruly short, dark curls framing her pretty face. She pulled on her boots that were so comfortable for driving and hastily ran a brush through her hair. It was funny not having to rush down to work and she couldn't help feeling a little bit sad. She looked around the room that had been her home for almost two years.

She had enjoyed her time working in this large rambling hotel in Keswick until that man had arrived on the scene. After finishing her course on hotel management at college, she had acquired a job in Ambleside in a much smaller hotel than this one. After only six months working there, she had been successful in her application as an assistant manageress here in the King's Head Hotel. She loved her work and got on well with both her employer and fellow staff members. When the manageress had left unexpectedly to start a family, Louise had been delighted to be asked to step into her shoes. Now, she felt leaving was the only answer.

"Hi, Lou. How's the head this morning?" Kate, her head waitress, asked, as Louise entered the staff kitchen. Louise smiled back at her.

"Not too bad now. Where's everyone else?"

"I expect they're having a lie-in. The others weren't coming in till ten o'clock. We're only siding up today and sorting the freezers out. Good night last night, wasn't it?"

"Too good!"

The hotel was closing for fourteen weeks while major renovation work and decorating were being undertaken. A skeletal staff was being kept on until the hotel re-opened in time for Christmas. Louise had decided to return home and had applied through an agency to work abroad. Kate was the only person she'd told about Martin. The situation had become almost unbearable and the fact that he was their boss's brother had made things more difficult. Louise couldn't bring herself to complain about his persistent attention. In fact, it almost amounted to stalking. The wedding invitation from an old friend back home in Dowerdale could not have come at a more convenient time.

She found it hard to imagine Richard married. His brother Neil maybe, but not Richard. It felt a little odd in a way, for as she'd been growing up there had always been a vague thought that they might end up together. They'd got on so well as children. She was quite looking forward to this break and spending some time with her parents. It was only after her Mother had been ill a couple of months ago that she'd realized how precious her parents were to her. She and Kate made themselves a bacon sandwich and went to sit in the now deserted restaurant.

"What time are you hoping to get away? asked Kate.

"Oh, around eleven, I think. When I've finished my packing and said goodbye to everyone. I'm driving leisurely home; maybe I'll have a bite to eat on the way. I told Mam not to expect me till mid–afternoon."

"Are you looking forward to your visit? It's a while since you've spent any length of time there, isn't it?"

"Yes, I suppose it will be a bit strange to begin with but I'm sure I'll soon adapt to the old ways. Anyway, I'll be hoping to hear from the agency."

"You will write and tell me how you come on, won't you?" Kate asked. Louise smiled at her companion. They had become firm friends, although very different in character. You would never catch Kate taking a hike up any of the fell-side walks, as her rather ample figure proved, and she certainly would never go near a horse. Her idea of an afternoon off was to put her feet up with a racy novel and have a box of chocolates close at hand!

"Of course I will." Louise smiled, her blue eyes sparkling. "I'm hoping that I might get the chance to ride. It's the one thing that I'd like to do again. Well, I'd better get on with the rest of my packing." She stood up to leave. Kate jumped up and hugged her.

"I shall really miss you. I'm sure if you'd told Harry how things were he'd have sorted his brother out." She blinked back a tear. "Good luck, anyway," she added, trying to smile. "I don't want to say goodbye in front of all the others." Louise returned the warm embrace.

"Thanks Kate. I shall miss you, not only as a friend but a great person to work with. Don't let my successor boss you around like I have done." That brought a big smile to her friend's face.

"Go on" Kate laughed. "I'll see you later."

Louise returned to her room and set about completing her packing. She thought about the time she'd spent here. It had been a very busy summer with all the rooms been taken most weeks as well as all the numerous functions they'd catered for. There'd always been plenty of things to do on her one day off each week and there had never seemed to be enough time to explore her favourite valley, Borrowdale. Each time she did manage to go there, she usually found something new to captivate and enchant her. Although she had made many friends, there was no special man in her life. Time enough for that, she thought.

As she tidied up her room, she tried to imagine what it would be like living back at home. She hoped she wouldn't find it too quiet. Hopefully it wouldn't be for long. It was certainly a very different way of life. Dad, who was Head gamekeeper on the local estate, would be very busy, as the grouse-shooting season had just got underway. The moors should be looking a picture at this time of year. Her mother had told her that they had a new 'keeper on the estate now. It always aroused interest when someone new, especially if they were young, came to live in the dale. She took one last look around the room and, picking up her cases, went down to the foyer. Now she would have to find Harry to pick up her references. He was busy in his office. She tapped on his half-open door.

"Good morning, Harry."

He smiled up at her over his dark rimmed glasses. "Hello Louise. I've just sorted all your papers out along with your reference," he said, handing her a large brown envelope. "We're all going to miss you, you know, but good luck in your quest to work abroad." He stood up and held out his hand. "Remember, there'll always be a job here for you if you need one."

"Thank you. Thank you very much," she replied, grasping the proffered hand. It was a shame that Martin wasn't more like his brother, for she really liked Harry. "I hope all the alterations work out. I must try and come back to see you all some time," she added, smiling. She bade him farewell and took her luggage out to her car before saying her goodbyes to other members of the staff. She pulled out of the hotel car park to a rousing cheer and left behind a sea of smiling faces and waving arms.

Oh well, that was that, then; the end of one era and the start of another. She pondered on the action she'd taken and hoped she'd made the right decision in going back to Dowerdale. She made her way through Keswick, taking the road for Ambleside. Soon she was driving along past the eerie waters of Thirlmere. It was her least favourite lake, always seeming dark and threatening. Perhaps it was because there had been a tremendous thunderstorm overhead the first time that she had driven alongside it. Today it looked almost friendly, with the towering crags reflected in its deep waters.

On she went, past the picturesque lakes of Grasmere and Rydal. Traffic was rather hectic as she made her way through the bustling town of Ambleside. Shoppers and tourists alike were vying for parking places in the limited areas and at times traffic ground to a halt. Even so, it wasn't long before she was clear and leaving the vast, blue waters of Windermere behind, taking the road to Kendal. Heading west, she crossed the M6 and, half an hour later, was high on the Pennines.

For once, there was no mist hanging on the fell tops and she could see for miles across the vast and bleak open moors. She decided to stop in the busy little market town of Hawes for a snack and drink. No point in having too much to eat for she knew her mother would be preparing a welcome home dinner for her and it would be a waste of time arguing about not being hungry!

Feeling pleasantly refreshed and her headache from the night before now totally gone, she carried on down the winding road through Wensleydale to Leyburn. Driving along, she smiled to herself as she mused on her last night at the hotel. There had been no residents in, of course, the last ones having left at the end of August when they'd unofficially closed. Harry had put on a buffet supper for their local customers who frequented the public bar, and all the staff. One of the bar lads had brought his guitar and singing had gone on until the early hours. They really were a great bunch that she had worked with and the locals provided some excellent entertainment, singing their own special brand of hunting and shepherding songs. Quite a night to remember!

It didn't seem long before she was leaving behind the stark open fells and stone walls, travelling now past green fields and hedgerows. Corn was already being harvested and in the fields huge round bales of straw lay waiting to be ferried home. Cows lay contentedly chewing their cud, enjoying the afternoon sunshine. Although traffic was rather heavy, there were no real hold-ups and having passed through Northallerton, she was well on her way back to the North York Moors.

No matter where she'd travelled or how happy she had been in a place, seeing that wonderful panorama of purple heather with the hills and valleys gave Louise a marvellous feeling of homecoming. She was sure it must have that effect on anyone who had been born and brought up in that wild and wonderful region.

Finally, she dropped down from the moors into the valley where she had spent all her childhood and soon could see the familiar spire of the village church, reaching high above the houses. Everything looked much the same in Dowerbridge as she drove slowly through. Children were out in the playground of the village school, which she herself had attended, no doubt playing the same games that she had played. Surely that was old Lily Baxter walking her beloved Westie? She smiled as she noticed the familiar form of Jack Watson sitting outside the Red Lion, puffing away on his pipe and wearing his old flat cap, slewed to one side. He always had a pint at lunchtime. He said it helped him concentrate on his Sporting Gazette. Life didn't change much in these places.

She crossed the river and, turning right, took the narrow lane leading up the picturesque valley of Dowerdale. The road followed the course of the stream for a while before gradually climbing out to higher ground further up the dale. Lanes branched off to farms nestled on either side of the valley and soon she passed the tall wrought-iron gates leading down to The Grange, or the 'big house' as it was often called. Memories came flooding back as she pulled in at a small lay-by a little farther on. She just had time to take a short walk down a well-remembered footpath to the stream. It was such a lovely afternoon and her mother wouldn't be expecting her back just yet.

She climbed over the style and made her way down the side of the field. The air felt sweet and clean and she really appreciated the beauty and serenity of her surroundings. As she went through the gate into the little copse by the stream she could hear the gushing of the small waterfall a few yards farther upstream. She reached the clearing and sat down on the grass by the huge oak tree, resting against its broad gnarled trunk. The canopy of green leaves shaded her from the hot glare of the afternoon sun. Swallows darted to and fro, catching insects above the water. Birds sang in the branches of trees and bushes that lined the bank side. It was so peaceful, with not a breath of wind. She closed her eyes and relaxed, listening to the stream as it gurgled over rocks and stones. She could hear a grasshopper clicking in the grass nearby and a tractor droning away somewhere in the distance. Her mind slipped back over the years and she could once more hear the voices of children. Her thoughts drifted to that summer twelve years ago.

Chapter 2

Childish laughter and squeals of excitement rang out above the sounds of the gushing water that summer's day twelve years ago. Louise almost slipped as she waded farther into the stream.

"Come on you two, it's time we were heading back home." A young lad in his early teens stood on the bank side. Brown tousled hair framed his suntanned face, emphasizing the dark brown eyes. Being the eldest, he always felt responsible for his younger brother and their tearaway neighbour.

"Oh, just a few more minutes, Neil. We nearly had it then," pleaded Louise from her knee-deep position in the water. "Look, there it is, Rich," she yelled, pointing to under the cam side of the beck. Her socks and trainers had been discarded on the grass and her denim shorts were none too dry as she splashed about barefoot in the water. Twelve year old Richard, the same age as Louise, raced down the bank side to where his pal was indicating.

"Go on Rip, get in," he urged to the energetic brown terrier as it flew past him and jumped into the stream, sending water flying up at Louise. The terrier dived under a tree root in the water, bounded over a rock and vanished under the overhanging bank side. A high-pitched squeal was followed by deep growling noises before Rip re-appeared, his little paws treading water as fast as could be. He scrambled up onto the grass, tail wagging furiously with his quarry in his mouth.

"Well done, Rip." Richard patted his beloved pet and was rewarded with flying sprays of water as Rip shook himself vigorously. The triumphant terrier dropped a huge brown rat at the feet of his master.

"Look Neil, we caught one," Louise exclaimed, splashing her way to the edge of the stream and scrambling out of the water. Her shorts were now soaked and most of her tee-shirt too. One side of her face was streaked with mud. Neil smiled at her jubilation. He didn't really mind her always being around. At least she liked doing the things that boys liked doing and Richard got on well with her. If he was honest he quite liked her really.

"Yeah, Rip did well," he answered her. Richard was holding up the unfortunate rat by the tail. "Rich, throw it away."

"No, I'm going to show Dad," he replied, his face beaming.

"I'll walk back to the oak tree with you," Louise said, as she pulled on her trainers.

"Would you like to come over for a ride tomorrow?" Richard asked, as they made their way back along the track. "It's Neil's birthday and Dad and Mam have a surprise for him." The boys' parents owned The Grange Farm and a few other farms in the valley, too. Keeping two ponies was quite within their means. Louise was mad about the ponies and with the help of Kathy, the boys' elder sister, had soon learned to ride. She wasn't as competent as Richard and certainly not up to Neil's standards. The brothers had been attending Pony Club since the age of seven.

"Can I? Yes, please! When I've done my jobs at home," she replied, her delight evident as she skipped ahead of them, sometimes backwards, sometimes forwards. "Do you know what the surprise is?" she queried. Strands of her wavy dark hair had escaped from their bunches and were blowing across her impish happy face. She was always thrilled when the boys invited her over to ride.

"No, silly, or it wouldn't be a surprise but we'll find out at ten thirty," Neil informed her, looking serious. He wasn't too keen on surprises. They had reached the oak tree where they parted company. The boys bade their young friend goodbye and continued on their way, heading for The Grange.

"'Bye, see you tomorrow," Louise called after them before turning and retracing her steps back up the course of the stream. She climbed over fences and ducked under the strands of wire dividing the fields as she made her way home. She pulled at the long heads of grass as she went along, parting them from the stalks and chewed at the soft tender stems. She picked up a broken twig and whacked the tall heads of the thistles, sending downy seeds flying everywhere. She stopped momentarily, a knowing smile on her pert little face, listening to the distinctive call of a woodpecker. Her knees were filthy from kneeling on the muddy riverbank and there was a trickle of dried blood on one of her legs where she'd caught herself on a briar. None of this bothered the carefree youngster. Eventually, she reached the path leading up the fields to the 'keeper's cottage where she lived with her parents.

Her father was just coming out of the feed-house as Louise arrived in the yard. He was followed by two black Labradors, their silky coats shining in the sunlight. His eyes lit up when they alighted on the young girl. George Bentley would be the last to admit that she got away with murder.

"Now, mi lass. What have you been up to?"

"Dad, guess what? We caught a rat down by the trout pool. A great big one." She stopped stroking the dogs to illustrate with her hands the exaggerated size of the unfortunate creature. "It didn't 'alf squeal when Rip got it." She continued patting the dogs as the words tumbled forth. "They've asked me to go riding tomorrow." She glanced up at her father. "Can I, Dad? Can I? It's Neil's birthday and he's getting a surprise." George found it difficult to say no to his little girl. He smiled down on her as she knelt on the cobbled stones, caressing the dogs.

"Aye, I expect so, lass. As long as it's all right with yer mother." She jumped up and threw her arms round him.

"Thanks Dad." Her face was beaming. "Do you want any help with the dogs?"

"Well, you could take that young'n out for a run. She just torments these two with her playfulness."

"Great. I'd better let Mam know I'm back first, though." She grinned cheekily at him in a knowing way and skipped off into the house.

Ellen Bentley was a devoted wife and mother who kept her domain spotless. Her sharp tongue was only surface deep though, for beneath the firm exterior lay a tender, loving heart. There was nothing she wouldn't do for her family. Young Louise had obviously inherited her mother's good looks for, despite having a son in his twenties and an extra inch or two round the waistline, Ellen was still a very attractive woman. All hope of having a second child had long gone when she and George had been blessed with their daughter. Ellen was preparing the evening meal when Louise burst through the door.

"Hi, Mam."

"Louise Bentley! What am I going to do with you? Just look at the state you're in. Where've you been?"

"I'm all right, Mam. I went for a walk down by the beck and met the lads from the big house. We caught a rat. Well, Rip did," she added gleefully. Louise ignored the gasp of horror from her mother and carried on. "I'm just going to take Bella out for Dad, before I do my jobs," and rushed back outside. Ellen sighed, shaking her head in a resigned way.

Louise loved Bella, the young cream Labrador. She was one her father had bred from his working bitch, Gina. Louise had been present at the birth of the puppies and George had let his daughter choose one to keep. He needed a replacement for one of his older gundogs. Louise had looked after the litter, once they'd been weaned, and hadn't been too upset as each of the other puppies had left for new homes. Louise had helped with the young Bella's initial training, teaching her to sit when told and walk quietly on a lead and had spent many a happy time encouraging the puppy to find and fetch her rubber bone when they played together in the field nearby.

Louise set off up the track to the moor with the boisterous youngster prancing round her legs. The young girl loved the moors and often took Bella with her when she went for walks. On her way back she went through the pine plantation, searching for huge cones to take home and save for Christmas. She had to scold Bella when she chased a rabbit, which fortunately soon found a hole down which to escape. Dad would not be pleased about Bella doing that. She knew that well trained gundogs didn't chase rabbits. She called the young dog to heel before making her way back home.

Next morning, Louise was up early and went out to help her father exercise the dogs. Louise loved to go with him, especially when she could take Bella. None of the dogs were allowed off their leads on the moors when the grouse and other birds were nesting but that was just in the springtime. At other times Bella loved bounding across the moor, and when the heather was in bloom would send clouds of pollen into the air which made her sneeze. Louise would hide in the deep ling beds, only to be jumped on by Bella, barking excitedly when she found her companion.

"Are you going to take Bella shooting on Monday, Dad?" she asked as they fastened them all back in their kennels.

"No lass, not ont' first days. Maybe next time out." The first shooting days of the season on the grouse moors were always a bit fraught with anxiety. Then things usually settled down as everyone got into the running of things.

"Can *I* come on Monday?" she pleaded. He looked at her eager face, knowing how she loved to be on the moors with him.

"Not this year. When you're a bit older you can come for a day." Seeing her disappointed face, he added, "How would you like to come round t'butts with me tomorrow, when you get back from t'Grange?"

"Oo, yes please." Once more her face was beaming. "Can I take Bella with us?"

10

"Aye, I reckon so."

Later, after coffee, Louise rushed upstairs to change ready to go riding. She pulled on clean jeans and chose her favourite blue sweatshirt. Ellen was giving her daughter a lift to The Grange.

"I have to go into the village this morning so I'll drop you at the gates." They soon arrived at the entrance to The Grange and Louise jumped out, thanked her mother and set off down the long driveway, which was lined with horse-chestnut trees. Clutching a birthday card for Neil in her hand, she half-skipped, half-ran down to the big house. As usual, Richard was watching out for her and went to meet her. He took her inside where his mother and elder sister, Kathy, were waiting.

"I'll go start tacking up the ponies, Lulu," he said, a secretive smile on his face, and went back out and across the yard. The old pet name often slipped out. As a toddler, Richard found difficulty in pronouncing Louise's name correctly and ended up calling her Lulu. The name had stuck with her over the years. Mrs. Nickerson was a tall, elegant woman with light brown hair swept back in a roll. She was an excellent horsewoman, having represented her county at Three Day Eventing in her younger days. She had taught all her children to ride and was very happy to encourage Louise. The blue eyes softened and smiled when she saw her sons' young friend, who beamed back at her. Grace had always had a soft spot for the gamekeeper's young daughter.

"Hello Louise; glad you could come."

"Hello Mrs. Nickerson. Hello Kathy." Louise thought the world of Kathy, who was almost as beautiful as her mother, having the same golden brown hair but with contrasting brown eyes, which she'd inherited from her father. At eighteen, Kathy seemed very grown up to Louise. Kathy was leaving at the end of summer for nursing college.

"Hi, Louise. I expect you'd like to borrow my riding hat? Mum says there's a pair of Neil's riding boots he's grown out of that you can wear. They're out in the tack room. Shall we all go and find Neil?" Louise could hardly contain her eagerness as she rushed ahead to the stable. The two ponies were tethered to rings outside. Richard was brushing the mud off Cloud, a stocky grey pony, thirteen two hands high. Louise went immediately to pat Cloud, as she knew this was the one that she'd be riding. Next to Cloud, standing patiently, was Fizz, a bonny bay pony with a white blaze down his face. He was a good hand higher than Cloud and normally would be ridden by Neil but when Louise was riding, Richard rode Fizz. Richard stopped his brushing and linked his arm through his pal's.

"Come on in here." He guided her to an open door in the building next to the stable. It had once been a pig sty but Louise knew it was now used for any sick animals on the farm. She stopped, rooted to the spot, and gasped in amazement at what she saw. Neil turned and smiled proudly at Louise. He was stroking the most beautiful horse Louise had ever seen. She stared, open-mouthed.

"Wow!" was all she could manage, her eyes glowing.

"Come and say hello to her," invited Neil.

"Is she *really* yours?" Louise could hardly believe that this was Neil's surprise birthday present. She walked over to Neil's side and stroked the smooth black coat that felt like silk.

"Wow!" again was all she could say. The mare stood at fifteen hands and looked every inch a thoroughbred. Her mane and tail had been expertly pulled. She had wonderful intelligent eyes with a white star on her face and one white fetlock. Coming back to earth, Louise found her tongue once more.

"I nearly forgot. Happy birthday, Neil." She handed him the card, glancing briefly at him before returning her attention to the mare. "Are *you* coming out with us today?" she asked eagerly, realizing that there were now three ponies. Louise normally only rode with Richard while Neil helped his father with the stock. Neil turned to Louise, taking the card from her hand, his handsome young face transfixed with joy.

"Thank you. Yes, I am." He turned again to the mare, his hand still stroking her neck. "Isn't she beautiful?" Even the normally undemonstrative young lad could not conceal his pleasure at this special gift from his parents.

Ten minutes later, the three young friends set off down the field to the track which forded the stream and headed up the road leading to the moors.

That summer holiday was the best Louise ever had. The three pals spent many happy days riding together, exploring all the tracks across the moors, crossing streams and climbing up steep stony hillsides. They rode over to the forestry plantations and cantered freely along the grassy rides. Sometimes they took a packed lunch, provided by Mrs. Nickerson, which Neil would carry in his back-pack and always found a place to stop near a stream so that the ponies could have a drink. The ponies were tethered to a tree or fence using string from their pockets. When this was done the three young riders could settle down to enjoy their picnic.

Some days they built small jumps in the wood behind The Grange, using fallen branches, and devised special courses. They would imagine they were competing in great competitions, awarding each other points. Needless to say Neil was nearly always the winner. These adventures were not without mishap but no serious injuries ever befell them.

Towards the end of August, they attended the local gymkhana and joined in all the pony games. Neil entered Star (as his beautiful horse was named) in the novice jumping class and rode home proudly wearing his rosette for having a clear round. One day before the end of the holidays, when Kathy was there to watch over them, Neil let Louise have a ride on Star. They were in the big field by the house and Louise was thrilled as she climbed onto Neil's horse for the first time. She trembled with excitement as Neil adjusted the stirrup leathers to the correct length for her. Proudly she rode the beautiful mare, her face aglow with pleasure.

"My, but you've improved these holidays," declared Kathy to the jubilant youngster, as Louise dismounted. "You handle her well." Louise went home *very* happy that day with Kathy's praise ringing in her ears.

Louise always had her jobs to do at home, of course, but as well as riding, she spent many days with the boys down by the beck. Sometimes they lay on the grassy bank overlooking the trout pool, watching those beautiful fish glide gracefully through the water or dart swiftly away when startled. They climbed trees, made rope swings on the branches and built dams in the streams. Other times, when Richard had Rip with him, they hunted for water rats but didn't have much luck in catching them. It was fun trying, though, and Rip enjoyed it, as he tore up and down the riverside, jumping in and out of the water, barking madly.

Chapter 3

The barking startled Louise. She opened her eyes, half expecting to see Rip but it wasn't the little terrier she saw. Not more than ten yards away from her was a black and white Springer Spaniel, watching Louise curiously, its head cocked to one side. It barked again, twice. Just then someone whistled from a short distance away and the spaniel bounded off. Louise stood up, rubbing her shoulder where it had been leant against the rough bark of the tree. She smiled to herself, thinking how her daydreaming had brought all her childhood flooding back. Checking that her keys were still in her pocket, she made her way up the footpath back to the road.

Louise continued in her happy frame of mind as she drove along the narrow lane thinking about her childhood. They had been good years, and it was only now that she realized just how lucky they were to have been brought up in such wonderful surroundings. She had seen very little of the boys since leaving school. They had all gone off to college. Kathy had gone first, to study for a career in nursing. Then Neil went to agricultural college and two years later Richard and Louise had gone to university. Richard was now a fully qualified accountant and had just recently been offered a junior partnership in the firm where he worked. This had encouraged him to fix the date for marriage to his fiancée, Sue, feeling his future would now be secure.

It would be good to see them again. Louise had met Sue once but only briefly. Now that she was home for a few weeks, she would have time to catch up with all the news. Soon she was crossing the cattle grid and pulling into the familiar yard at home. The dogs started barking, as they did when any strange vehicle approached the house. She barely had time to get out of the car before a welcoming voice greeted her.

"Hello love, good to see you." Ellen Bentley enveloped her daughter in a huge hug.

"Hi, Mam. How are you?" asked Louise, returning the warm embrace.

"I'm fine, thank you, and even better for seeing you. C'mon, I've got the kettle boiling. You can bring your cases in later." Louise followed her mother into her old home. The well remembered sight of Wellington boots, waterproofs, walking sticks and dog leads met her as she entered the porch. The smell of home baking drifted through the kitchen door. There was something very reassuring about it all. Yes, it was good to be home.

An hour later, George Bentley arrived home from work and the pleasure on his face at seeing his daughter was very evident. He was a short but strong man, his tanned complexion showing that he spent most of his time outdoors. The sleeves on his green checked shirt were rolled up past the elbows and braces supported his plus fours.

"Now, mi' lass. You had a good drive over, then?" he asked, hugging her warmly.

"Yes, not bad at all, thanks, Dad. How're things with you?" Louise asked, kissing him affectionately on the cheek. Her father sat down in his carver chair and began unlacing his boots.

"Oh, can't grumble, you know. Busy as ever but it's made a big difference having young Tony around."

"Is he your new underkeeper?"

"Aye. He has a bit to learn but willing enough. He's living in Crag Cottage. Nickersons did it all up last year. You'll meet him Monday if you come out with us. We're shooting again." He stood up and picking up his boots took them out into the porch.

"She's come home for a rest!" interrupted her mother, laughing. She was busy setting the table. "She won't want to go traipsing all over the moors." Louise hadn't actually thought about going beating but it did sound rather appealing. She hadn't done any beating since leaving school.

"Oh, I don't know, Mam. If it's a day like today it'll be grand up on those tops. How's the shooting going, anyway, Dad?"

"Not bad lass. We had two canny days this week but it needs to be a bit cooler for t'birds to fly better. We'll see how they go on Monday." Even though it was summer time, George Bentley still looked forward to his 'meat and two veg' dinners and all three of them tucked into a hearty meal of shepherd's pie with fresh greens from the garden. George wasn't interested in growing flowers but he was very proud of his vegetable patch. Ellen then produced a delicious apple crumble served with ice cream. By the time they'd finished eating, the dogs were letting everyone know that it was their mealtime. Louise offered to go out with her Dad but he wouldn't hear of it.

"No, plenty of other days for that. Besides, they won't want to go far. I've had them out with me most of today going round t'butts.

You stay and have a natter with your Mam. I'm sure you'll find plenty to talk about. I know what you women are like," he teased, adding, "not to mention that there's a wedding coming up!"

"Go on with you," chided his wife. "Come on, Louise. We'll take a drink and go sit in the garden. Might as well enjoy this lovely weather while it lasts. We can do the dishes later."

Louise followed her mother outside. She was quite surprised at how comfortable she'd felt being back with her parents. Perhaps she'd made the right decision after all and felt greatly relieved at not having to be constantly looking over her shoulder. It was a beautiful evening as the slowly setting sun cast long shadows across the dale. Although not a great gardener, Ellen liked her flowers and the neat borders were a blaze of colour, with the fragrant perfume of stocks, sweet peas and evening primroses permeating the still air. Swallows were darting to and fro, chattering madly, stopping momentarily to rest on the telegraph wires. The two women made their way to the old rustic seat and relaxed, at ease in each other's company.

After Louise had brought her mother up to date with all the latest news from Keswick, (she omitted her real reason for leaving) and the prospects of her new employment, the conversation inevitably turned to the forthcoming wedding and the Nickersons.

"How are they all down at The Grange? I haven't seen them since the funeral and didn't have a lot of chance to talk that day," asked Louise.

"No, it was a shame you had to rush back to work. Still, it was good that you managed to come for the day. Grace seems to be coping very well and Richard, of course, has Sue. I think it's been very hard for Neil, especially with taking on the responsibility of the farm so young. He certainly works hard but I know he misses his Dad a lot."

"Yes, I'm sure he does. Must have been an awful shock for Neil – well, all of them when Mr. Nickerson had his heart attack. He wasn't that old, was he, Mam?"

"Philip? No, he was younger than your Dad," Ellen replied. The silence that fell between them wasn't uncomfortable as they each dwelt on their own thoughts. Louise felt great sadness as she thought about what they all must have gone through. She couldn't bear to think of what it would be like to lose her father. She would have to go and visit Mrs. Nickerson and Neil. Louise turned to the rest of the family.

"How's Kathy?" she asked.

"Keeping well but she was quite devastated at the time. She was always very close to her father but I suppose she had plenty of things to do that helped her through. She came to visit quite a lot in the early days but with two little ones to look after and Rob working all hours at the hospital, it was never easy."

"It will be good to see Kathy again and I'm looking forward to seeing the children," declared Louise.

"Yes, young Rebecca starts school after Christmas. I bet they'll be getting excited about the wedding," replied her mother. Kathy had met her husband, while working at the same hospital in Scarborough. It had been love at first sight. Louise had been quite surprised when she was first introduced to Rob. He wasn't at all the kind of man she would have expected Kathy to fall for. Hiding behind his spectacles and a neatly trimmed ginger beard was a lovely person, who was sensitive and kind with a wicked sense of humour and he absolutely worshipped Kathy. The joy felt when their first child arrived was tinged with sadness. The baby girl was diagnosed with Spina Bifida. It had taken a while for Kathy to accept the truth of baby Samantha's condition. However, with Rob's knowledge and her own practical nursing experience, they had soon come to terms with Sam's disability. The little girl was now six years old and although confined to a wheelchair, was very bright and full of life. She had responded well to the physiotherapy treatment, both at the hospital and at home.

Rob was aware that if you have a child born with this condition, there is more chance of its happening again, so he and Kathy decided not to take that chance. Two years after the birth of Samantha, they were successful in adopting a little girl, Rebecca.

"That reminds me, I thought we might go shopping on Saturday," her mother continued, smiling at her daughter. "New clothes and all that!" The conversation drifted on to more frivolous affairs as the sun set ever lower.

Not used to lying in, Louise was up in good time the next day and after breakfast set off up the track to the moor. Having consulted her father on which dog she could take, she was accompanied by Donna, a granddaughter of Bella's. She was a cream Labrador and very much like her grandmother in nature, too. At two years old, Donna was showing great promise and enjoyed her work. George had told Louise that if she got on well with Donna, she could take the young dog on the moors on Monday.

It was a clear fresh morning as Louise climbed up the hillside and through the plantation, out on to the open moor. The shades of pink and purple heather stretched endlessly before her, its honeyed perfume filling her nostrils. Curlews called out in alarm as they noticed her presence and a cock grouse cackled out a harsh warning call to his family. Donna behaved very well and remained at heel to Louise's bidding. Yes, she would go beating on Monday. It felt so good to be back on the moor with its familiar sights and sounds and the air so fresh and clean.

As of old, Louise once again felt in awe of this vast beauty around her and thought how privileged she was to have this wonderful freedom. Much as she loved the grandeur and majesty of the fells and mountains of Lakeland, she realized for the first time that this was where she felt she truly belonged. It felt like a home-coming in every sense of the word. She had a great respect, as well as love, for these wild expansive moorlands. They weren't always bathed in sunlight with heat-waves rippling across the distant skylines like they were today. She knew their darker moods, when they were wrapped in shrouds of dense mist, swirling menacingly across each hill and gully, transforming the terrain into an eerie alien land. She'd seen them wreathed in blankets of powdery snow with the howling winds causing blizzard conditions, whipping up deep drifts in the lee of every mound and hillock. Even the hardy grouse sought shelter in the deepest ling beds when faced with such arctic conditions. She loved them as they were today, a sea of purple foam, stretching away to the distant horizon.

Later in the day, Louise was in her bedroom finishing her unpacking when the 'phone rang. Her mother's voice called up the stairs.

"Telephone, Louise." She rushed downstairs, wondering who would be calling her, and picked up the 'phone.

"Hello?"

"Louise? It's Neil. Heard you were home."

"My, but news travels fast. I only arrived yesterday." There was pleasure in her voice as she spoke to her old friend.

"Ah, yes, but we knew you were coming. Nothing stays a secret round here, or had you forgotten? Mother asked me to call you to see if you'd like to come down for tea on Sunday. She'd love to see you. Well, we both would," he added. Louise smiled at his afterthought.

"Thank you. I'd love to come. I was just saying to Mam that I planned to visit you. I shall look forward to it."

"Good."

"Will around four be okay?" asked Louise.

"Yes. Fine. We'll see you then. 'Bye for now."

"'Bye." Louise hung up the 'phone. There was a difference in his voice somehow. She couldn't quite make out what it was but then a lot had happened since she'd last spoken with him. She hoped he hadn't changed too much.

Chapter 4

On Sunday afternoon Louise found herself driving down the dale to The Grange. The weather was still glorious and for once she'd forsaken her jeans for a short cotton skirt and sleeveless blouse. She didn't want to feel out of place. Grace Nickerson always looked smart and elegant, even when working in the garden, where she spent a great deal of her time. Louise stood on the step and rang the bell. It was Neil who opened the door.

"Hi! Come in. Mother's just been called to the 'phone." Louise followed him through into the large, comfortable lounge. She received quite a shock on seeing Neil. He'd changed, appearing broader than she remembered and although very tanned from working out in the open so much, there was a haunted look about him. The hollowed cheeks made him appear older than his years. In fact, if she were honest , he looked rather handsome in a Heathcliffe sort of way.

"Louise, how lovely to see you." Grace returned to the room, arms outstretched, and kissed Louise on the cheek in a warm embrace.

"You too," replied Louise. "You're looking very well."

"Thank you, dear, but I do have a little help these days. Can't get away with it like you. Isn't that right, Neil?" Feeling slightly embarrassed, Louise passed a swift glance in Neil's direction but he just winked at her before replying.

"Oh, I'm sure Louise uses make-up sometimes, especially now that she's grown up so much!" he teased. Oh well, it was good to know he felt he could treat her like his little sister still. Neil looked almost like his old self when he smiled like that.

"That was Richard on the 'phone," said Grace, turning to Louise. "When I mentioned that you were here, he said to ask you to give him a ring. He wants you to go over to see him and Sue before the wedding. Remind me to give you his number before you leave. Now, let's go through and have tea. We want to hear all your news."

The meal passed very pleasantly as they chatted about the forthcoming wedding. It was taking place in Millford, their nearest town, followed by the reception at Stavely Manor, on the outskirts of the town. Neil told her about the house that Richard had bought in Millford, where he now worked. Grace wanted to know all about Louise's plans for working abroad.

"There's not a lot to tell yet but I'm hoping to be offered a post in

Italy. I've never been abroad much and thought the experience would be good for me. I'm supposed to be brushing up on my Italian, just in case, but haven't done much so far," she added. After tea, Grace insisted on doing the dishes herself, when Louise offered to help.

"Go and show Louise the new game larder, Neil. I'm sure her father's told her all about it." Outside the sun was still shining and the air was warm as they crossed the yard to the new building that housed the game larder.

"We also have a utility room adjoining it. The guns now lunch here. It seems to be working out fine." Neil was opening the door into a light and airy, well equipped and spacious room with tables and chairs. At one end was a serviceable kitchen area with a small cloakroom and toilet alongside.

"I understand that Colonel Barrington paid for all this," said Louise.

"Yes. He's developing the pheasant shoot and felt it would be more convenient all round," Neil informed her. Colonel Barrington owned all the moors that her father managed and also had the shooting rights on the Nickerson's farms as well as those on the tenanted farms that he owned. As they emerged from the utility room, a sheep dog came trotting over, tail wagging, towards Neil.

"Now, Tess, how are you, old girl?" Neil bent down and stroked the collie.

"She'll be retired now, with the sheep all gone?" said Louise. They had wandered over to the gate at the end of the yard, overlooking the bottom pastures.

"Yes." He paused a moment before continuing. "I couldn't part with her, as well." There seemed to be almost a crack in his voice as, arms resting on the gate, he gazed out over the valley. Louise moved closer, laying a hand comfortingly on his bronzed arm. He turned his tear-filled eyes momentarily to hers then buried his face in his forearms. Louise moved her arm round his broad shoulders, not sure what to say.

"It's okay, Neil. It's better to let it out. Everyone has to grieve." She could sense the pain and grief he was suffering and found it hard to hold back her own tears. Presently, he raised his head and brushing away the tears, managed a weak smile.

"Sorry about that. That's the first time I've really let go since Dad died. I suppose by holding back you half believe it isn't true." He put his arm round her shoulders, giving her a gentle squeeze.

"Thanks, Louise."

"That's okay. I'm glad I was here. That's what friends are for," she smiled back at him.

"It's true, you know, what they say. There's no friend like an old friend. C'mon, let's go back and join Mother. I'm sure she'll be ready for a glass of wine."

Shortly after they'd returned to the house, Neil excused himself, as he had an appointment with Roger, the other gamekeeper who looked after the pheasant shoot. After Neil had left, Grace and Louise settled down with their wine. Louise decided not to mention what had occurred outside.

"Dad says that Neil's coping with the farm alright?"

"Yes, he's doing very well, really. It wasn't easy to start with. It was all such a shock," she replied, "but he seems to be settling into it now." She was gazing out of the window, a faraway look in her eyes.

"And how are things with you, or is it still too painful to talk about it?" asked Louise.

"Oh, I'm doing all right most of the time. I suppose it takes a while to get used to not having someone around." She hesitated a moment before continuing. "I'm not sure some days how I feel." It seemed to Louise that Grace needed to talk, so she encouraged her.

"How do you mean?"

"Well, a marriage isn't always as it appears to other people. Philip and I had the usual ups and downs like most other couples do but it went further than that."

"You always seemed so happy together, like Mam and Dad," remarked Louise. Grace smiled at her young guest.

"Not everyone's as lucky as those two. They're *still* in love with each other."

"Weren't you?" asked Louise, a little surprised at what she was hearing.

"Oh, maybe, once. Maybe I was just in love with love," Grace added wistfully. Louise smiled at that comment.

"What's amusing you?" Grace asked curiously.

"Just something Mam once told me when I was still at college. I was mad about this second year lad and was asking her how you know when it's for real. After trying to explain about the different kinds of love she said, 'It's all right being in love with love but don't make it permanent'. I didn't really understand what she meant."

"You will one day." She paused a moment, as if deep in thought

22

then began again. "I suppose things were fine in the beginning. Then the children came along and we were always busy with the farm but soon I knew I wasn't happy in my marriage and Philip had sensed there was something wrong." She paused again, an anguished expression on her face. Louise reached for the older woman's hand.

"You don't have to tell me all this, you know." Grace took Louise's hand in both her own.

"I've never told anyone before but I feel I need to tell someone and it wouldn't be fair to discuss it with the children. It's been such a burden all these years. You always seem so sensitive to other people's problems. Do you mind if I continue?" she asked.

"Not at all, and you know it will never be repeated to anyone else," Louise assured her.

"I knew it was my fault, of course, so I discussed it with Philip. Although we slept in the same bed, we might as well have been in separate rooms. I couldn't expect him, a young healthy man, to live like that so I agreed that he should look elsewhere and as long as he was totally discreet, I wouldn't complain. I never knew if there were any liaisons or not but if there were it never came to my knowledge. He continued to show me loyalty and respect in every other way and that was how it appeared to the outside world. He was a wonderful father to the children and we remained very close friends." Her gaze was drawn again to the window and a silent tear slowly trickled down her cheek. Louise stood up and put a comforting arm round her shoulder.

"You must miss him terribly," she half-whispered. Grace pulled a handkerchief from her bag on the table and dried her cheek.

"Yes, I do," she sighed. "More than I thought possible but I suppose I'll get used to it, in time. Thank you for listening, Louise. I hope you don't think me disloyal telling you all this but I have never before felt able to discuss it with anyone else." Louise sat down once more and was pleased to see a smile return to Grace's face. She really was still a beautiful woman.

"Not at all. Anyway, you're still young and beautiful. One day you might really fall in love."

"Oh, Louise, ever the optimist. You haven't changed at all. It's so good to have you around again. Let's go and have a look round the garden."

Later, when Louise was travelling back up the valley, she was recalling the events of the evening. Not quite what she had expected but she'd enjoyed her visit, nonetheless. Engrossed in her thoughts and not expecting to meet anyone on this quiet road on a Sunday evening, Louise was surprised by a pair of blazing headlights bearing down on her. They appeared, as if from nowhere, approaching at great speed. She slammed on her brakes and skidded into the grass at the side of the road. The vehicle, a rough looking lorry, went tearing straight past, narrowly missing Louise's front wing. Shaking slightly, she tried to pull back onto the road only to find that the car refused to go forward. She daren't go backwards in case she slid into the gutter.

Swearing to herself, she got out to see what the trouble was. The back wheel had slipped into a deep rut off the edge of the road. She hadn't her 'phone with her and was thinking that she'd have to walk the rest of the way home and drag her father out, when another vehicle came round the bend towards her and slowed down. Feeling hugely relieved, Louise went over to speak to the occupant, thinking it would be someone local that she would know. In the lights of her car she could see it was a blue pick-up truck but before she reached it a young man jumped out and came to meet her.

"Now what have we here? Did you stop to count the stars or something?" he teased in a broad Irish accent. Louise was completely taken aback. She hadn't seen anything so good-looking in a long time. The stranger was tall and slim with very short black hair and the bluest eyes she'd ever seen. His denim jeans were skin-tight and his sleeveless top showed well-muscled, tanned arms.

"Hello. No, I, er," she stuttered, "seem to have got stuck. That lorry practically ran me off the road."

"Well now, 'tis a good job I happened by then, isn't it?" he said, his broad smile lighting up his face and showing a set of super-white teeth. "And where were you heading for?" he inquired.

"The 'keeper's house, up the dale," replied Louise.

"Ah," he said, in a knowledgeable sort of way. "The beautiful Miss Bentley." He grinned wickedly at Louise who was completely at a loss.

"You're not from round here. How do you know my name?" she asked. His reply was what she herself had told Neil earlier in the week.

"News travels fast round here." He seemed determined to keep her in the dark, so in desperation she tried again.

"Should I know you?"

"Anthony McGuire ma'am, at your service." He feigned a mock

bow and held out his hand. She accepted the firm handshake.

"I'm Louise."

He promptly raised her hand to his lips. "'Tis a pleasure to meet you, to be sure," he said. Louise found it hard not to laugh. She'd never met anyone quite like him.

"I'm glad you stopped. Do you think you could help me get my car back on the road, please?" The young man took a look round her car and assured her they would soon have it pulled out. He went back to his vehicle and after turning it round in the nearest gateway, backed it up to Louise's car. Using a tow-rope that he found in the back of his truck and with Louise behind the wheel of her car, he soon had her back on the road. After unhitching the rope he came round to the driver's door and Louise wound down the window.

"I can't thank you enough," declared Louise, gratefully.

"Oh, I'm sure you can," he replied, a twinkle in his blue eyes. Louise coloured up and wondered for a minute what he might say next. "Come and have a drink with me at the Red Lion?" he asked.

"I'd love to but it will have to be another time. I must get home tonight. I'm going beating tomorrow and don't want to be late," she informed him, smiling.

"Beating?" he asked, curiously. "Would you be meaning the carpets?" Louise wasn't sure how to take him. Surely, he was having her on. She tried to explain.

"I'm going grouse-beating on the moors. You know, bird driving." He still looked nonplussed. Louise tried to explain to him what beating involved. "You carry a stick with a plastic flag attached and keep in a straight line with the other beaters across the moor," she told him. He appeared not to understand at all. Oh well, she thought, he was obviously new to these parts.

"I'm sure it sounds wonderful. Maybe we can have that drink some other time, then?" he suggested, eyes sparkling as he spoke. "I'm sure to see you again soon," he added, a bemused expression on his face.

"Yes, I'd like that. And thanks again for coming to my rescue." She waved through the open window as she pulled away. Louise was almost home before realizing that she hadn't asked him where he was staying. He seemed to know who she was. She felt quite excited at the thought of seeing him again. Only the porch light was on when she arrived home. Her parents had obviously gone to bed. After getting a glass of milk, she tiptoed quietly up to her room.

Chapter 5

"Louise!" Her mother's voice woke her from a deep sleep. Goodness, she must have overslept. She jumped out of bed immediately and went for a quick shower, calling to her mother as she went.

"Okay. I'm up now." Soon, dressed in her green stretch cords and sweatshirt, she hurried downstairs and joined her mother in the kitchen.

"I've made you some bait. Do you want tea or coffee in your flask?" asked her mother.

"Oh, thanks, Mam. I'll do my flask. Has Dad gone?"

"Yes. He's taken Donna with him for you in the Land Rover but said to tell you to be sure to take a lead."

"Fine." After breakfast, she put on her walking boots and rummaging in the porch cupboard, she found her old battered baseball cap.

"You're not wearing that old thing, are you?" asked her mother in surprise. Louise grinned back at her as she laced up her walking boots.

"Why not? I'm not going to a fashion show." Picking up her lunch bag and car keys she made for the door. Suddenly remembering, she turned to her mother.

"Remind me to ring Richard when I get back. I have to see him before the wedding. 'Bye!" She grabbed a dog-lead on the way out and was gone. Her mother smiled to herself as she heard the car pulling away.

Once more Louise was driving through the large iron gates down to The Grange but this time it was a hive of activity. There were vehicles, dogs and people milling around. She drove through and into the field beyond, where the beaters all parked their vehicles. Louise noticed a blue pick-up, like the one that had helped her the previous evening and thought that she would have to ask her Dad if he knew who her rescuer might have been. As she made her way back to the yard, in search of her dad's Land Rover to get Donna, she was greeted by many of the other beaters. Most she knew and a few she didn't. A variety of gundogs were wandering about and others were on leads with their owners. Most were Labrador Retrievers and Springer Spaniels but there was the odd terrier and Cocker Spaniel.

As Louise entered the yard again, she spotted Neil coming through the farm gate on his quad bike. He'd obviously just got back from his morning round of the stock. She crossed over to have a quick word with him.

"Hi, Neil."

Switching off the engine, he looked up and gave her a welcoming smile. "Hello. Are you off on the moors then?"

"Yes. Couldn't resist, I'm afraid. Your Mam all right?"

"Yes. She really appreciated your company last night. Seems to have done her the world of good."

"I'm pleased. I enjoyed my evening, too."

"You must call again and I'll try and arrange to be home next time."

"I'd like that." She smiled at him as she pulled her cap down more firmly on her head. "Well, I'd better go. See you later." She turned and went off to find the Land Rover. Neil's gaze followed her as she crossed the yard, an unreadable expression in his eyes.

Louise spotted her father talking with Roger and another 'keeper, all wearing the familiar green-tweed, plus-four suits. She walked over towards them. The third keeper, wearing a twin-peaked type cap, looked vaguely familiar to Louise. He turned to face her when she reached the group and she got quite a shock as she recognized her Good Samaritan. She stared in disbelief as the colour rose in her cheeks.

"Now, Louise," her father greeted her. He turned to the two young men with him. "Roger, I think you know, and this is Tony." The young man offered his hand to her.

"Pleased to meet you, Louise," he said, a mischievous glint in his eye and not a trace of the Irish accent. "I've heard a lot about you. Your dad said you'd want to be out with us today." Louise took his outstretched hand, cringing inside at what he must have thought of her description of beating. This time he didn't kiss her hand, just shook it firmly. Louise said the first thing that came into her head.

"You don't look like a 'keeper." Then remembering her manners added, "Pleased to meet you, too." Wanting to get away, she hurried on. "Must go and get my dog. The trailer will be going soon." She turned and fled towards the Land Rover, grateful at least that he hadn't mentioned their encounter the previous evening. A convoy of vehicles was coming down the drive; Range rovers, estate cars and other four track vehicles, good – the guns were arriving and that meant Tony would not be able to follow her. She felt mortified. How could he have led her on like that? She would have to make sure she didn't step out of line today and give him an excuse to tease her again.

In the huge, covered trailer being pulled by a tractor, she sat near the back and talked to Roger's wife, Liz. Tony was at the front by the window, directing the driver, ready to set the beaters off at various points. Clutching her flag in one hand and Donna's lead in the other, Louise tried to make normal conversation but inside was wondering how she could have been taken in so easily. She was relieved when Tony called her name.

"Louise, you go with Roger's gang. He'll keep you right." He winked at her as she walked past him. She smiled sweetly and said nothing as she stepped out of the trailer. She had never been so embarrassed as when her father had introduced her to Tony, after what had happened the previous evening.

There was a fresh breeze blowing up on the high moors as the beaters made their way across the heather to where they would line out to commence the first drive. They had to wait in their positions quite a while before the whistle blew for them to start. There was a spring in Louise's step as she set off, flag held aloft, through the heather. Donna bounded to and fro ahead of Louise, scenting out the grouse which flew off down the moor away from the line of waving flags. White, fluffy clouds were skimming across the sky, occasionally blotting out the morning sun. While making sure she kept in line with her fellow beaters, Louise encouraged Donna to seek out the grouse without letting her get too far ahead. The grouse flew well, going with the breeze towards the shooting butts.

Louise felt privileged to be out on a day like this and enjoyed the wonderful smell of the flowering heather, and the fantastic views all around her. A hare, disturbed from its slumbers bounded away across the moor. A bunch of sheep, startled by this invading army, hastily departed back along a track in follow-my-leader fashion away from the beaters. Louise recognized the haunting notes of a pair of golden plovers as well as the curlews that called and circled overhead.

As the line of beaters drew ever closer to the row of butts, the sporadic banging of the guns became louder and the acrid smell of gun smoke drifted in the breeze. When the beaters reached a distance deemed to be within gunshot range, a horn was blown. This was to intimate to the guns who were shooting that they could only shoot away from the line of beaters. When this happened, Louise called Donna close to her side. She didn't want the embarrassment of having her dog run in near the butts and pick up a shot grouse before the final whistle to end the drive was blown.

Two more drives were completed before lunch after which the guns piled into their vehicles and went back down to The Grange to eat. Louise went to get her bag from the trailer and joined the other beaters. They sat in groups on the course heath grass and heather by the side of the track. The hot sun was still beating down and she was more than ready for her can of beer, which was provided by the shoot for each of them. She sat near Liz and another girl who took the opportunity to work her spaniel when she could manage a day off work. They chatted amiably as they ate their sandwiches. Some of the dogs, now less boisterous after their hard work of the morning, lay panting in the heather. Others wandered among the beaters, hoping for tit-bits.

When she'd finished her lunch, Louise went in search of her father's Land Rover.

"Come on, Donna. We'll go find you a drink." She knew from experience that there would be a drum of cold water and a bowl in the back. She was trying to tilt the heavy water container over without spilling, when the now familiar voice of Tony startled her, making her splash water everywhere. He was standing right behind her.

"This is what you're at? Here, let me help you." He reached in front of her, lifting the drum with ease. Louise was very aware of his nearness as his arm brushed hers. She had been taken completely unawares and stepped back out of the way. She could feel herself blushing and didn't know why he had this effect on her.

"Thank you," was all she could manage. He turned, a big smile on his face, before setting the bowl of water on the ground for the grateful dogs. A black and white spaniel was eagerly lapping up the water with Donna. Louise thought the spaniel looked familiar but couldn't place it. Oh well, maybe she'd seen it in the field this morning.

"My pleasure. That will be two visits to the Red Lion you owe me now," he added jokingly.

"I don't think I should come at all after the way you wound me up last night," Louise retorted but there was a smile on her face. It was impossible not to smile when Tony was around.

"I guessed you were the kind of girl who could take it. So when will I have the pleasure of your company for a drink?" he asked, the Irish accent suddenly returning.

"What's with the accent?" Louise queried, ignoring his question.

"Come out with me and I'll explain all," he coaxed.

"You don't give up, do you?" she grinned at him. "I'll think about it and let you know tomorrow. And it's only because I'm curious," she finished.

"I'll accept any reason," he smiled, flashing those whiter than white teeth. "Oh, here's your pay packet. I almost forgot why I was looking for you." He handed her a brown envelope. "C'mon Rufus, time we were off. I can't stay chatting up young girls all day." He winked at Louise, turned and strode away, the spaniel trotting at his heels.

They completed three more drives in the afternoon. After the second one, they had quite a time to wait, while the guns travelled on to the next row of butts. Roger asked Louise if she would like to go and search for a bird that the gun in the end butt thought might have come down over the bank side.

Louise set off through the heather, sending Donna ahead of her to hunt out the area. Over the brow of the hill was a large area of waist-high bracken and she encouraged Donna to search in it. As Louise watched, she could hear the young dog forcing her way through the dense stalks of the bracken. She smiled in amusement as, every now and then, Donna kept jumping up, head above the tall green fronds, in order to see Louise. Donna was just seeking reassurance that she was searching in the right place. After several minutes, with Louise frequently urging Donna to 'seek it out,' she was delighted that her persistence had paid off as the young dog appeared with the dead grouse in her mouth, her tail wagging in delight. After taking the bird from her proud companion, Louise made her way back to the line of beaters, just in time to set off for the last drive.

It was almost five o'clock when Louise pulled out of the field at The Grange and set off up the dale for home. She was tired but content and had really enjoyed her day back on the moors. She hadn't seen Tony again. He and her father would be late off the moor after seeing to the guns before taking all the grouse back to the game larder. There, the birds would be sorted, the young, (all those less than a year), from the old and hung up ready for collection by the game dealer. It would be an hour or more before her father would be home. She would have time for a leisurely bath before dinner. She hoped she wouldn't be too stiff in the morning. It was one thing to go walking on good even footpaths but quite another to trample through knee-high heather beds over uneven ground and through patches of sieves, avoiding all the holes, stones and boggy patches! Later, feeling much refreshed, Louise had time to ring Richard before laying the table for dinner.

"I've arranged to go over to Richard's tomorrow evening, Mam, so I'll just have something light to eat." Louise was looking forward to seeing Richard. "Dad will be late in again, won't he?"

"Yes, he will. I could take you and drop you off, as I know where Richard's house is. It's really time that I visited Gran, not that she'll remember when I was last there."

"Is she getting worse?" asked Louise. Her Gran was in a home in Millford.

"Afraid so but at least she still recognizes me. That way you could have a drink with Sue and Richard."

"What about Dad's dinner?"

"Oh, he's not helpless, you know. I'll leave him a casserole or something in the oven."

As she set the table she thought about Tony. She would have to let him know tomorrow about going to the Red Lion. She'd decided she would go with him on Wednesday evening. She wasn't sure whether it was a good idea or not but told herself she was curious about his past. The future she wasn't so certain about.

Chapter 6

Next morning Louise was up in good time and was pleased to find she wasn't too stiff. In the kitchen she found her mother filling her father's flask.

"Hi Mam."

"You're up bright and breezy. Did you sleep well?"

"Yes thanks, like a log. Must have been all the fresh air. Looks like another fine day."

"Yes. Hope it doesn't break before Saturday for the wedding." Ellen was packing her husband's lunch into his bait bag. "I'll just pop this out for your dad. He'll be off soon." Louise helped herself to cereal before making her own sandwiches. She didn't usually bother much with breakfast but she felt quite hungry. The fresh air must have sharpened her appetite, too. Soon, she was driving down the dale, looking forward to another day on the moors.

Apart from a quick hello in the beater's trailer, Louise didn't see much of Tony until lunchtime. He again managed to find her on her own when she was giving the dogs a drink.

"We'll have to stop meeting like this," came the soft lilting Irish voice. Louise turned to find him standing close behind her.

"You startled me. I was miles away," she said. She could feel her heart beating just a little faster.

"I hope you were thinking about our date." He was smiling broadly.

"Sorry. No, I wasn't," she told him.

He feigned a sad expression. "You disappoint me. Well, it must have been something good from the expression on your face."

"Actually, I was thinking about my visit tonight to see an old friend."

"And when is it my turn, or is there a long queue?"

"Of course," she teased, "but I could go for that drink tomorrow night if it suits you." His flashing smile returned.

"Fine. I'll pick you up around eight." He handed her a pay packet, pulled the front of his cap down and turned away towards where the other beaters were lunching.

The afternoon went well apart from when Louise stepped into a boggy hole and soaked one foot. She hadn't watched where she was going when looking for Donna, who'd disappeared into a large patch of bracken. Louise then squelched every alternate step for the rest of the day. It was a good job it had been a warm day.

After a much-needed bath, Louise, dressed in jeans and pale blue shirt, joined her mother for tea. Soon they were setting off in the car for the drive into Millford. Her mother handed her some flowers that she had picked from the garden. Louise loved the delicate assorted shades of the sweet peas and their perfume.

"Mmm, " said Louise, burying her nose in the fragrant blooms. "Are you taking these for Gran? She'll love them."

"I hope so. She won't be able to see them very well but she'll appreciate their lovely scent. Was that Neil on the 'phone earlier?"

"Yes. He's asked me out to dinner on Thursday. Wants to tell me all about the plans for the farm. We didn't really discuss it much on Sunday as he had to go out." They chatted on, and it seemed in no time at all they were pulling up outside a neat semi-detached on the edge of town. Her mother pointed to a red brick house on their left.

"That's the one. Number nine." Louise saw a small lawn in front of the house with a path leading up to a bright green door with the name 'Woodlea' on it. She jumped out of the car.

"Thanks, Mam. See you later." With a spring in her step, she hurried up the path and knocked on the door. No answer. She knocked again and waited a while before trying the door. It opened and she walked into a small hallway leading through to a pleasant, welcoming room.

"Hello, anyone home?" She heard footsteps rushing down the stairs and the beaming face of her old pal burst into the room. His unruly hair, still damp from the shower, curled around his forehead and his eyes lit up when they saw Louise.

"Richard!" exclaimed Louise, arms outstretched.

"Hi, Lulu, wonderful to see you." He took Louise in a huge embrace, swinging her off her feet. Then releasing her he held her at arms length, saying, "You look great. I've been really looking forward to us meeting up again."

"Me too," she replied. "It seems ages since we spent any time together".

"I know. Have a seat, please. I'll get us a drink." He was unable to hide the delight he felt at seeing his childhood friend. "Glass of wine be okay?

"Yes please, red if you have it." Louise settled into an armchair by the fireside and looked around the cozy yet modern room. It obviously showed a woman's touch.

"Where's Susan?" she asked, as Richard handed her the glass of wine. He made himself comfortable on the settee opposite.

"Oh, she'll be along later. She goes to a keep-fit class on Tuesdays. You have met, haven't you?"

"Well, only just, at your father's funeral. I was sorry I couldn't stay around long that day. We were introduced but that was about all. So, are you all excited as your big day draws near?" asked Louise.

"Nervous, maybe," he grinned boyishly at her.

"Well, here's to your happiness. Mind, I must say I'm a bit disappointed," she added, seriously. "I always thought you would marry me." For a moment he looked crestfallen, then realized that she was only teasing. He laughed.

"Wouldn't have worked. We know each other too well. Besides, I love you as my friend. I hope you will remain so."

"Of course," Louise answered. "I wouldn't want it any other way." They laughed and talked, reminiscing about their childhood and remembering all the good times. Time passed quickly and they were on their second glass of wine when a car pulled up outside. Richard jumped to his feet.

"That'll be Sue." He looked straight at Louise, a serious expression for once on his amiable countenance. "I do hope you like her."

A girl a couple of years younger than Louise entered the room. A slim, not very tall figure but with curves in all the right places. Long black hair was tied back in a ponytail and a pair of dark eyes glanced first at Louise then softened as they fell on Richard.

Richard made the necessary introductions. Louise smiled and held out her hand.

"I'm so glad to meet you again. I hope we'll have more time to get to know each other now that I'm back in Dowerdale."

"I feel I know you already. Richard talks so much about you."

"I hope it's good," laughed Louise.

"Couldn't be," joked Richard, "not with the things you used to get up to when we were young." They all laughed and Richard poured a drink for Susan.

"I'm only having one or I'll undo all the good I've done this evening," she said, thanking Richard.

"I wouldn't have thought you had a problem with your weight," said Louise. "You look in excellent shape."

"Thank you, you're very kind but I have a terrible weakness for sweets and I'm desperately trying to keep to my size twelve for Saturday." She was quite striking looking, in a Latin sort of way, thought Louise. She had excellent bone structure and a generous mouth.

"I'm sure you'll look wonderful on Saturday, won't she, Richard?" The conversation drifted to the wedding and other things. Sue was giving up her flat in Scarborough, which she'd been sharing with a friend.

"I'm moving the rest of my stuff here on Thursday," she informed them.

"You mean there's *more?*" cried Richard.

"Just be careful what you say or I'll bring my parents as well."

Richard raised his hands in the air. "Okay, okay, I surrender. Bring what you want." An hour passed by and it seemed like no time at all when there was a horn beeping outside.

"Gosh, that must be Mam. The evening's flown." Louise jumped up and hugged Richard. "It's been great meeting up with you both. See you on Saturday." She turned to Sue, took hold of her hands and kissed her on the cheek. "I'm glad Richard met you. I'm sure you'll be very good for each other. And good luck on Saturday." She wished them both goodnight. Richard and Susan waved from the window as Louise climbed into her mother's car. Susan clasped Richard's hand as he put an arm around her shoulder, a happy smile on his face.

"I like her," Susan admitted.

"I knew you would," Richard replied, "but why the solemn look?"

"Well, I was afraid I wouldn't. Knowing how you feel about Louise and the way you talk about her, I've been jealous without even knowing her." Richard turned towards his fiancée and cupped her face in his hands.

"You silly girl," he said, pulling her close to him, "You're the one I want to marry." She lifted her face to his.

"I'm so glad, because I love you very much."

The following evening Louise pondered on what to wear. Her mother had shown surprise when Louise informed her where she was going.

"Got a bit of a reputation, that one, you know."

"Mam, I thought you didn't listen to gossip."

35

"Well, I don't normally but it came from Joan Horton, who cleans at the Red Lion. Says he has a different girl every time he's out."

"There's nothing wrong with that, is there? He's not secretly married or anything, is he?" asked Louise.

"Not that I know of. No-one seems to know much about him. Mind, he did have good references and your Dad speaks well of him."

"You worry too much, Mam, but thanks for your concern anyway." She'd given her mother an affectionate hug before she'd gone upstairs to get ready. Maybe she'd find out a bit more about Tony this evening. She eventually settled on a matching skirt and blouse in soft gentle shades of green. She brushed out her hair and applied a light touch of lipstick. The dogs started barking so she presumed that was Tony arriving. Full of anticipation, she hurried downstairs and went out to greet him.

"Hello there. You look delightful, like a breath of spring." He smiled as he held open the door of his pick-up for her. Louise noticed the odd grouse feather and a couple of spent cartridges lying on the floor. "Sorry about the mess in here but I did make sure there were no dead birds lying around." Louise grinned back at him.

"Don't worry. I haven't forgotten what 'keepers' vehicles are like." Ten minutes later they were pulling up in the pub car park.

"Go find us a quiet table while I get the drinks. Was it a glass of wine you were having?" he asked as they entered the bar. It was still fairly quiet with lots of spare seats. Louise chose a table in the corner and they were soon settled with their drinks. Conversation flowed easily as they discussed the days shooting. Tony seemed surprised by the knowledge Louise had of the shooting business.

"Well, I've grown up with it, haven't I? When did you get into keepering? There's no grouse shooting in Ireland."

"That's true. I suppose I'll have to start at the beginning."

"Well, it was part of the deal," Louise chided him.

"I spent most of my childhood in Ireland." He smiled. "They were good times for me but not so happy for my mother. Apparently she met my father while at college in Liverpool. She lived near Northallerton. Her family were farming people, in fact they still are, but they were rather strict and when my mother wanted to skip college for marriage, they wouldn't hear of it. So, to cut a long story short, when she realized she was pregnant, they got married and fled to Ireland.

"Where did they go? Did they have a home?" Louise was intrigued by his story.

"My Irish grandparents, who are wonderful people, took them in and eventually gave them a tied cottage on the farm. That's where I was born and raised but apparently my father was not for being tied down and after a year or so did a runner."

"How awful. Can you remember him?"

"No, not really. But my grandparents made up for him and you don't miss what you've never had."

"But what about your mother? In a strange place with a baby to rear?"

"I guess it must have been tough on her. She used to receive payments every now and then but eventually these dried up and after about five years, she filed for divorce and even Grandpa McGuire said she was better off without him." He paused and took a long drink from his beer. For once the engaging smile was absent. It was clear that speaking of these things had brought back many memories.

"I'm sorry if it's too painful. I never meant to intrude." He looked up and smiled at her.

"It's okay. It's probably for the best. I guess no one's ever asked before." He took another drink. Louise didn't know whether to carry on or not but she was quite fascinated by his story and curiosity got the better of her.

"When did you come back to England?"

"After I started school, my mother took a part-time job in the village. She never got in touch with her parents, thinking they would disown her, but she used to write to an old school friend. By the time I was eleven, and changing schools, she'd saved up enough money to pay for a passage back here. We stayed with this friend in Masham until mother found a flat and started a job as a secretary."

"Didn't she try to contact her parents?"

"No. Her pride wouldn't let her after all that time."

"But you, have you never met your other family?" He rose, his empty glass in his hand.

"Oh, yes, but that's another story. We've talked enough about me. Is it another glass of wine you'll be having?" It was weird how easily he slipped into the Irish brogue.

"Yes please." When he returned he insisted on Louise telling him about her life.

"It's really very mundane after listening to you." Louise told him of her childhood, her days at college and work in the Lake District.

She mentioned briefly that she might be going abroad to work. The evening passed swiftly and Tony suggested they leave around ten as he had to be up early. As they were making their way to the door, they were met by a rowdy bunch of lads, including Neil and Richard, all laughing and talking. Suddenly, a voice Louise recognized shouted out.

"Hey, Lulu, are you going to join us?" Richard sounded much the worse for wear. "Who's this you've got with you? C'mon and join us." As they tried to make their way past, Louise glanced at Neil who was looking less than pleased.

"Leave it, Rich," he said to his brother. "Louise is on her way home." He nodded, in an acknowledgement to Tony.

"She can stay for one. She looks beautiful tonight," added Richard, who was rather unsteady on his feet, and Neil took his arm. Tony had been standing quietly by while this was going on but as he tried to get past he spoke to Richard.

"She's just as beautiful when she's asleep." Richard looked at Tony, then Louise, disbelief written all over his face. Louise blushed to her roots and fled outside, noticing as she did so the expression on Neil's face. He'd obviously heard, too. Louise heard Richard complaining that they could have stayed for his stag night.

Once outside, Louise could barely contain herself. She waited until they were in the privacy of the pick-up. She was furious.

"Why did you say that?" she demanded. Tony was smiling at her in an amused way.

"Say what?"

"About seeing me asleep?"

"Because it's true and…" he wasn't allowed to finish.

"You've never seen me asleep. You let them think I've slept with you." Her voice was rising angrily.

"I would have explained if you hadn't rushed out like that."

"Explain! How can you explain a lie?"

"But I *have* seen you asleep and very beautiful you looked, too." He could see that Louise was close to tears. He took hold of her hand.

"Look, I'm sorry. I never meant to upset you but I thought he was annoying you."

"Richard? He's one of my best friends – Neil's younger brother. He couldn't upset me." She pulled her hand free and brushed away a tear. Calming herself, she continued. "You haven't explained yourself yet."

"I was walking home last week by the footbridge when I came across a beautiful young girl, sat leaning against the old oak tree, her eyes closed. I thought she must have been dreaming for her face was smiling. I didn't want to disturb her but I think maybe Rufus did." Louise closed her eyes remembering. *That* was where she'd seen that spaniel. So he hadn't lied. She opened her eyes to find Tony watching her, that wide smile back on his face.

"I've never met Neil's brother before. I suppose I should have spotted the likeness. Will you forgive me?" he asked, as he started up the engine. How could she not?

Chapter 7

Louise awoke early and enjoyed the luxury of a lie-in. Inevitably her thoughts returned to the previous evening. Thinking back, in the cold light of day, she didn't really know why she'd got so upset. Tony had been rather sweet when he'd dropped her off. He'd kissed her lightly on the cheek and asked if they could do it again sometime. Louise smiled to herself. So much for his reputation. Her thoughts turned to the evening ahead. She would have to ring Neil, as they hadn't fixed a time for going out.

Although the nights were pulling in, it was still daylight as she travelled down the dale to The Grange. She'd offered to drive down and take her car so that Neil could have a drink, seeing as he'd chauffeured Richard and his mates the night before. She was a little early but Neil must have heard her car on the gravel as he was outside before she'd turned the car round. He opened the door on the driver's side.

"I'll drive there," he said, smiling. Louise thought how handsome he looked – his dark tanned arms showing up against a crisp, cream shirt. Funny really, she'd never thought of him as being handsome before. He was just Neil. She returned his smile as she got out and walked round to the other side.

"Thanks, Neil. Where are we going?"

"I thought we'd drive over the moors to Layton. I've heard the food's very good there in the local." It was a lovely evening as they drove down the valley to Dowerbridge before climbing up the steep bank on the narrow road across the moors. Passing the Red Lion in the village reminded Louise of the previous evening. She thought she ought to mention it and pondered on what to say.

"How did the stag night go? Hope Rich wasn't feeling too bad this morning."

"Oh, he roused himself eventually. He slept over at home with us as he had the day off today to help Sue move the rest of her stuff. I hope we didn't spoil your evening. I didn't know you knew Tony that well."

"I don't." That made things sound worse. Louise could feel the colour creeping into her cheeks. She felt she ought to offer some sort of explanation. "I owed him a favour." Neil smiled, one eyebrow raised quizzically.

"I hadn't realized you were so generous with your favours."

"Look, I never…" she started angrily.

"Hey! It's your life!"

Louise was silent. She turned and stared out of the window. If that's what he thought, why bother to explain? If she had looked at Neil she would have seen the huge grin on his face and realized that he'd just been teasing her. For the rest of the journey she tried to concentrate on the views. They pulled up in the pub car park and Neil came round to open her door.

"Let's forget about last night and just enjoy this evening," he said, helping her from the car. She was annoyed with herself for feeling so churlish. As long as they were still friends – that was all that really mattered.

The food was indeed very good and they soon drifted back into their old familiar companionship, the talk of the previous evening all but forgotten. They had coffee brought to them in the lounge bar, where a log fire blazed.

"I wanted to tell you of our plans for The Grange, if you're interested," Neil offered.

"Of course I'm interested. Please do."

"Well, as you know, the sheep have all gone. There was too little return for all the work I was putting in and I couldn't manage it all on my own after Dad died." He paused, no doubt reflecting on the last few years, working with his father before his death.

"Do you miss them – the sheep?" Louise asked. He looked up and smiled.

"No, not really. I always preferred working with the cattle. Sheep can be so stupid."

"So what are your new plans then?

"Well, as we're constantly being told to diversify I've decided to open up a livery service. I've discussed it with the local hunt and they seem to think there's plenty of demand. Also, more people are buying holiday cottages in the countryside and want to take up riding, as well as others in the villages that don't have land."

"Sounds like a great idea. What does your Mam think about it?"

"She's fairly keen and has even talked of starting to ride again. She's offered to do the book-keeping side of it, too, along with the farm accounts."

"Could be just what she needs to pick up her life again."

"Yes, I thought that. The plans have been passed and building work starts very soon. It will be situated at the end of the five-acre, with a separate entrance off the road and ample parking for the horse trailers and cars. I'm sure it'll work fine." He smiled at Louise, the enthusiasm for this new venture evident in his face.

"I do hope so. Talking of riding, I'd love to have a go again. Do you know anyone with a horse that I could borrow or hire?" Louise asked. Neil grinned broadly at her.

"Didn't Mother tell you? We still have old Star. She hasn't been ridden for a while but she's sound enough. I'll get her shod, then perhaps Mother will have a go, too, if you ride her out first." Louise's face shone with excitement.

"I'd love that. I haven't ridden for ages." Neil smiled affectionately at her. Louise thought how easily they had slipped back into the old familiar friendship. The drawn look had left his face and she was glad. They reminisced about their pony rides and gymkhanas and the time flew by.

As they were travelling back over the moors to Dowerdale they were discussing the wedding.

"You must come down tomorrow evening to see Kathy and Rob," Neil suggested. "They've managed a rare weekend off and I know Mother would love you to come."

"I'd love to but I don't want to intrude on your family get together."

"Don't be daft. Anyway, you *are* family, or so it always seems."

"Thanks Neil," she replied, giving his arm an affectionate squeeze, his reply making her feel warm inside. "I'd love to see the children, too." It was almost midnight when they pulled up at The Grange. Neil took her hand.

"Thanks for tonight, Louise. It's the first time I've really enjoyed myself since Dad died."

"I'm glad. I've had a great night, too." She smiled up at him as he took her hand in his and then he leaned over and kissed her on the cheek before getting out of the car.

"See you tomorrow then?" he asked.

"Yes. And thanks for a lovely meal."

"My pleasure." He closed the door and stood watching the car until it was out of sight.

Sunlight was streaming through the window when Louise awoke on Saturday morning. Good, she thought, a fine day for the wedding. As she showered and dressed, she thought about the previous evening at The Grange. She'd had a chance to catch up on the news with Kathy, who was hoping to return to work part-time after Christmas. She'd also found herself alone in the kitchen with Richard, who'd popped over for an hour, leaving Sue to get ready for her big day. He'd put a friendly arm round her shoulder and said,

"Sorry if I messed up your evening the other night. I'd had quite a bit to drink."

"So I noticed!" She grinned at him. "We'll excuse you. After all, it was your stag night. Tony had to be up early or we might have stayed on a bit. I hadn't realized that you two had never met."

"Well, you certainly didn't waste any time getting to know him. Love at first sight, was it?" he asked, laughing, moving away from her and started hunting in his mother's cupboards.

"Hey, we've only just met and were having a friendly drink, nothing more."

"Now don't get mad, I'm only teasing. Neil was a bit mad, though. Good looking guy, that Tony. Can't say I blame you for falling for him... those biscuits must be somewhere here." He was looking in several tins.

"Rich, I've told you, we've only just met. And by the way, I haven't slept with him."

"Yet!" He winked at her cheekily and had to dodge a fake punch on the nose from Louise. "Ah, at last." He'd finally found the right tin. "It had to be chocolate chip biscuits for those nieces of mine."

"Oh, I give up," laughed Louise. "Come on, let's get back to the others."

Later, as she travelled down the dale with her parents, she thought about the wedding. It must be a bit scary getting married, although Richard hadn't seemed too worried last night. She studied her parents as she sat in the back seat. Her father looked almost smart, not in his plus-fours for once, and her mother always turned out well for these occasions. Marriage had worked for them. She hoped Richard and Sue would be as happy.

Louise and her parents arrived in good time and were seated in a pew a few rows behind the family guests. Richard was chatting away to his best man, not looking at all nervous. Neil looked very dashing as he escorted his mother, elegant as always, to their seats at the front. Kathy, in a cream two-piece, followed them with young Rebecca, and even Rob looked quite respectable in his dark grey suit, as he pushed Sam's wheelchair down the aisle. The little girl spotted Louise and gave her a big grin. She and Rebecca had been very excited the previous evening and had insisted on showing Aunt Louise their outfits – and the silver horseshoes that they were going to give Auntie Sue at the reception. Louise's face clouded over as she thought about Sam. Life could be very cruel sometimes. Thinking about Sam's enthusiasm for life, it seemed to Louise that the youngster coped better with her disability than did those close to her.

Louise glanced around at the other guests as they awaited the arrival of the bride. Her gaze fell on a large white hat, trimmed with black, in the pew opposite. Its owner was a blonde young woman, a similar age, Louise guessed, to herself. As they all rose to the familiar music announcing the arrival of the bride, Louise thought what a stunning outfit the blonde girl was wearing, showing off a perfect figure.

The reception was held at Stavely Manor, and after the wedding lunch and all the speeches, the guests moved into the adjoining lounge bar. Louise was having a word with Grace and Neil when she noticed the girl with the large hat approaching them, accompanied by an older gentleman. The girl spoke to Neil.

"Hello, you must be Richard's brother." She smiled at him beguilingly. "Sue never told us how handsome you were, did she, Daddy?" she added, turning to the man at her side. Her father was tall and slim with dark hair, greying at the temples. He was quite distinguished looking, with a strong jaw line but kind eyes. He turned, with a look of affection, to his daughter.

"No, dear." Facing the others, he said, "I do apologize for this intrusion. Let me introduce us properly. I'm Colin, Sue's uncle, and this is my daughter Melanie." He held out his hand to Neil. "Neil, isn't it?" Neil took the proffered hand.

"Yes, that's right. Pleased to meet you. This is my mother," and placing a hand on Louise's shoulder added, "and this is our neighbour, Louise." After the introductions Colin turned to Grace with a smile.

"I understand you're farming up in Dowerdale. It must be years since I had a ride up there."

"Well, you must come up again sometime and visit us," suggested Grace. Melanie couldn't wait to reply.

"I'd love that. I've never visited a real farm. Can we go before I return to London, Daddy?" Louise got the impression that whatever Melanie wanted, as far as Daddy was concerned, Melanie would get.

44

She seemed to have eyes only for Neil, and Louise was rather pleased to see Kathy approaching with the girls. She laid a hand on Neil's arm.

"I'll see you later, Neil. I'll go and give Kathy a break." To Melanie and Colin she added, "Nice to have met you," and walked to meet Kathy.

"Kathy, shall I take these two outside for a while? We can go down to the lake." Rebecca started jumping up and down excitedly.

"Can we, Mummy?" she pleaded.

"Please, Mummy," Sam joined in. Kathy looked at Louise apologetically.

"There's really no need, Louise."

"I don't mind at all. You go and join your family – you don't see them often enough." She took the wheelchair and with Rebecca skipping alongside headed for the exit. "Come on, you two; let's see if the sun's still shining. We might see some ducks on the water." Along the hallway they met a waitress who must have overheard Louise's comments.

"Are you going to the lake? Would the girls like some bread for the ducks?" She was young and pretty and smiled at the girls. They responded with their usual enthusiasm.

It was pleasantly warm as they made their way down the paths between the flowerbeds and shrub boarders. Sam was clutching the packet of buns given to her by the friendly waitress.

"Who was that lady talking to Gran and Uncle Neil?" asked Sam. "The one with the big hat?"

"She is a cousin of your Auntie Sue's," Louise replied.

"She's a bit posh," quipped Rebecca. "Did you see her fingernails? They were *huge* and *purple*." She pulled a face.

"Well, she comes from London, so I expect it's very fashionable. I'm sure she's quite nice, though." Louise wasn't sure who she was trying to convince. They were approaching the water and all thoughts of 'posh ladies from London' were dispelled as the girls caught sight of the ducks and a beautiful pair of swans. Swallows were darting to and fro above the water, catching insects, and birds were singing in the trees and bushes nearby. Louise sat on a bench watching the girls throw bits of bread to the greedy mouths fighting over each scrap. Looking above the trees to the west she could see the distant hills and moors. It was so peaceful. No wonder this place was such a popular holiday haunt. The girls were enjoying their time by the water, so

Louise delayed going back in to rejoin the guests as long as possible.

"Come on Louise – time you were off," her mother called up the stairs. Louise grabbed her jacket and with one last quick glance in the mirror, dashed downstairs where her father was waiting to run her down to The Grange.

"You look lovely, dear. Have a good time," said her mother.

"Thanks, Mam," replied Louise as she followed her dad outside.

"Weather held just long enough for them," he commented as she got into the car. It was just damp enough to have the wipers on.

"Well, doesn't matter now. It was great day, though, wasn't it? Sue looked wonderful and everything went really well. Thanks for running me down, Dad. I'll ring you when we get back to The Grange." They chatted amiably and in no time at all they were pulling up in front of the Nickersons' home.

"See you later, Dad." Louise shut the car door and after a quick wave ran round to the back porch out of the rain.

Neil opened the door for her. "Come in, Louise, we're almost ready – just waiting for Kathy; you know how it is with you girls." He led her through to the lounge to join Rob and Grace. Sam was propped up on the settee, with Rebecca next to her, studying a book. Sam's eyes lit up when she saw Louise.

"Look, Aunt Louise, Gran bought us a new farm book and it has cows in just like Uncle Neil's. You look nice."

"Thank you, Sam," replied Louise.

"She always looks nice," added Neil, winking at Louise.

Rebecca joined in. "Tomorrow, Uncle Neil is taking us on the quad bike to see the new calves. I hope it's not raining." Just then Kathy entered the room, looking radiant, her long hair loose for once.

"About time, too," exclaimed Rob. "Must say it was worth all the effort, though," he added, giving his wife's hand a quick squeeze. He bent to kiss both the girls. "Now be good for Gran, you two, or there'll be no quad ride tomorrow." He left the room to bring the car round to the front while Kathy said goodnight to the youngsters. It was still raining as they all went outside.

"You sit in the front, Neil. There's more room. Louise and I will go in the back," suggested Kathy. It was almost dark when they pulled up at the hotel for the evening reception. Neil offered Louise his arm as they entered the lounge bar where they were welcomed by Richard and Sue. Music was playing and guests were mingling, laughing and talking in groups. Floor space had been cleared for dancing and at the far end a long table was laid with an enticing looking buffet. After purchasing their drinks at the bar, the four new-comers made their way to a vacant table. It was only when they were seated that Louise noticed who was at the next table. Melanie, in a very revealing, slinky white dress, which showed off her perfect tan, was sitting with her father and Sue's parents. She didn't waste a moment in claiming Neil's attention. Louise turned to Kathy and Rob.

Kathy was telling Louise about the progress Sam was making with her physiotherapy treatment.

"She really enjoys her sessions in the pool, and I was wondering about enrolling her in an RDA group. She seems to have such an affinity with animals and I'm sure she would love it."

"I think you're right. Has she ever seen Star? Neil's getting her shod and I'm hoping to take her out a bit. Maybe we could get her in tomorrow and see how Sam reacts," suggested Louise. Rob thought this was a good idea, so they arranged a time.

Soon after all the guests had arrived it was time to eat. Later, the dancing got under way and, having enjoyed a few glasses of wine, Louise was in party mood. She sought out Richard for a dance.

"Hasn't sunk in yet that you're a married man," Louise teased. "Have you enjoyed it all?"

"Wonderful – I feel very lucky. Everything has gone like clockwork. What do you think of cousin Melanie?"

Louise pulled a face. "Don't know. She's certainly got the looks and figure but I don't know if she'd fit in round here," she answered. They could see her, arms entwined round Neil's neck, a few steps away.

"Well, she may want to try, the way that she's pursuing our Neil," Richard laughed. "She usually gets what she wants but then she's used to it. Her mother died when she was young and her father has tried to compensate for that by rather spoiling her." They joined a group of other friends, some of whom played cricket in the local team, and it wasn't until much later that Neil came and asked Louise to dance.

"Enjoying yourself?" he asked.

"Yes, it's been great fun. I've been catching up with loads of people I haven't seen for ages. And you? Melanie seems to have taken a shine to you."

"Oh, she's very charming but not really my type."

"And what is your type?" asked Louise. Neil raised one eyebrow quizzically.

"Let me think now – brunette, about five foot six, bit of a tomboy, fiery but tender hearted..." he was smiling at Louise as she interrupted him.

"If I didn't know you better, I might take you seriously," she laughed. She had never seen him so relaxed and happy. As they made their way back to the table Melanie came over to them, laying a hand on Neil's arm.

"Neil, I thought you must have gone. Can we have that dance you promised me?" she said in a pleading voice, turning him back on to the dance floor.

Much later, Richard and Sue made their farewell to everyone and guests started to drift home. Louise was one of the last to leave and when she got in the car was surprised to find Neil in the back. She was tired and a bit drowsy with the wine and closed her eyes, music still ringing in her ears.

"C'mon sleepyhead, you're home." Neil's voice startled her. She realized she was leaning against him, her head on his chest with his arm around her shoulders. She opened her eyes and sat upright.

"Gosh, I'm sorry. I must have fallen asleep." Realizing where they were, she exclaimed, "Rob, you shouldn't have come all the way up here. Dad would have come for me."

"Don't worry," he replied, "Neil telephoned. It saved your dad turning out." Neil had got out and was opening the door for Louise. He helped her out and walked her to the back door.

"You okay?" he asked.

"Mm, fine, just tired," she smiled up at him.

"Goodnight then." He cupped her face in his hands and kissed her gently on the mouth before he turned swiftly and was gone. Louise waited until the car had pulled away, then went inside.

Chapter 8

Louise was laying the table for dinner and paused a moment to gaze out of the window. It was still dull, with mist hanging on the moor tops. She was thinking how lucky they'd been yesterday with the weather. The ringing of the 'phone intruded on her thoughts.

"Can you get that, love?" her mother called from the kitchen. Louise went to pick up the 'phone and recognized Neil's voice.

"Is that you Louise? Neil here." He paused a moment. "I er, am ringing for Kathy." Louise gasped inwardly. Goodness, she'd forgotten all about going to The Grange. Neil continued. "She asked me to let you know that they won't be here this aft. Rob got a call from the hospital, some kind of emergency, and they have to go back straight after lunch."

"That's a shame but there'll be another time."

"Yes." Another pause. "Louise, I'm sorry about last night."

"Sorry?"

"I shouldn't have done what I did." So she hadn't dreamt it. Was he now regretting it?

"Oh well, it was nothing." That wasn't quite what she meant to say but she didn't want him feeling guilty.

"I must dash now – I'm taking Rich and Sue to the airport. See you sometime."

"'Bye, Neil." She put the 'phone down and returned to the dining room, a puzzled look on her face.

"Fancy a walk out up the moor?" her father asked when they'd finished lunch. "The fog's lifted a bit and I've some butts to check for tomorrow."

"Yes. Fresh air will do me good after last night's merry-making," his daughter replied. Suitably attired, Louise climbed into the Land Rover and crunched on an apple as they took the road up the valley. They soon reached the open moor and turned off up a track to where the first row of butts stood. Louise jumped out and went to let the dogs out of the back. It was much cooler than when they'd been out shooting and the air felt damp against Louise's face as they went from butt to butt, inspecting them. Most were fine. There was the odd spent cartridge, which had been missed on the last shoot day, and the occasional sheep droppings, which needed removing. Once, she remembered, when she'd been with her father, they'd discovered a

49

dead sheep, which had taken shelter in the butt in its final hours before dying. That wouldn't have made a pleasant sight for the fee-paying guns. The dogs bounded around in the heather, tails lashing when they came across the scent of a grouse. A curlew called out above them, concealed from view by the mist which swirled menacingly around them. They'd soon all be leaving the moors for the winter.

When all nine butts were examined, Louise and her father made their way back to the Land Rover and drove on to the next row. After that, George dropped Louise off to do a row on her own and he took the vehicle farther up the moor to do the last row. She set off with Donna down the semblance of a path to the far end of the butts and worked her way back up the row.

The moors looked very different today. Puddles of water stood everywhere after the night's rainfall and the dampness hung on the spider's webs, stretched across the heather stalks like fairy shawls. The purple flower of late summer had faded to a pale insignificant brown. Louise could barely see to the next butt ahead of her as the mist had intensified and the shadowy silence was broken only by the harsh call of a grouse as it flew off when disturbed by Donna.

When she'd completed the row of butts she climbed up onto the last one and sat on a stone on top to wait for her father. The fog was swirling around in the light wind, making it feel rather ghostly, but Louise felt no threat from her surroundings. She knew the dangers of getting lost on the moor in the thick fogs, that could descend so rapidly but still she felt drawn to the moors in all their mysterious and ever changing moods.

Musing on life, and how some things never change, she knew that these moors would still be the same today as they had been for centuries, ever since the disappearance of the ancient forests. If it had been a clear day, she knew the view from her isolated position would be just the same as it would have been hundreds of years ago. She wondered if another girl had ever sat there contemplating what life might have in store for her. Her thoughts returned to the previous evening as she tried to make sense of her confused feelings.

Suddenly, Donna, who had been sitting close to Louise with her head resting on Louise's lap, stood up, tail wagging. Then Louise heard what the dog had heard – the rumble of the Land Rover coming down the track. She climbed down and when her father pulled up, put Donna in the back with the other dogs and jumped into the front.

"Hope it clears in the morning," said her father.

"Will it be too dense to shoot if it's like this?"

"Aye, beaters 'd never see each other. I remember one year, we were on t'second drive, up on Highfield Moor, when t'fog cam in that sudden, two lads on t'end o't line got lost and ended up down on t'Layton road."

"They were lucky – I mean that they found the road."

"Aye, they were." Her father chuckled. "Got their legs pulled a bit but it can be pretty frightening if you get lost in t'fog." George Bentley, never one short of a story to tell, kept Louise amused until they reached home.

Next morning was wet but at least the rain had washed the fog away.

"You'll need your waterproofs today, mi lass," her father said, as he collected his bait bag from the kitchen. Louise was still eating her breakfast.

"Yes, and my wellies," Louise replied, "but at least we'll be able to see where we're going."

The first day passed without incident and Louise didn't see much of Tony. She stayed in the beaters' trailer both lunch times, out of the rain. On the second afternoon it had actually stopped raining when they emerged from the trailer and she found herself with Tony as they walked out to their positions for one of the drives.

"I've a favour to ask you, Louise."

"Another drink at the Red Lion?" she queried. He grinned broadly.

"That would be very nice but no, just coffee at my place." Louise wasn't sure if he was serious or not.

Tony continued. "Your father says you're up on computers?"

"Well, I can get by. Why did he tell you that?"

"I was wondering if you'd come over and help me out?"

"I've not heard that one before," she replied.

His smile widened. "No, I'm serious. Your father wants me to take over the records. Shooting numbers, burning acreage, vermin and such like. You see, I started classes while at my last job but left in the middle when I came here."

Louise eyed him curiously, half believing his story. "Have you *got* a computer?" she asked.

"Yes, I bought a second hand one when I was doing my classes but haven't done much since and my printer has never worked here either. I don't think I've got the right touch."

"And you think I have?" she asked, without thinking what she was saying.

"Oh, I'm sure you have," was his quick reply. Louise avoided his face, feeling the colour rush to her cheeks.

"Well, I suppose I could, if it will help my dad. When were you thinking of?"

"What's wrong with tonight?"

"Er, nothing I suppose."

"Good. That's settled." He looked around the moor. "You stay here; I'm going further down the line." Louise smiled to herself as she watched him march off through the heather with the other beaters, his long legs making light of the deep ling beds. She wasn't sure what she felt about him but she certainly found him interesting and told herself that she was curious to hear the rest of his story. The signal was given to start the drive so she concentrated on what she was doing and didn't see Tony again until the end of the day. He was counting grouse into the game trailer when she went to put Donna in her father's vehicle.

"What time shall I come round tonight?" she asked, as she shut the Land Rover door.

"Oh, not before seven. It'll be late before we arrive back at The Grange and get the guns their brace of grouse and the rest of the birds sorted and hung." He was concentrating on his work but looked up and smiled briefly.

"See you later then," Louise replied, before running off down the track to catch the beaters' trailer.

As Louise lay in the bath, she contemplated the evening ahead and thought about Tony. He was good company and did have a certain effect on her. Probably had the same effect on all the girls he dated – but this wasn't a date, was it? Would she rather it was? Louise couldn't answer herself. She towelled her hair and let it dry naturally, pulled on a sweater and jeans and felt much better. It had been hard work today. Walking in wellies and waterproofs always seemed more tiring.

As she drove down the valley, rain was again falling. She noticed as she passed The Grange that work had started on the stables. She wondered how soon the first horses would be arriving. She continued until she came to the right turn-off which took her over the river crossing and then climbed up the winding road to Crag Cottage. She hadn't been up here for ages, not since she'd ridden past on the way to the moor on the ponies with Neil and Richard years ago.

The cottage nestled into the bracken-covered hillside, sheltered behind by a copse of tall pine trees. It certainly looked a lot better now than how she remembered it. New windows and fresh paint everywhere and even a new garden fence but it didn't look as if much gardening went on! The familiar pick-up was parked in the yard and Louise pulled up beside it. She ran to the front door and knocked loudly.

"Come in, come in, out of the rain," Tony greeted her, looking very attractive in dark jeans and a short-sleeved black top.

"Thanks. What a night. Gosh, it's warm in here," Louise said, taking off her coat and looked around the neat kitchen, surprised at how tidy it was. There were modern units with a small pine kitchen table in front of the window and parquet effect tiles on the floor but no fire. "You must have central heating?"

"Oh yes, all mod cons. They did it properly when they modernized it. It's a bit small but suits me fine. Here, give me that – it's rather damp." He hung her coat over a chair back and placed it by the radiator. "Come on through." He led the way into a cozy lounge with an open fire blazing away.

"What a delightful room," she said, going over to the fire.

"I don't light the fire every night as the heating is adequate, only for guests!" She smiled at him while admiring the brown leather chesterfield suite. There was a television in the corner and hi-fi unit on a small cupboard on the back wall. The room had a masculine air about it – no flowers or smell of perfume – but felt warm and inviting. There were pictures, mostly landscapes and animals, hung on the walls and a few that Louise presumed were family photographs adorning the mantelpiece, on either side of a beautiful oak-cased clock.

"Do you have another room for your office?" asked Louise, thinking there didn't look to be space for one from the outside.

"Ah, this will surprise you." He walked over to what looked like a floor-to-ceiling cupboard on the wall opposite the window but when he opened the doors revealed a computer station surrounded by fitted shelves. "The space was wasted under the staircase, so I pulled out all the old woodwork and Roger came and helped me construct all this. He's much better at DIY than I am."

"I'm impressed. Are we ready to start, then?"

"Sure. I'll just make us both a coffee first; I didn't have time for a drink after my dinner tonight. We were later than usual off the moor. A lot of the guns were buying grouse on top of their usual brace."

Soon they were engrossed in the complex yet intriguing workings of the computer world. It was very peaceful with just the mouse clicking away between all the questions and answers and the gentle ticking of the clock. The double-glazing on the windows made it impossible to hear the rain lashing against the outside glass of the window. Tony proved an apt pupil but got extremely frustrated when he couldn't remember the sequence of moves. To help him, Louise, having re-downloaded the software for his printer and got it working properly once more, printed off lists of instructions. Time passed quickly and Louise was surprised when she glanced at her watch.

"Gosh, how the time's flown. I'd better be getting back home. Promised Mam I'd be back early."

"So soon?" Tony asked. "Will you come back another night and guide me through the setting up of these charts, please?"

"I'm sure you'll manage okay but I suppose I can."

"I'll tell you what. The next time you come I'll cook dinner for us, as a thank you." He flashed that engaging smile at her. "Say yes, please?" he begged. Louise succumbed as she made to leave.

"Okay then. Beginning of next week when there's no shooting?" she asked. They were in the kitchen and Tony was holding her coat for her.

"Fine, I'll look forward to it, and many thanks for tonight." He opened the door for her. "Good grief, you'll have to run for it. It's tanking down." Louise made a dash to her car through the pouring rain, shouting goodnight as she went.

Chapter 9

The rain was much heavier now than when she'd driven down. With the wipers on fast and no white lines on the road, visibility was bad. Cautiously, she made her way down the winding road towards the river. As she neared the crossing at the stream she was appalled at what she saw. It must have rained continuously all the time she'd been at Tony's. The water over the ford had risen almost three feet and was far too deep for Louise even to think about attempting to cross. Cursing herself for not thinking about the river rising, she realized that she would have to turn round in the gateway, and return up the lane and go the long way round. She had to open the door to see where she was reversing and got thoroughly soaked in doing so but managed, without getting stuck on the soggy grass, to complete the maneuver. It was only then that she realized with a sinking heart that she was low on petrol.

"Damn. You idiot, Louise," she scolded herself. Why hadn't she remembered about the river flooding so swiftly or how low she was on fuel? She'd been going to fill up after visiting The Grange on Sunday but of course she hadn't been to The Grange. There was only one thing she could do – go back to Tony's. She'd have to ring her parents, too. For the second time that night she found herself pulling up in Tony's yard. She locked the car and ran to the door, knocking on it loudly. The rain was lashing across her face as she knocked again, harder. Suddenly a dog started barking, – it had obviously heard her frantic banging on the door. After what seemed like an eternity the door finally opened.

"Good grief, girl, come in quick." Tony beckoned her inside, swiftly closing the door. "I was upstairs. Have you been knocking long? Here, give me that," he said, taking her wet coat. "Nice of you to come back and see me. What happened?" he queried. Louise tried to explain. She felt such a fool about both her mistakes.

"I meant to fill up on Sunday but went round the butts with Dad and forgot to go to the village. I should have remembered how fast the beck comes up." She looked quite forlorn with water running down her face.

"Hey, cheer up; it's not the end of the world. Here, take this." He reached for a towel on the radiator. "Dry your hair and I'll put the kettle on. You'll have to stay here and we'll sort something out in the morning. Don't look so worried – you'll be safe on the settee," he grinned at her.

"I'll have to ring home. May I use your 'phone? I couldn't get a signal on my mobile."

"Yes, go ahead." A short while later, sitting in front of a roaring log fire with a mug of hot coffee in her hand, Louise felt much better. She'd kicked off her shoes and was curled up on the leather settee. Tony came and sat next to her.

"Please, don't let me keep you up. I'm really sorry for putting you out this way. I'll be fine here with a rug."

"No problem," he mused. "Somehow, I don't feel like bed after all and can't think of better company for a late night chat." He smiled that flashing smile of white teeth and settled back into the settee. Louise was conscious of his gaze and a little unsure of the situation in which she found herself. She was desperately thinking of something to say.

"If you really don't want to go to bed just yet, maybe you could tell me the rest of your story," she smiled at him.

"Why do you want to know about my life?" he asked, stretching his long legs out before him.

"Curiosity, I suppose. Having led such an ordinary life, I find it fascinating hearing about other people's lives." Louise watched the flickering flames from the burning logs as she sipped her coffee, trying to imagine Tony as a young lad. "Where did you live when you came to England?"

"We came one July, after school finished, and stayed with this friend of Mother's in Masham. Mother had booked me in at a school in Northallerton, so as soon as she found a flat to rent, we moved there."

"Must have been strange, not knowing anyone."

"Certainly took some stick about my accent but I liked sport and that helped me make friends. I did miss my grandparents and the country way of life but mother bought me a bike that first Christmas which made a big difference. After that, every weekend almost, I used to go with two other lads on long rides out into the countryside. It was great. Sometimes we went fishing and in the summer months we camped out. They were good mates." He paused, obviously thinking back to those happy days when growing up in the Yorkshire countryside.

"What about your family? How did you find them?" asked Louise. Tony stood up, taking their empty mugs.

"Fancy a beer? All this talking's making me thirsty."

"A beer would be fine, thanks," she smiled. He went off to the kitchen, returned with two glasses, a couple of cans and settled himself on the settee.

"I'd been mulling it over for a while but didn't know what to do. The only thing I knew for sure was my mother's maiden name and that her folks farmed somewhere near Bedale. Shortly after we came to Masham, I'd overheard my mother's friend talking to my mother. She said something like 'it's not a million miles to Bedale, Rose. Couldn't you go, just for the bairn's sake?' but my mother muttered something about 'too late now' and nothing else was said." Louise tried to imagine what it must have been like, not knowing who your family were. She'd been very lucky being brought up in a happy family environment all her life. She looked across at Tony and smiled.

"So what *did* you do?"

"One Saturday morning I decided to try and find them. I'd already made a list of all the Robinsons around Bedale from the telephone book so I set off on my bike with my tent and my list. Mother thought I was with my mates, same as always. After several disappointments I pitched my tent by the river Swale and decided to try the last two places the next morning. It never crossed my mind that they could have moved or even died. I set off, bright and early next day, thinking I was never going to find them. I'd ridden several miles when I rode into this farmyard. A dog barked and a collie sheep dog came trotting towards me. Then a bloke came out of a large barn wearing an oil-streaked overall and a spanner in his hand. He smiled at me as he brushed his dark hair back from his face. The dog was sniffing round my legs. 'Now young man – don't worry, she won't hurt you – what can I do for you?' I remember thinking that he looked okay and that even if this wasn't the right family, he might be able to help me. I propped my bike against the side of the barn and removed my rucksack, laying it on the ground near my bike. In my best Yorkshire, which I was quite adept at by now, I started, 'Well sir, I'm looking for someone'. He frowned, a puzzled look on his tanned face. 'We've 'ad no strangers through 'ere, lad,' was the response I got. I tried again. 'No, I mean someone special. Do you know a Rose Robinson?' For a moment I was a bit scared. The smile left his face and he just stared at me. Then he said slowly, 'What do you want with her?' I remember thinking, he must know of her. I wasn't sure then what to say. I'd waited so long to find out about my family and now it seemed kind of unreal. 'Nothing,' I said. 'I was really looking for her parents.' He stared at me for what seemed like ages, then, laying aside the spanner in the barn, said, 'I think you'd better come inside lad.'

"I followed him into a large kitchen, his boots sounding loud on the tiled floor. At the far end was a huge cooking range, where a lady of ample proportions had her back to us and was making a pot of tea. 'I was just going to call you, Robert.' She turned, her short grey hair framing a face that was etched with sadness but smiled when she spotted me. I could see my mother in her straightaway. 'And who might this young man be? Would he like a cup of tea, too?' I had noticed the slices of fruit-cake on the table and as it had been a long time since breakfast I was only too glad to accept. She poured out two mugs of tea and passed them over. The man, Robert, spoke again. 'This young man wants to know if we know Rose Robinson's parents.' The woman went ashen and sat down, pulled a hanky from her pinny pocket and pressed it to her mouth. 'What's happened?' she managed in faltering breath. 'Is… is she dead?'

"I realize now how awful it must have been for her. She'd never heard from her daughter in fourteen years. I did my best to explain to her who I was. At first she just stared at me, unable to take in what I was telling her, then slowly a smile came back to her face and tears trickled down her cheeks. 'After all these years,' she whispered. Then she stood up and came to me, holding out her arms. 'I'm your grandmother. Welcome home,' she said. I couldn't believe it and just sat there, open-mouthed. She took hold of my hands, pulled me to my feet and kept saying, 'Welcome home, lad.' I couldn't say anything."

Louise brushed the tears from her eyes, overcome with emotion. Tony took her hand and squeezed it gently.

"Hey, come on. That was a happy day!" he smiled at her. "That, as they say, was the start of a beautiful friendship. I began visiting and slowly got to know my new family – my grandparents, my uncle Robert, who worked on the farm with Grandpop, as I always called him, and another uncle, Frank. I stayed with them regularly and had a room of my own, and my Gran spoiled me rotten. I went as often as I could without my mother finding out, till one day I had to tell her.

My Gran and Grandpop asked me to. They wanted to see their daughter. My mother, who by then had a new man in her life, was very reluctant to go but eventually she did visit them and an uneasy peace was made. After my mother married, I continued to visit the farm and stayed many weekends and most of the holidays. Soon, it was as if I'd never been away from the countryside. I became great friends with my uncle Frank, who was a gamekeeper, and after he got married I often stayed with him and his wife, where they lived on an estate near Leyburn. When I left school he helped me get a job in 'keepering and the rest is history." He still had hold of Louise's hand and standing up he pulled her to her feet. "And now, young lady, enough bedtime stories, I need some sleep." Louise looked at her watch.

"Goodness, I'd no idea it was so late. I'm sorry. I'll just use the bathroom, please." He showed her the way and then went to find a duvet for her. When Louise came down, he was putting a guard round the fire. He straitened up, smiling.

"Right, I'm off to bed," then added, "Do I get a goodnight kiss?" and taking her silence as consent, he tilted her chin with his hand and kissed her firmly on the mouth. "Goodnight, Miss Bentley. See you in the morning."

After a restless night Louise rose early and had the kettle boiling when Tony came down. After gulping down his tea he went off outside to see if he could find some petrol.

"There's a bit in this. It might just get you to the garage." He was carrying an old plastic container and a funnel. "Some left over from moor-burning last spring. It needs filling up again – we'll be starting burning soon if the weather dries up."

Louise rang her mother again before leaving to let her know she'd be coming round the long way. Her mother had a message for her. She asked her to call at The Grange on her way back, as Neil had been ringing and wanted to see her. It was still only eight o'clock when Louise pulled up outside the Nickersons'. She went round to the open back door and shouted. She was surprised to see Neil coming out of the house.

"Hi, thought you'd still be round the stock," she greeted him. He smiled at her as he invited her in.

"I go earlier these days with so many of the cows nearing calving. I'll make us a coffee. Mother's having a lie-in. Picked up some bug at the wedding and isn't quite over it yet." He had his back to Louise

59

as he spooned coffee into two mugs.

"Mam said you had a message for me?"

"Yes. She told me you were staying the night with Tony." He paused, as if waiting for Louise to say something. Louise offered no explanation. "I didn't know..." he started, then stopped.

"Didn't know what?"

"Nothing, it doesn't matter." He turned round with the mugs. "Stavely Manor rang for your number. Apparently they'd mentioned to Rich that their manageress is leaving unexpectedly at the end of the month. He'd suggested to them that you might help them out temporarily. They couldn't find your number so rang here. I gave it to them. I hope you didn't mind."

"No, of course not. Dad's number comes under the estate number," she explained. "I suppose I should think about it. Doesn't look as if anything's going to come from abroad. Anyway, I don't feel that bothered about going away now." She picked up her mug and didn't see the expression on Neil's face. He turned and added more milk to his coffee. When he next spoke the smile was back.

"Oh, by the way, I had Star shod the other day so you can come and take her out when you like."

"I'd love to. I'll ring you when I'm coming." They chatted about the stables, which were slowly taking shape, while they drank their coffee, then Neil said he would have to get on as he had some straw arriving and wanted to sort the big shed out. Louise stood up to go.

"Do you think I should go to Stavely?" she asked.

"No harm in going to see about it, is there?" he answered. "Do what you think's best, Louise."

Chapter 10

Louise parked her car in the large car-park at the back of Stavely Manor and, after checking her lipstick in the driving mirror, gave her hair a quick brush through, then got out of the car and made her way round to reception. Pearl Collins had sounded very pleasant on the 'phone yesterday and seemed to be taking it for granted that Louise would be starting work for them.

"Good morning. How can I help you?" The woman behind the desk looked up from the task of filing her nails and smiled at Louise. Her auburn tinted hair that was cut in a short, pageboy style clashed with the pink-rimmed spectacles that she was wearing. Louise greeted her.

"Hello. I'm Louise Bentley. Mr. Collins is expecting me."

"Oh yes. Could you go through to his office, second on the right," she indicated down a passage to the left. Louise found the right door and knocked gently.

"Come in, come in." Louise entered the small but neat room and was greeted by a thick-set man with more hair on his moustache than on his head. Why was it, she wondered, that men losing their hair on top seemed to want to preserve it on their faces? She vaguely remembered seeing him around on the day of the wedding. Eddy Collins held out a chubby hand to Louise.

"Sit down, please." He let go Louise's hand and started fussing about with papers on his desk. "So glad you could come in today – was most relieved when Mr. Nickerson told me about you." He went on to explain to Louise the predicament in which he and his wife had found themselves. His manageress was having to leave unexpectedly, as her mother had been taken ill and there was no-one else to care for her disabled father.

"In short, she wants to leave as soon as possible. I understand you've been working over in Keswick." His rounded face broke into a smile. "Beautiful country – my wife and I spent our honeymoon there." Louise agreed with him, then went on to tell him what she had been doing.

"Well, we'd be most grateful if you could help us out." He explained the various shifts that Louise would be expected to work and terms of pay. She didn't give it much thought before deciding

61

she might as well give it a go.

"We have three more weddings before Christmas and, as well as all the usual guests on holiday, we start with the shooting parties at the end of the month. I'm sure you'll soon get into the running of it. My wife Pearl, whom you met in reception, will cover for you on your days off." After agreeing to start the following Monday, Louise left.

As she drove back home, she pondered on whether she was doing the right thing. She did need a job and as nothing had come from her other application it would be fine for the time being. She wasn't sure she wanted to go abroad now but didn't really know why she didn't.

Next day she decided to nip down to The Grange and arrange a time to have a ride. Grace greeted her as she pulled up at the big house.

"I was in the garden when I heard your car coming down the drive."

"I just popped in to see Neil about taking Star out." She smiled at the older woman. "You must be feeling better – Neil said you weren't too good the other day."

"Oh yes, thank you, dear. Just one of those forty-eight hour things – must have picked it up at the wedding. Neil will be back soon. He went back round the stock as there are several more cows due any day. Come in and have a coffee while you wait." They went into the kitchen and Louise perched herself on a stool by the large kitchen table. They chatted about the wedding while Grace tended to the coffee.

"Yes, it was a great day, wasn't it? You seemed to be getting on well with Colin," Louise teased, as she helped herself to a biscuit from the barrel on the table.

"I think it was more his daughter's doing. Melanie made sure they got an invite to visit the farm. Oh, there's the quad bike now," Grace added, reaching for another coffee mug. Two minutes later Neil walked into the kitchen, smiling at Louise when he saw her.

"I thought I could smell coffee. Thanks, Mother," he said, accepting the drink. "Well, no longer a lady of leisure, then?" He raised a quizzical eyebrow at Louise.

"How did you know?" Louise asked, surprised.

"Ah, news travels fast. You should know you can't do anything round here without everybody knowing about it," Neil grinned at her. His mother intervened.

"I told him, Louise. I saw your mother in the village yesterday.

She said you were starting on Monday."

"Yes, that's why I came today – to see if I could take Star out tomorrow, as we're shooting again on Saturday. Would that be okay, Neil?"

"Yes, of course. Tell me what time, and I'll bring her up an hour beforehand. I expect there'll still be some of Kathy's boots kicking around that you can borrow." They fixed a time and, having finished her coffee, Louise made to go.

"See you tomorrow then," she said, beaming.

"Doesn't seem like five minutes since you were all riding the ponies," mused Grace, a tender smile on her face. "She's grown into such a lovely girl, hasn't she?" Neil was staring into his mug.

"Mm? yes... yes she has."

Next morning, Louise couldn't believe how excited she was at the thought of her impending ride. It was ages since she'd been on a horse. Grace came out with a riding hat when Louise arrived at The Grange.

"This should fit you, and I left some boots in the tack room. Neil brought Star in an hour ago." She smiled at Louise. "You will be careful, won't you?"

"Yes, of course, but I don't think Star could misbehave at her age anyway." She took the hat and after thanking Grace made her way over to the little stable. Neil was nowhere around. She took a brush and made sure there was no mud on Star's back where the saddle would fit. It didn't matter too much about her legs. She brushed out the long black mane, which hadn't been pulled for quite some years, as best she could, and after cleaning out her feet, tacked her up. It was funny how she put on the bridle without ever thinking about what to do. Star nuzzled her face and Louise again enjoyed the familiar smell of being close to a horse.

She gathered the reins, put her foot in the stirrup and pulled herself up into the saddle. It felt good as she set off at a steady walk down the old familiar track to the stream. She'd forgotten just *how* good it felt to be back riding. The air was clean and fresh after all the rain, and the gentle breeze caressed her face as she climbed up onto the moor. Patches of bilberry were already beginning to change from their fresh bright green to crimson shades of autumn and it wouldn't be long before the bracken, too, started exchanging its mantle of green for gold. Louise revelled in the peace and solitude, alone with her thoughts, as she rode along the well-marked track, surrounded by an endless vista of browning heather. She pondered on the latest turn of events in her life. It wasn't what she'd expected when she left Keswick.

Conscious that Star hadn't been ridden for quite some time, Louise decided that after about a mile on the moor top she'd ridden far enough and turned off down a sheep track making her way back towards the valley. Once down on the level where the track ran along the edge of a field, Louise squeezed Star into a trot. She responded happily and Louise enjoyed the lovely smooth rhythm that the old horse still produced.

Neil spotted the horse and rider as they came into view and stood and watched them approaching, a faraway look on his face. Louise waved to Neil when she spotted him by the gate, her face radiant. He smiled back at her as he opened the gate and followed her into the stable, where Louise began taking off the saddle and bridle.

"Thanks, Neil. That was wonderful. I'd forgotten how great it is to ride up on the moors. You should try it!"

"I'm glad you enjoyed it. You must do it again when you've got the time."

"Oh yes, please. I'd love to."

"Well, you never know, we might have another job for you when the stables are up and running. You'd better get in shape!" he teased.

"I don't know about that," Louise replied. "The horses would have to be fairly quiet."

"We'll see. Go and have a word with mother, I'll take Star back." He clipped a lead rein on Star and set off down the field. Louise pulled off her boots and was lacing up her trainers when she heard a car approaching on the gravel. As she crossed the yard towards the house, she recognized the young woman getting out of a blue sports car. This time she was wearing a bright red blouse, matching three inch heels and tight black leather pants. The happy expression faded from Louise's face.

"Oh, I see who it is now. Didn't I see you at the wedding?" The new arrival eyed Louise up and down, noticing the dirty smudge on her cheek and the black horse hairs clinging to her shirt and jeans. "I didn't know you worked for Neil," she added. Louise took a deep breath, feeling at a distinct disadvantage.

"I don't. I've been out riding." She didn't have to explain herself, so why was she feeling she had to do so.

"Oh." Melanie paused. "I thought you had to wear special clothes for riding?" She turned as she spotted Neil coming towards them.

"Neil, darling, how lovely to see you again." She went right up to him and offered her cheek to be kissed.

"Melanie, this is a surprise," he replied, obliging.

"You said to come and see you, and here I am. I stopped in the village and they directed me here," she said. Neil turned to Louise.

"Are you having a word with Mother before you go, Louise?" Before she had time to open her mouth, Melanie interrupted.

"Oh, I'm sure she'll want to go and get cleaned up first," she said, casting a disdainful glance at Louise, adding, "won't you, dear?" Louise was furious and got into her car.

"Another time, Neil. I'll be in touch," and with that she slammed the door and drove off at speed, sending gravel flying as she did so. By the time she reached home Louise had calmed down and recovered some of her former feeling of happiness. She went straight up for a quick bath and then enjoyed telling her mother about her ride over a bite to eat.

"I'm glad you enjoyed it. You won't have much spare time now, will you?"

"No, but I'll have my days off. I'm off into town this afternoon to get my hair trimmed and I need to call in at Stavely. I forgot to ask about uniform. Do you need any shopping doing?"

"I don't think so, dear. Oh, you could call at the cleaners and pick up your dad's suit. Are you going beating tomorrow?"

"Yes, might be my last chance," she replied.

Next day was fine and dry, and Louise was glad to be out on the moors again. She would miss this feeling of freedom and space when she started work but was glad that she wasn't leaving the area. She managed to get a word with Tony as they were walking back to the trailer for the last drive.

"And how's my special teacher?" he asked jovially.

"Fine, thank you. I've been hoping to get a word with you today. I'm starting a new job on Monday," Louise informed him.

"What? No more exercising on the moors? I shall miss my favourite beater. Still, you won't be giving up on the computer lessons, I hope."

"No, I'll have to ring you and fix a night, as I'm not sure what hours I'm doing 'til I see the work rota. I know I have to work alternate weekends but that means I'll get time off during the week."

"I'll look forward to hearing from you, then. In the meantime, do you fancy having a ride over to Layton tonight? Apparently there's some live music on. Roger was telling us at lunchtime. He and Liz have got babysitters and are going. I'm sure we could all go together." Safety in numbers, thought Louise, but why should she feel she needed safety? Was it herself she was afraid of or Tony? She decided she quite fancied a night out.

"Why not? Yes, I'll go," agreed Louise. They had reached the trailer and Louise climbed in, wondering if she'd made the right decision. Somehow, she just found it too difficult to say no to Tony.

Louise was unlocking the door of her car in the field back at The Grange when Liz came rushing up to her.

"Glad I've caught you, Louise. Roger says he'll drive tonight, so if you come down to the village for eight, we'll pick you up outside the Red Lion. We'll ring Tony and let him know."

"Are you sure?

"Yeah. No problem."

"Okay, I'll be there, Liz."

"Must dash – got the bairns to pick up. See you later," Liz called over her shoulder as she rushed off.

There was already a good crowd in when they reached the inn and the two girls only just managed to find a seat. Louise recognized a few other people present and more were arriving all the time. It wasn't long before the group started playing and things got very noisy. Although Tony and Roger tried to stand near where the girls were, it was impossible to have any sort of conversation, so Louise just got in the mood of the music, a mix of country and rock. As the evening wore on she found herself singing along with Liz to all the numbers that they knew, really enjoying the evening.

It was almost midnight when they turned out into the night, and for the first time that autumn there was a touch of frost in the air. The night was clear, with an almost full moon shining. As when they'd come, Liz got into the back with Louise and they continued singing some of the more familiar numbers they'd heard, which brought some derisive comments from the front occupants.

"We weren't thinking of making a career of it," laughed Louise.

"They were good though, weren't they?" Liz said, "The group, I mean. I'd go and see them again." Soon they were back in Dowerbridge. Tony and Louise got out and made their farewells. Tony's truck was parked near the road at the side of the pub.

"Where's your car?" he asked, linking his arm through Louise's.

"I put it in the back car park."

"I'd better see you safely to it then." They made their way round, and Louise hunted in her bag for the keys and put them in the lock. Tony turned her round to face him, smiling, and put both arms round her. As he bent to kiss her, Louise found herself responding and was left rather shaken at the emotion she felt. He released her, saying,

"Goodnight, Louise. Drive home safely."

Chapter 11

When Louise looked out from her bedroom window, the sun was rising over the rim of the valley and she noticed a touch of frost on the grass outside. Autumn had arrived. She took extra care over her appearance and applied a light touch of make-up. She knew how important first impressions were and wanted to feel right when meeting her new fellow staff members. She'd enjoyed her days at home but was looking forward to the challenges of this new job.

"You look very nice, love," her mother commented as Louise entered the kitchen. "I've just boiled the kettle. Tea or coffee?" She was busy packing up her husband's bait box.

"Tea, please. I'll do it. Dad not gone off yet?"

"No, he's messing about in the buildings, sorting out fire beaters and a petrol drum. He's hoping that after the frost lifts they'll be able to start heather burning."

"Well, things certainly would have dried up a bit yesterday." Louise had taken advantage of the sunny afternoon and taken Donna for a walk up on the moor. There had been a definite feel of autumn in the air, and she'd noticed the bracken already starting to turn golden in the more exposed places. Ten minutes later she was ready to leave.

"See you later, Mam."

"'Bye, Love. Hope all goes well." Louise was just unlocking her car when her dad appeared from the buildings.

"Mind how you go now, mi lass. There's been quite a frost and the roads could be a bit icy in places."

"I'll be careful, Dad. 'Bye."

Louise's first day went very well. She met most of the staff who were on duty, and Adrian, the bar manager, showed her round the place, explaining the daily routine as he went.

"Don't worry about Pièrre. Like most chefs he can be a bit temperamental but is good at his job, and he seems to work the rest of the chefs okay. You'll be consulted by him about the menus, which are changed every three weeks or so. Pearl's better for knowing, and will oversee all the residential side. Eddy lightens up when he's with the customers. You'll no doubt spend quite a bit of time with him in his office. Before I do the brewery order each week we'll get together and work out the wines needed for the restaurant. That's normally Tuesdays, so we'll be meeting up tomorrow and that will give you some idea of things. Anything you want to know and don't want to bother the boss with, feel free to ask."

They discussed the general routines of the place and various duties of different members of the staff. Louise knew from past experience that she'd be expected to cover in emergencies and help out in any department. "Eddy's pretty accommodating but can't stand people turning up late for shifts. Pearl's not in today but I'll get Emma, our head waitress, to take you round the guest rooms and show you the staff quarters. We'll go and get a coffee, then find Emma, as I'll soon have to open up the bar."

The rest of the day went very quickly, and Louise felt she would soon get into the swing of things. There were a few couples in for morning coffee and more customers in for lunch. Emma, a cheerful redhead, chatted almost non-stop to Louise as she went about her work but had a very professional approach with the customers.

"Popular time of year for older people. They know the children are back at school and they come for a run out into the country. Lots come in October and even November if the weather's good. The autumn colours can be quite amazing some years, here, in the grounds." She had a certain lilt to her voice which Louise was unable to place. "There's one couple from Leeds who come and stay a week every year just to enjoy the autumn scenery. Very nice they are. Are you from round here?" Louise filled her in briefly with her background as they laid the tables in the small dining room. It overlooked the garden and was where the residents had their evening meal.

"But you're not local, are you?" queried Louise.

"Well, I am now but I was born in Wales – my parents moved up to Yorkshire when I was three, so I almost class myself as a Yorkshire lass." She grinned at Louise, showing a dimple in one cheek. "My Father is Welsh and has never lost his accent. I suppose it rubs off a bit on me. You're not on tonight, are you?" she asked.

"No, but I will be tomorrow night."

"Pièrre will be back then. He makes me laugh," said Emma. Louise thought that Emma would probably see a funny side to most things. Louise liked her infectious giggle and easy approach to life. "Some of the other girls are a bit wary of him when things get hectic and he starts screaming in French at them. Well, that's it in here. I'm

69

going for a quick bite to eat. I'll see you tomorrow." She gave Louise that lop-sided grin and went off to the kitchen. Louise made her way to the office, where she spent the last hour of her shift with Eddy, discussing the work rota and other duties, before making her way home to Dowerdale, happy with how her first day had gone.

Louise settled in well at her new job and the week went by quickly. The weather stayed fine most of the week, and her father and Tony got in three good days moor-burning before the rain returned. They were shooting again Friday and Saturday but although Louise had the weekend off she elected to stay at home, clean her room and sort some clothes out to take to work. She'd agreed with Pearl to accept one of the staff rooms at the hotel for when she finished late and was on breakfast duty the next day. Also, there wouldn't be the worry of getting in to work when the weather got bad. In a way she wasn't sorry to be missing the shooting, as Saturday turned out very wet in the afternoon.

Sunday was still damp and drizzly but Louise accepted her father's invitation to go down to The Grange with him, where he was meeting the game dealer. Tony often saw to the grouse being collected but had gone off the previous evening to visit his relatives on the farm.

"His Grandpop hasn't been so good lately, and Tony wanted to go and see him," explained her dad. "I told him to stay until Monday unless the weather improves drastically, and I can't see it doing that now." They pulled up in The Grange yard near the game larder and Louise went round to the back door of the house.

"Anyone home?" she called, knocking on the open door as she walked into the back porch. Grace appeared, smiling at her visitor

"Hello, Louise. This is a nice surprise," she greeted Louise. "Come in."

"Dad had to meet the game dealer, so I thought I'd pop in to see you. How's things?" They made their way into the kitchen and Grace put the kettle on.

"Oh fine. Neil hasn't come back from doing the rounds yet but I expect he'll be back soon. How has the new job gone?" she asked. Louise told her all about work and then asked how the honeymoon had been.

"Very good, I think. Neil picked them up on Tuesday. I haven't seen them yet but have spoken on the 'phone. We're meeting them for lunch today, so I hope nothing's wrong with the stock. Neil should have been back by now."

"I've finished my coffee. I'll go and see," volunteered Louise.

"But it's pouring down."

"I'll borrow your wellies and get my waterproofs from the Land Rover. Maybe there's a cow calving." Five minutes later Louise was making her way through the muddy gateway out of the yard and heading to the bottom pastures, where she knew the cows were most likely to be. As she neared the far end of the pasture, she could see some of the cows but no sign of Neil. Then, as she made her way between the blackthorn trees and gorse bushes, she spotted the quad bike above a steep sloping part of the field. She headed towards the bike, then went down the slippery bank side, and there at the bottom behind a bed of gorse was Neil, jacket off and sleeves rolled up to the elbows, knelt near the back end of a cow that was stretched out on the ground. He looked surprised when Louise called his name.

"Having trouble?" she asked.

"Could say that," he grinned. His hair was wet through and shirt and sweater soaked as well. "Why do they pick the worst days to calve and always places farthest from home? She was already down and wouldn't budge from here but she's having difficulty. I think the head's back."

"What can I do to help?" asked Louise.

"Can you drive the quad?"

"Well, sort of. I've driven Dad's but not for a while."

"I'm sure you'll manage. Take it back to the farm and in the big implement shed, if you look behind the muck spreader, you'll find the old sheep trailer that goes on the quad. Get some straw from the stock shed to put in it and see if you can find a rope. They should be hung up in that old stone barn next to the little stable where we put Star the other day. I may need to rope it."

"Okay, I'll give it a go." Louise sounded more confident than she felt.

"Come back the long way, through the bottom gate – it might not be so muddy. Less chance of you getting stuck," he called after her. Louise climbed on the bike, managed to start it and set off back up the field. She was facing the rain and her hair was soon wet through, as her hood blew back. She needed both hands on the bike to control it as it slipped about on the wet, muddy field. She just hoped she wouldn't get stuck, and each time it looked tricky she bravely revved up a bit more. This was not her favourite form of transport. Eventually she made it back to the farm, jumped off and ran to the house to explain to Grace what was happening.

"Goodness, Louise, you're soaked," she exclaimed.

"No, I'm fine underneath, really, but I must hurry. Tell Dad where I am, please." With that she turned and ran back to the bike and drove it round to the big shed to look for the trailer. She found it as Neil had said, behind the muck-spreader. It was covered in dust and cobwebs and filled with a pile of empty plastic feed bags. She lifted these out and after several minutes, tugging it first one way then another, got it pulled out to yoke on to the bike. 'Won't be dusty for long when I get it out there in that weather', she thought, . She could hear the rain falling on the roof and it sounded to be heavier than ever. The pin was stiff and she had to find a bar to knock it out and cursed out loud when she caught her hand. Eventually she managed to get it hitched to the bike and drove round to the end of the stock yard for the straw. She was about to set off back down the field when she suddenly remembered the rope. Jumping off again, she ran back and found a wagon rope, also covered in dust and cobwebs, where Neil had told her it would be. It was a good job she didn't mind spiders.

She tried not to be scared as she made her way back down to the bottom gate and through into the pasture. The bike seemed to slip even more as the trailer jolted around from side to side, rattling along behind her. She was very relieved when she finally made it back to Neil, who was anxiously waiting for her return. She collected the rope from the trailer and, as she slithered down the bank side, was pleased to see that there were two feet showing from the labouring animal. It moaned loudly as it tried in vain to push out the unborn calf.

"Well done, Louise. I hope we're not too late." Taking the rope he set about securing it round the protruding hooves.

"Did you find the head?"

"Yes, it's forward now but she's got weak and is going to need some help. Here, take this end and when I say, pull as hard as you can." Louise took the rope and positioned herself behind Neil. It was difficult getting a grip on the wet, muddy grass and she had to dig her heels into the ground. She could barely feel her hands they were so cold but she wrapped the rope round them and when Neil shouted, as the poor animal again strained, she pulled with all her might. "Again," Neil encouraged each time the animal tried to push and they heaved against the rope. "Good, keep going, it's coming." Louise was puffing and blowing, using all the strength she could muster while she dug her heels in further and pulled on the rope. The cow gave an almighty bawl out as the head emerged. "Phew! Just hold a minute – right – now gently," as the poor animal gave another laboured moan and the rest of the calf's body slithered onto the soggy wet ground. Neil set about rubbing the motionless big bull calf.

"Is it alive?" Louise gasped, still getting her breath back.

"I hope so." Suddenly the calf shook its head and let out a wail. Neil jumped up and hugged Louise, a broad smile on his face. "Yes," he beamed, "we've saved him." He kissed her wet face with water dripping from his hair, not noticing the tears of joy mingling with the rain running down her cheeks. There was something very special about the miracle of new birth. Louise had felt the same when any of her Dad's bitches whelped. It amazed her how each newborn puppy, without being able to see, knew instinctively where to go to look for food.

The calf was making no attempt to stand as Neil removed the rope, so he dragged it round in front of its mother and she began to lick it. Still its feeble efforts were getting it nowhere.

"I hope *she'll* get up now." Neil sounded anxious as he looped up the rope. "I'll take the bike round the end of these bushes and bring it back on the bottom to get closer. If she sees us taking the calf in the trailer she might be encouraged to try and stand." Minutes later they'd lifted the slimy shivering calf on to the straw in the trailer. When Neil jumped on the quad and drove a few yards away, the mother made a huge effort and bawling out to her new-born, heaved herself to her feet. Neil smiled back at Louise, giving her the thumbs up. She smiled back at him, a very satisfied smile.

"Keep going," she called, "I'll walk behind." Slowly, the bedraggled party made its way back to the warmth and shelter of the stock yard, where Neil laid the calf on clean dry straw in a pen, attended by its mother.

"I'm sure he'll soon be on his feet. I'll come back and check when I get out of these clothes." As they came back into the yard, near the house Louise noticed a black saloon car.

"Damn!" uttered Neil, "I forgot we're going out to lunch. Where's your car, Louise?"

"I came with Dad. He must have gone. Whose is that car?"

"Don't worry, I'll take you back as soon as I've showered and changed," he replied, avoiding the question. They entered the back kitchen and stripped off their wet coats and leggings. Louise was quite dry underneath but Grace was appalled when she saw them both.

"Heavens above, Neil, you're soaked. And look at you, Louise." She reached up into a cupboard and handed a towel to each of them. "Did you save the calf?" Neil finished washing his hands in the sink and, beaming, turned to his mother.

"Yes, a fine bull calf, with Louise's help."

"Neil, what have you been doing?" Louise recognized the voice before she emerged from the towel with which she was vigorously rubbing her hair. Glancing up she saw Melanie, looking exquisite as usual, in a slinky black dress, her hair expertly coiled round the top of her head and her face looking like a model's from the front page of Vogue. Neil spoke first.

"Hello, Melanie. Sorry I'm going to be a bit late. What time are we meeting up with Rich and Sue, mother?"

"Twelve, but the table's not booked until one."

"Good, because I have to run Louise home when I've cleaned up. You go along and I'll catch you up later, in time to eat. Excuse me, I need a hot shower." He moved past Melanie and disappeared upstairs. Melanie looked crestfallen.

"Come on in, Louise. What you need is a hot drink while you wait for Neil," said Grace. Louise followed her into the kitchen. Colin appeared from the lounge, surprised to see Louise.

"Hello there. Did you get caught in the rain?" he asked.

"Yes, you could say that. We were calving a cow." Louise smiled but her feeling of happiness had suddenly diminished.

Chapter 12

Neil seemed rather preoccupied as he drove Louise home. He was now dressed in a suit and pale blue shirt with matching tie and smelled of aftershave. The picture he presented was very different from the one Louise could still envisage; wet, cold and muddy down at the bottom of the pasture.

"I'm sorry I've spoilt your day," offered Louise.

"Not at all. You haven't. On the contrary; you've helped make it. I'd sooner not have gone out to lunch today but Mother expected it." Silence fell again. Louise wondered why he'd arranged to go, if that was the case but kept her thoughts to herself. She tried again.

"How's the work coming on at the stables?"

"Very good. We're hoping to be ready for the first horses in a couple of weeks. I advertised a while ago and have already had quite a few replies. I've decided I'll need someone else to help run it, as not all the enquiries are for self-livery. Mother's agreed to help out and do all the paper work but I need a stable manager, so have advertised for that, too."

"Sounds exciting. You're going to be kept busy."

"Yes. I could do with getting it all up and running before the stock come in. The living quarters above the tack room aren't going to be ready by then but I suppose if they can't travel we could find them accommodation locally." They were pulling up in front of the Bentleys' cottage.

"I hope your mother's kept you some dinner."

"Oh yes, she makes sure I eat properly when I'm at home," replied Louise, laughing. "Thanks for running me back." Louise got out and shut the car door, not wanting to delay him further. Neil smiled and waved before turning the car and disappearing down the lane.

Next day, Louise was kept very busy and didn't get her lunch until after three o'clock. One of the girls had rung in sick and Louise found herself helping out with the chamber-maiding. Mondays were always busy, as quite a few of the rooms were change-overs after the departure of weekend guests. She did a stint on the main bar at lunchtime, followed by a spell in reception, covering for Pearl, who had an appointment at the dentist. While having a quick break before starting the evening shift at six o'clock, she managed to give Tony a quick call. After enquiring after his grandfather and family she suggested coming over to do the computer work the following night.

"That will be fine. Can you make it for seven and I'll cook your dinner as promised?" Louise laughed, realizing he'd actually been serious about cooking for her.

"I'll do my best. See you then. 'Bye."

It was late when she finished work that night and Louise went straight up to her room. She would have to be up early, as she was on breakfast duty. The next day was just as busy. After breakfasts were served, she had a meeting with Pièrre about the new menus and also details about the shoot dinners which were starting the following Saturday. Next, she had her weekly chat with Aiden about the wine order for the restaurant before helping with the lunches. As well as casual customers in the main restaurant, there was the annual luncheon party of the local Women's Guild in the small dining room. They stayed to have their meeting afterwards, which meant that Louise didn't get the tables re-laid for the residents' evening meal until nearly five o'clock, making her later home than usual.

It was just after seven when Louise pulled up outside Crag Cottage. Tony greeted her at the door in jeans, a short sleeved shirt, a navy and white striped apron and his usual flashing smile. Her heart was beating a little faster than normal as she recalled the last time she'd seen him.

"Hello there. Come on in."

"Sorry I'm a bit late. Couldn't get away from work on time. You look the part, anyway," she teased, trying to sound casual. She followed him into the kitchen. "Mm, that smells good. Hope I haven't spoiled it."

"Not at all. I allowed us time for a drink before eating." The meal was excellent. Louise was quite impressed with his efforts of grilled gammon, new potatoes and French beans. He even produced a mandarin cheesecake for desert.

"Before you ask – no, I didn't make it. I treat myself every now and then to one of these from the supermarket." They sat at the table chatting while they finished their wine, then Louise helped with the washing up and Tony told her about his weekend away at the farm.

"Shall I make us a cup of coffee to take through while you go and boot up the old machine?" asked Tony, the chores completed.

"Please, that would be good. No sugar for me." The next two hours passed quickly as Louise explained how to create and fill in the charts. She was surprised how well Tony had remembered the work she'd done with him. He produced some sheets of paper with the heather-burning facts and figures from the previous season.

"Your father gave me these. Could we have a go at a few to make sure I know what I'm doing?"

"Sure, why not." Louise showed him where to put the dates, the acreage burnt and the exact location.

"I'm sure you'll manage very well but if you get stuck, just give me a call." She stood up to go.

"Will you stay for another drink before you go?"

"No thanks. I'd better not when I'm driving."

"Not even a coffee," he coaxed. She sighed in resignation, unable to resist his persuasive smile.

"Oh, all right then, but I don't want to be late." Half an hour later he saw her to the door.

"Thanks for all your help, Louise. I hope I get stuck on something," he grinned, putting his hands on her shoulders.

"I'm sure you won't. Thanks for dinner. It was lovely."

"The pleasure was all mine. Goodnight, Louise." He bent and kissed her on the mouth – a long lingering kiss.

"See you soon." He released his hold on her.

"Goodnight." Louise smiled and turning quickly away, made for her car, not wanting Tony to see the effect his kiss had had on her.

Ellen Bentley was busy in the kitchen when her daughter came down the next morning. She turned and smiled at Louise.

"'Morning dear. Have a good evening?" Louise had arrived home the previous evening to find her parents already in bed.

"Yes, fine thanks. The work went well. Dad should soon have all his records up to date in print."

"And dinner?"

"Yes, that was good too. I would never have thought that Tony was the cooking type, but then, I suppose he's had to fend for himself a lot in his life." She made herself a drink, put some bread in the toaster and sat down at the table. Her mother turned to face Louise.

"Almost forgot, Neil rang last night."

"Did he say what he wanted?"

"No, only that it wasn't important. He might ring again today." She looked at her daughter quizzically, unable to read the expression on her face. Suddenly Ellen's face changed, breaking into a broad smile. "Oh, by the way, didn't get the chance to tell you last night. I received a rare letter from your brother yesterday. Says he might be in England just after Christmas and will try and get up to see us." Louise hadn't seen Nick for almost two years. Because of the big age gap between them, she felt she didn't really know him very well but it would be great to see him again. She stood up and gave her mother a big hug.

"I bet you're pleased about that, Mam?"

"Yes, I am," she replied, embracing her daughter. "Fancy a day's shopping? I feel like spoiling myself."

"Why not?" replied Louise, infected by her mother's happiness.

"Make that two gin and tonics and a double whisky please, m'dear. Now then, who hasn't got a drink?" The tall imposing figure of Colonel Barrington, standing by the bar, was trying to attract the attention of all his fellow shooters to get their drink order. Eddy was supposed to be here but still hadn't appeared, and so it was left to Louise to serve them. She'd heard Eddy on the 'phone as she'd passed his office but didn't think he could still be talking. Aiden wouldn't be on duty until the evening shift started at six o'clock.

"Ice and lemon?" she enquired of the Colonel.

"Just ice in one. You're new in here, aren't you?"

"Yes." Louise was taking the tops off the tonics and placed them by the glasses of gin. She looked up and smiled at her customer. The neatly trimmed moustache was now mostly grey, with only a hint of the once bright copper tones. She'd met him a few times at her father's in the past but he obviously didn't recognize her and she hadn't time to explain just now.

"Put all this round on the tab, will you. I'll come and sort the wine with you later." Louise had recognized a couple of the other gentlemen. They were farmers in the area but the rest were strangers to her. Most wore cords or moleskins, and some, like the colonel, were in plus fours. She smiled to herself when she saw the familiar green velvet waistcoat the Colonel was wearing, and wondered if it was the same one he always wore. She couldn't remember seeing him not wearing it. Perhaps he had them specially made.

"Alistair, what would you like?" A slim man, younger than all the rest, who had his back to the bar, turned and rested his penetrating gaze on Louise. He'd obviously changed out of his shooting garb in the car park, for he was smartly dressed in black blazer and grey trousers. His black hair was parted and flicked back from a deep brow above a long thin nose and hollow cheeks.

"What have we on offer?" The thin lips parted in a cynical smile and his cold grey eyes never left Louise's face. "I think a pint of bitter would go down very well." Louise could feel the young man watching her as she pulled his pint. She avoided looking at him as she passed the beer across the bar. Just then, Eddy came rushing through from the back to join Louise behind the bar.

"Hello Colonel. Good to see you again. Has Louise been looking after you?" He held his hand out across the bar and the Colonel shook it firmly.

"Yes, splendidly. How's that gem of a wife of yours?" Eddy laughed, as was expected, at the Colonel's attempt at witticism.

"Good, good, yes, she's fine. And yourself, keeping well I hope? How did the shooting go?" Louise was at the till entering up the drinks while this small talk between Eddy and the Colonel was taking place. She could feel Alistair still watching her, and started to head for the kitchen to let Pièrre know that the guns would be ready to eat shortly. As she turned from the till, Alistair moved along the other side of the bar and held a hand out towards Louise.

"Alistair Colleridge. Pleased to meet you, Louise." She shook the outstretched hand and struggled with a smile. She was aware of his eyes focusing on her trim figure, as if he could see right through her top. She quickly made her excuses to leave.

The dinner passed without incident and Louise managed to avoid any further conversation with Alistair. While they were busy with their main course she had a chat with Eddy, who was most apologetic about being late through to help.

"It was that blooming Saville woman. I just couldn't get off the 'phone. She changes the plans for that wedding every time she rings. First it was the placing of the tables, then it was the tables themselves – 'perhaps we should have all round ones.' The next call she wanted to change the menu, again. Today it was the choice of drinks for the welcome and the toast. Next time she rings I'll pass her on to you or Aiden."

"Thanks very much," said Louise, a hint of sarcasm in her voice but with a smile on her face. "Tell me," she continued, "Who's the arrogant looking young man with the shoot party?"

"Alistair? He's the Colonel's nephew. I understand that some of the guns are none too happy at him being there. Still, that's not our problem. They're good customers at a slack time of year."

"Does he live locally?"

"No, but often stays at Bamford House with his uncle at weekends during the shooting season. Works in London a lot, I understand." They were well out of earshot of the diners, who were at the far end of the restaurant away from the bar. Louise glanced across at them and noticed the Colonel looking their way.

"I'd better go and check everything's okay," said Louise and she walked down the room towards the diners. As she did so, she was aware of Alistair's turned head, and could feel his eyes on her.

"Yes, everything's excellent as always," replied the Colonel. "Could we have another bottle of the red, please, m'dear? The conversation was shooting talk and it was impossible not to hear snatches of it.

"Terrific high bird you took at Ing's Dell, Frank."

"Yes, rather surprised myself when I brought that one down. Old Bill had a good right and left at Crow Banks and Ned dropped a woodcock on the last drive ..." And so they went on but when Louise was uncorking the wine at the service table close to them the conversation had turned to horses.

"Next Friday, you say," the Colonel remarked.

"Yes," replied his nephew. "Thought I'd take him cubbing on Saturday and join you later. The hounds are out over near Layton. Bit of a trek with the trailer but I want to see what he's made of. I could really do with finding a good livery somewhere local for the season." So, thought Louise, he was into hunting as well. She might just be able to send Neil another customer.

When the meal was over and some of the guns were leaving, Louise managed to get a word with one of them – a farmer whom she knew, who lived in the next dale.

"Louise, isn't it? How you youngsters grow up. How's your father keeping? I haven't seen him for ages."

"He's fine, thanks. He'll probably be out with you one of these Saturdays. I couldn't help overhearing at dinner that Mr. Colleridge was looking for a livery in this area. I don't know if anything was said today but Neil Nickerson at The Grange is opening up a livery stable very soon."

"No, it wasn't mentioned as far as I know, but then we weren't up as far as The Grange today. I'll certainly mention it to Alistair. Give my regards to your father, won't you?"

"Yes, of course. We'll look forward to seeing you all next time."

Chapter 13

Louise managed to grab a quick coffee before the residents started to arrive in the dining room for their evening meal. Emma was on duty and in charge of the main restaurant, and the first guests who were dining there had already arrived. They were fully booked in the restaurant for the evening, so it was all systems go in the kitchen.

It turned out to be one of those hectic evenings, and as it progressed Pièrre's voice was reaching crescendo proportions. His black curly hair was clinging to his perspiring brow.

"Where are table eight? Why they not in yet? Louise, try and get them in, and the ten on table two should be here by now. Where is Emma? – her meals are ready." He was putting the finishing touches to four dinners as Emma came rushing through the swing doors holding a plate.

"Can you do this steak a bit more? The lady asked for it well done and says it's pink!"

"Does she wish for me to cremate it?" he spluttered in his broken English and gave instructions to one of the other chefs. Louise returned to the bar to tell the party of eight that their table was ready and fortunately they followed her through to the restaurant. After seeing them to their table, offering them water and giving them a wine list, she returned to the kitchen. The intercom buzzed. It was Pearl in reception.

"Louise, can you spare a minute, please?" Louise had just answered and switched off when it buzzed once more. It was Pearl again.

"Can you take four more in the restaurant?" Louise hardly dared ask Pièrre.

"Can we take another four, Pièrre?"

"Now? Look at the time! What do they think this is – a roadside café? Will there be a free table soon? If you can fit them in, yes, but no more tonight." Louise answered Pearl, then went in search of Emma. She found her setting up coffee trays.

"Emma, have table three had their sweets yet?

"Yes, I'm just about to take their coffee."

"Will you ask them if they'd like to have their coffee in the residents' lounge, please? We need their table – ask Becky to reset it for four." Becky was the young pretty waitress who had provided the bread buns for the girls on the day of the wedding. And so the evening went on with Pierre screaming more French than English.

It was after ten o'clock before the last of the meals were served and most of the diners had had their coffee. Louise and Becky were laying the breakfast tables in the residents' dining room when Emma came through the door, her usual cheery expression on her face.

"Nearly done, Louise? There's a couple in the bar asking for a word. Go on, I'll help finish off here."

"Thanks, Emma. I'll drop these off on my way." Louise gathered up an armful of table napkins and casting a big smile at the two girls, left the room. After taking the linen to the laundry room she made her way through the crowded bar and eventually spotted Richard and Sue seated at a small table in the corner. Richard stood up and kissed her on the cheek.

"Hi. Busy night, isn't it?"

"Yes, just a bit." Sue made room for Louise next to her.

"Sorry there isn't a chair." She smiled at Louise, who flopped gratefully on to the seat.

"Thanks, this is fine," said Louise. "Can't stay long as we haven't finished yet. Good to see you both, though. How's things?" They chatted about the honeymoon and the farm. Richard was most enthusiastic about the changes back home.

"I was on the 'phone to our Neil the other day and he was saying how well the building work's going. He says they're hoping to start someone in the stables very soon. Things are definitely changing up there. Melanie called at our house tonight; she was on her way up to The Grange. Maybe she fancies the job."

"You must be joking. Anyway, I thought she was going back to London," said Louise. Sue shrugged her shoulders.

"You know Melanie. Nothing's ever definite. Anyway, she was asking about tickets for the Hunt Ball. She was a bit secretive when Richard asked her who they were for."

"Yes. Said we'd find out in time," added Richard. "Are you going, Lulu?"

"Hadn't really given it much thought," she lied. "It depends how busy we are and what shift I'm on." She stood up. "I'll have to be getting back to work. I'll catch up with you both again soon, I hope. Thanks for calling in." She smiled and took her leave of them. Later, when she finally got finished after bringing all the residents accounts up to date, she made herself a hot drink and took it up to her room.

As she prepared for bed, she pondered on what Richard had told her. Melanie obviously hadn't given up on Neil if she'd been up to The Grange again tonight.

It was a cool damp afternoon with mist on the hills as Louise made her way home. She was glad that she had the rest of the day off. It had been a hectic weekend. She had an excuse to call in at The Grange and see what it was that Neil had been ringing for. Maybe it was the Hunt Ball.

She pulled up in the yard and made her way round to the kitchen door, knocking on it loudly. There was no reply, so she tried the door, which opened, knocked again and called out. She heard footsteps approaching. Good, someone was home.

"Hello, my dear, this is a nice surprise. Come on in," Grace greeted her warmly. "Sorry, I was upstairs, sorting out some clothes for the jumble sale next week. Have you come from work?"

"Yes, just called in on my way home. Hoped I might catch Neil." Grace was filling the kettle.

"We'll have a cuppa while we wait. Neil's gone round the stock, so won't be back for a while." She set the tea things and some buttered scones on a tray as she talked. When it was ready she picked up the tray.

"Come on, we'll go through to the lounge, seeing as it's Sunday," she smiled at Louise. They settled down with their tea and when the subject of the stables came up, Louise told her about Alistair.

"Yes, we need to be up and running soon, as we've had some bookings confirmed. Neil is interviewing some applicants for the stable job this week, so we're hoping one will be suitable. It's all getting a bit hectic as he's taking some beasts to the suckler sale on Tuesday, which means he'll be sorting stock out tomorrow and there's a planning officer coming on Thursday. Something to do with the drive access and the first horses arrive next weekend."

"Gosh, things are moving forward fast. How's Neil coping?"

"Not bad, really. He'll be pleased to see you. He was just saying this morning that he hadn't managed to get hold of you the other night and he doesn't like to ring you at work." She paused to take a drink before continuing. "He was out last night."

"Oh, where was that?"

"He went to the theatre in Scarborough. Melanie had these tickets for a show and talked him into it."

"That would make a nice change for him," Louise managed.

"I suppose so but he didn't have much to say about it this morning. Probably got too many other things on his mind at the moment and he has another cow due any day."

"How's the calf doing that I helped with?" Louise asked, glad of the change of subject. Grace smiled at her young visitor.

"Oh, he's doing fine." They'd finished their tea and Louise stood up, running a hand casually through her hair.

"I'll go and see him while I wait for Neil."

"Yes, you do that. Neil shouldn't be long now." Louise crossed the yard and made her way round to the huge barn housing the cattle. Scrutinizing the pens, her eyes shone with delight when she recognized the cow with its offspring that she'd helped to deliver. The calf seemed much bigger though, now that he'd filled out and his coat was dry and shiny. The mother lowed gently to him as he scrambled to his feet from his warm comfy bed of straw. Soon he was guzzling hungrily from the milk-laden bag.

"Hello there." Louise jumped on hearing the familiar voice behind her and, turning, saw Neil standing a few feet away.

"Gosh, you startled me," she beamed at him.

"Yes, I could see you were enraptured. Fine young animal, isn't he?" Neil said, coming to stand by her side.

"Mmm, amazing, isn't it, and just a week old." They stood watching in silence as the sturdy bull calf satisfied itself with his mother's milk. Neil put his arm round Louise, giving her shoulders a squeeze.

"We did a good job there, didn't we?" Louise nodded in agreement, a warm satisfied look on her face. A moment later Neil removed his arm and moved aside, pushing his hands in his overall pockets, looking down at the ground. Then, looking up, added, "That reminds me, I tried to ring you." Louise turned and smiled at him.

"I know. That's why I called in today. I'm on my way home from work." She waited expectantly. Neil's gaze returned to the cow and calf in front of him.

"I wondered if you would come out for a meal with me again." He turned once more to face her. "My way of saying thank you for all your help last weekend." The expression on Louise's face gave away her disappointment. Neil hurried on. "It's okay if you don't want to. I'll understand." Louise blinked. He didn't understand at all. She wasn't sure that she did, come to that.

"No, I'd love to," she replied. "When?"

"Well, when are you next off?"

"Wednesday. I was hoping I might come for a ride on Star during the day. We could go out for a meal in the evening."

"It's a deal. Come on, Mother will be wondering what's kept me," he said, casually taking her by the hand as they walked back towards the house. Louise popped in to say goodbye to Grace before continuing her way up the valley. She had mixed feelings as she mulled over things in her mind. She was both sad and happy. Happy that Neil had asked her out but sad that he wasn't taking her to the Hunt Ball. He must have agreed to go with Melanie.

As she drove into the yard at home, she was surprised to see Tony's familiar, blue truck. He didn't usually come round on a Sunday. She went inside where her mother was making sandwiches.

"Hello, love. You're back in time for tea. Busy weekend?" Louise flopped into her father's carver armchair.

"Yes, but I'll be fine when I'm washed and changed." She smiled at her mother, adding, "I see Tony's here. Is everything okay?"

"Yes, fine. He came over to collect some fire beaters that need fixing. The new shafts arrived yesterday, so Tony's taking them back home. It's a job he can do when they can't get on with anything else. I've asked him to stay for tea."

"Really? That's very nice of you."

"Well, I thought I'd better get to know him a bit better seeing as how you two seem to be such good friends!"

"Well," Louise laughed, "he is rather handsome, isn't he? Have I time for a bath before tea?" she asked.

"Yes, of course. Dad said they'd be in about five." Half an hour later, dressed in jeans and sweatshirt, Louise felt refreshed and came downstairs to find her father and Tony laughing at one of her father's stories. Tony looked completely at home and relaxed in their modest kitchen. She'd forgotten that Tony had been working here quite a while and would know her father pretty well. They would have spent hours in each other's company, working together on the moors. After tea Tony raised his tall frame from the table and thanked Ellen for her hospitality.

"Your baking is almost as good as my Gran's," he teased, flashing that attractive smile at her.

"Well then, I shall just have to keep practising, won't I?" she replied. Tony looked across at Louise, who was enjoying this friendly banter.

"Fancy a short walk up the moor? I'm taking the dogs for their exercise." Louise was taken by surprise.

"Er, well, why not? The fresh air will do me good. I'll take Donna, shall I Dad?"

"Aye, might as well, lass. It will be one less for me to take out."

The rain had stopped as they set off up the track by the wood on to the moor. It was cool with a fresh breeze blowing, which had dispersed the earlier mist patches.

"Most of our summer visiting birds will soon be gone," commented Tony, as they reached the heather-clad moor. "No more goldies and curlews calling to us." They had been walking in companionable silence, enjoying the freedom and rugged beauty of their surroundings. It felt strange to Louise, for she had only been on the moors with Tony previously on shoot days, when he was always concentrating on the job in hand. She felt, for the first time, at ease in his company. She supposed that they had quite a lot in common really.

"It's marvellous how they know when it's time to leave and then return again in the spring." She paused. "All but the grouse. Such majestic creatures, aren't they?"

"Yes, regal rulers over their own small domains. Look, over there." He pointed to a cock grouse standing proud and alert on a hillock of bilberry, showing off his bright red comb and wattles, his dark feathered coat glistening in the fading sunlight.

"Seems such a shame that they have to be shot."

"I agree." He thought a moment. "But, you know, in a strange way, it's because of the shooting that we are able to encourage their survival. That's how I feel anyway. That I'm helping a special species to survive in an unpredictable world." He looked around for the dogs. "Time we were getting back. It will soon be dark." He whistled up the dogs and they turned right-handed, taking a well worn sheep-track back down the steep hillside.

Chapter 14

Next morning on her way to work Louise called at the village to post some letters for her mother and fill the car up with petrol. As she came out of the Post Office, she noticed an unfamiliar red mini car parked close by. Inside was a girl Louise did not recognize, which was unusual in the quiet little village so early in the day. As she was walking past the stranger's car to reach her own near the filling station, the driver of the red mini got out and approached Louise. She was tall and slim with short brown hair and expressive eyes.

"Excuse me, are you local here?" the visitor asked.

"Yes, can I help you? Louise offered.

"Maybe. I heard there were some stables in the Dowerdale area. Do you know where they are?"

"Stables?" Louise looked puzzled, then suddenly it dawned on her what the young girl meant. "Oh, of course. You mean the new ones at The Grange."

"I expect so. Can you direct me there, please?"

"They're not actually open yet but I can certainly tell you where to find The Grange. Go over the bridge there and when you reach the fork take the road to the right, continue up the dale about two miles and you will see the large iron gates on your left at the entrance to the drive at The Grange."

"It sounds rather grand," the girl replied, with a friendly smile.

"No, it's not really – just a working farm, and the family are really nice people. Do you ride?"

"Yes." She stepped towards her car, opened the door and turning to Louise added, "Thanks for all your help."

"You're welcome. I'm just off to work in Millford but I live up the valley past The Grange so maybe we'll meet again. 'Bye." Louise rather hoped they would. She liked the look of this open-faced friendly girl who was now seated in her car with the window down. There was something vaguely familiar about her and Louise felt she must have seen her before somewhere. She was about to walk away towards her own car when the girl spoke again.

"Oh, I forgot to ask. What was the name of the family?" Louise turned and answered her.

"Nickerson."

Louise kept thinking about the incident as she drove to work. The girl had looked most surprised when Louise had said Nickerson. She'd obviously heard about the stables from someone and was presumably expecting to hear a different name. Louise wondered where she might have seen her before. She looked only a few years younger than herself so she supposed it could even have been at college. Maybe she was moving into the area and looking for a livery for her horse.

Louise arrived at work just as Eddy and Pearl were setting out on their day off. They were going to the races for the day.

"You've got a meeting at three this afternoon with a charming lady," Eddy informed her with an amused expression on his face.

"Do I know her?" asked Louise.

"You'll wish you didn't when you meet her," said Pearl, adding, "It's the delightful Mrs. Saville."

"Don't let her manipulate you, like she does me," said Eddy. Louise couldn't imagine Eddy being manipulated by anyone. "Just tell her we have to have everything finalized today. Good luck!" and off they went. Actually, the meeting went much better than expected and all the wedding details were completed. Her two days went quickly and it wasn't until she was driving home that she remembered the attractive young girl with the boyish figure and short cropped hair that she'd met the previous morning. She wondered if they would meet again.

Wednesday morning was bright but cool, and Louise was looking forward to her ride.

"Been a frost down in t'valley bottom," her father said when he came in for his breakfast. "Should be a fine day though, according to t'forecast."

"You'll be hoping to do some burning, then," his wife replied.

"Aye, we should get a go today. There might be a 'phone call from t'bloke delivering t'grit. You'll have to try and get hold of me if it's coming today."

"Well, you should be able to get a signal up on the moor," Ellen answered, handing him his plate of bacon and eggs. Getting a signal on mobile 'phones was a bit hit and miss in parts of the valley.

"Oh! and can you ring t'Fire Service? There's bound to be someone who reports a fire on t'moors."

"Which moor will you be on, Dad?" asked Louise. "I'm taking Star out today and wouldn't want to get too near your fires."

"Have you nowt better to do than ride about t'moors?" he teased, winking aside to his wife. "We'll be right over on Layton side, well away from where you'll be, mi lass."

An hour later when Louise arrived at The Grange she was greeted by an incessant bellowing of cattle. Of course, Neil had taken some of the stock to the suckler sale yesterday. The cows, whose young had gone to the market, would be baling for their calves for a couple of days. She found Grace baking in the kitchen.

"They're having a cake stall on Saturday at the jumble sale," she explained. There were two fruit cakes and a large ginger loaf cooling on a wire tray on the table.

"Mmm…, those look good." Louise perched herself on one of the kitchen stools. "Got the cattle away all right then?"

"Yes, not too bad. Young Billy came over from Crag Farm and gave Neil a hand. The wagon was here before six as he had two other loads to collect after ours." Grace was placing two more baking tins in the oven. She stood up, turned to her young companion, smiling. "Nice morning for a ride."

"Yes, I'm lucky, aren't I? I'll go and bring Star in, then I thought I might have a look round the new stables."

"You do that. They're looking good. I think Neil's still feeding up. He has someone coming today to help with the new fencing round the parking area. The timber arrived yesterday."

As Louise collected the head collar and rope from the old stable, Tess appeared, her tail wagging.

"C'mon then, you can come with me." She patted the old dog affectionately and they set off together down the pasture. She spotted Star grazing down by the side of the copse near the stream and called to her. Star raised her head when she heard Louise's voice and came trotting up the bank. Louise soon had the head collar on and led the old mare back to the farm. She could hear a tractor buzzing somewhere round the back of the cattle sheds, so presumed Neil was still fothering. Not all the cattle were inside, just those that had recently calved. The spring calvers and all the in-calf heifers were still outside in the fields. As soon as the weather changed and the grass stopped growing, they, too, would all be coming inside for the winter months.

After tying Star up, Louise made her way past the game larder round to the new block. There were several workmen busy at various tasks. Two were hanging doors onto the loose boxes and another was fixing power points and switches where loose electrical wires were sticking out of the newly plastered walls. It all looked very clean and bare. Soon it would look and feel very different. There would be the sound of horses chomping on their food and shoes clip-clopping on the cement floor as they went in and out of their boxes. Instead of the smell of new timber it would be horses, fresh hay and cleaned leather. Louise wandered around, trying to picture it all as it would be very soon and wondered what kind of horses were coming.

As she arrived back in the yard, a wagon was coming down the drive. Louise recognized the name on the side of it as a firm in Northallerton that sold agricultural tools, small machinery and other farm related equipment. He pulled up, and winding down his window, called out to Louise.

"Can you tell me where you want this lot unloading?"

"Just a moment. I'll go and find out," and she ran into the house.

"Can you find Neil, please?" Grace replied to her query. "I don't want my cakes to burn." Louise went back out and explained to the driver and then went in search of Neil. She found him on the quad bike, just about to set off down the pasture.

"Oh good, it'll be the stable equipment." He jumped off the bike and returned to the yard with Louise. "It's the feed bins, barrows and stable tools. I was getting a bit anxious about them getting here on time." He smiled at Louise before rushing off to direct the driver. "Enjoy your ride, maybe see you later." Louise went to groom Star and get ready for her ride.

Louise left the farm and headed down the field to the track by the stream. The old horse was enjoying herself and Louise let her canter for short spells where the going was good and level. There were no flies to annoy her and she flicked her ears back and forth as she listened to Louise's voice. The onset of autumn was certainly evident. Black, shiny clusters of berries hung from the elderberry bushes and even some of the green berries on the holly trees were starting to turn pink. The hedgerows gave way to stone walls as Louise headed up a green lane leading to the open bank side, covered in the now dying bracken, already turning golden brown. A hare jumped out from almost underneath Star and fled away across the bracken, startling Louise, but the old mare never even flinched.

Louise felt more confident than she had on her previous ride and was able to relax and enjoy herself. She thought back to something Neil had said as she trotted along the track on the open moor. Maybe she *would* feel confident enough to ride another horse, should the opportunity ever arise.

As she rode she could see the familiar plumes of smoke rising in the distance where her father and Tony were burning the heather. Looking around, she could see more smoke where the 'keepers on neighbouring estates were also burning. Occasionally the peaty, pungent smell of burning ling drifted across to her on the breeze. She knew that her father quite enjoyed this controlled burning, carried out in the winter months when conditions were safe. He'd explained to her how it benefited the grouse, as new heather would soon re-grow, providing young nourishing shoots for them to eat.

The smell always brought back memories of that dreadful time when there was a huge moor fire in that long hot summer they'd had when she was still at school. It had taken ten days to bring it under control. As well as crews from several fire stations and the game keepers, many local farmers had helped too. Extra water had had to be carried in huge bowsers, as the streams on the moor had all dried up. Long trenches, several feet wide, were dug with large tractors some distance from the edge of the burning moor as a fire break, in the hope of stopping the raging flames. The men worked for hours on end beating the flames and digging out the burning peat as the fire worked ever deeper into the ground.

Louise remembered how each morning when the fire crews returned to help for the day, her father had come back home, exhausted, blackened and reeking of burning peat after spending all night working on the fire. His eyes were red and sore from the hot dust and smoke, the skin on his face scorched and his lips cracked and dry. He always got straight into the bath and her mother would take him a mug of tea while he relaxed in the water. He only got a few hours sleep before he had to get up, try and eat some dinner and then, with a re-filled bait bag, return to the hot, smoky, dusty conditions of the ravaged moor. Louise had fed and exercised the dogs for her father each day throughout that exhausting time.

Long after the flames were extinguished, small spirals of smoke could be seen all over the decimated land, which only a few weeks earlier had been a purple haze of heather in bloom. She'd gone in the Land Rover with her father to keep watch one night. It had looked eerie and unreal, like an alien planet. Patches of burning earth glowed red in the darkness and when the wind blew in gusts it was like seeing miniature fireworks exploding, as sparks of lighted peat flew into the air. Since then, people had been warned about the dangers of lighting picnic fires and being careless with cigarette ends when visiting the moors. No-one knew for sure what had started the fire but everyone had their own idea.

Louise turned off on to a steep cart track that slanted down the bank side. It was rough and stony, with bracken growing on either side, and she let Star pick her way carefully down between the rocks and boulders. Here and there a few stunted trees were trying to grow. One of these had branched out across the track and Louise had to lie forward over Star's neck to duck underneath it. At the bottom of the bank was a fence, with a small hand-gate leading into a plantation. It had once been a natural forest but had been taken over by the Forestry Commission and now had large areas of planted trees for felling though some of the original hard-wood trees remained. Louise managed to negotiate the gate without having to dismount and set off along the soft, grassy track.

Some places were quite boggy and Louise had to steer Star round these very carefully. Larch needles were already falling, forming patches of orange carpet where they fell. Rabbits scurried away as she rode along, and a young roe deer, startled by this intrusion, bounded across the track in front of Louise and disappeared among the undergrowth. It was very peaceful and quiet apart from the gentle rustling of the leaves high up in the trees and the occasional snap of a twig under Star's hooves. Here and there on the edge of the trees grew clumps of broom, their dried seed pods rattling in the breeze. The earthy smell of damp grass and decaying leaves was quite strong, and as they rode through a small clearing in the trees, Louise was aware of the distinctive musky smell of a fox that had obviously passed through earlier in the day.

Once out of the plantation and on a good firm track Louise urged Star into a canter until they reached the gate at High Ghyll Farm. Here, a bridleway went through the fields back down the dale. She let Star walk the last half mile to cool down, knowing she couldn't turn her out hot and sweating now that the weather was cooler. After arriving back at The Grange feeling happy and invigorated by her ride, Louise un-tacked Star and gave her saddle-patch a good rub down before leading the old mare back to the field.

When Louise arrived back in the yard, there was a black saloon car near the house, which she thought was like Colin's. Louise was sure Grace had said that Melanie had returned to London. She quietly slipped in at the back door to replace her riding hat and, seeing no sign of Neil anywhere, jumped into her car and drove home.

"Enjoy your ride, love?" Louise and her mother were sitting at the kitchen table, having a bit of lunch.

"Yes, it was smashing, thanks."

"So what did you think of the new stables, then?" Louise looked surprised. "Grace rang," her mother explained. "She wondered if I wanted my jumble picking up, as they were sorting it all through before sale day. We chatted quite a while until she realized what time it was. Said she had company arriving and would have to change."

"Didn't say who it was, did she?" Louise asked casually.

"No. Why?"

"I thought it looked like Colin's car in the drive." Louise stood up and started to clear the table. Her mother studied her daughter but said nothing. Later that evening, as Louise was going upstairs to get ready for her night out with Neil, the 'phone rang.

"I'll get it, Mam." Five minutes later she returned to the kitchen, looking rather downcast.

"Everything all right, love?" her mother asked.

"Yes, I suppose so." She paused a moment, then asked, "Was there any dinner left? I'm not going out now. Neil's got a cow calving."

Chapter 15

It was a sound Pippa Johnson loved. Horses contentedly crunching on good crisp seed hay. Not the soft meadow hay they'd used on the farm but long strands of sweet smelling sun-dried grasses. She walked down the centre of the large covered shed that housed the horse boxes, plastic bagged haylage, baled hay, straw and the tack and feed stores. She was checking on her charges for the last time that day.

First Rollo, the big chestnut, who was not too fast but dependable and had plenty of stamina. She'd ridden him out that afternoon and noticed a back shoe was clipping a bit. Good job the farrier was booked for next week. She patted his big strong neck, then closed his door and went into the next box.

Minstrel, a grey gelding who jumped like a stag when in the right mood, caused her more work than the other two put together. Who would have a grey? Every morning she'd spend up to half an hour washing off the stains from his hind quarters where he'd lain during the night. She'd hosed off the worst of the mud on his legs today when her bosses had returned from their day's hunting. Then she'd had to towel his legs well, especially his heels, as he was prone to mud fever. She checked his heels and adjusted his rug slightly before going on to the third box.

Sceptre, her favourite, a dark bay mare, was fast and intelligent, even if at times she was a bit unpredictable. She nickered softly as Pippa entered her box and nuzzled up against the young girl's neck when she stroked the soft, silky skin. Pippa loved the feel of the horses when they were clipped out. Their coats weren't bristly as one would imagine but soft as velvet, like moleskin.

She closed the last door and went into the feed store to measure out their hand food ready for morning. Next she put sugar-beet to soak in three buckets for the following day. As she closed the door, she whistled up her dog, Gyp. Her little Border terrier had been hunting around near the straw bales, ever hopeful of scenting a rat to hunt.

"Come on, Gyp! Bed time." Pippa smiled when she saw him appear, head cocked to one side as if to say 'do we have to go already?' She called him again and he diligently came trotting towards her. She switched off all the lights before going out into the chilly night air and closed the big sliding door shut. She noticed two other cars parked in the driveway of her bosses' house as she drove up the yard. Her bosses, a young couple in their thirties, had a large social circle and often had friends round. Although they had been hunting today, it was not a regular practice. Their main activity was entering point to point races, and in order to qualify for these events the horses had to have been hunted a minimum number of days each season. They also took part in some Cross Country and Eventing when they could fit it in. Time was limited, though, as they both worked full time to fund their expensive hobbies and pay for the mortgage on their fine home. Pippa loved working with the horses, and the advantage of being able to ride these wonderful animals more than compensated for the odd hours her job entailed.

As she drove back the short distance to the home she shared with her step-father, Pippa contemplated her future. Now was probably a good time for a change, if she was going to act on her mother's letter. She swallowed hard. Thinking about her loss still evoked great sadness, and although it had been the anniversary of her mother's death last week, time had made little difference to how she felt.

She parked her mini behind her step-father's car on the short drive outside the neat semi on the outskirts of York. After locking her car, she entered the small porch at the side of the house and tugged off her boots. Gyp promptly went straight to his water bowl for a drink, then followed Pippa into the lounge. The terrier went across to the man seated in an armchair, received his customary stroke, then went and curled up in his basket at the right of the fireplace. A welcoming fire blazed in the hearth, with iridescent tongues of flame leaping from the black coals. There was a half empty glass of whisky on the small table between the arm chair and settee opposite. A television was playing in the corner. Derek Johnson removed his spectacles, looked up and attempted a smile.

"All done for the night?" he asked, switching off the television.

"Yes, they're all settled. You don't have to switch off, Dad."

"It's all right, I wasn't really watching." His gaze returned to the glowing flames. Pippa was concerned for him, knowing how much he'd adored her mother. They'd been married nineteen happy years, and Derek was the only father Pippa knew. She had been born six months after that fateful accident. That had been two years before Derek, the shy, unassuming bachelor, had entered their lives.

"Fancy a night cap? I'm having one," she asked him.

"No thanks, love, I'll not bother." He reached for the glass on the table. Pippa went through to the kitchen and put the kettle on. She heard the clink of glass and worried about the amount he was drinking. It had only started after her mother died. He said it helped him sleep. She took her hot drink through and sat down opposite Derek. They were both deep in thought, the methodical ticking of the mantle clock the only sound breaking the companionable silence. As Pippa reached forward to place her mug on the table, she noticed, half hidden under a magazine, a letter.

"Is that Sophie's handwriting?"

"Mm? Oh, yes, it came today. You can read it."

"What's her problem this time?" Pippa knew from past experience that her sister only wrote when something was wrong or she needed something. She picked up the envelope and drew out the single sheet.

 Dear Derek,

She had always refused to call him Dad. Although only six when their mother re-married, she'd always called Derek by his name.

 I was wondering if I could come home again for a short
 while. Things are not good at the moment here.

Things rarely were in her haphazard life, with her on-off relationships.

 I got rather depressed again last month and had to go
 back on my pills. Greg's been rather beastly, saying I
 should have got over it by now.

He was a new one – it had been Oliver at the funeral.

 I don't mind sleeping in the back room, just till I feel
 better.

Pippa read to the end and placed the letter back on the table. Well, that helped her to go ahead with her plans. She would feel better knowing Sophie was around to keep an eye on Dad – or would it be the other way round?

She and Sophie were as different as the proverbial chalk and cheese. Although Pippa was four years younger than her sister, she had always felt to be the protective one. Sophie never exercised (not that she was overweight, just the opposite in fact), hated animals and changed her men almost as often as she changed her mind. The sisters didn't even look alike. Sophie had her father's dark hair and sallow skin, never really looked very healthy and at school had always seemed to be ailing something. Pippa on the other hand had been a strong robust child, always active. Pippa smiled as she remembered her mother complaining good naturedly that Sophie's hand-me-downs always pinched across the shoulder on her. She'd always been an outdoor girl, enjoying sport at school, and had spent most of her school holidays at the farm a mile away on the edge of town. She still had her old push bike in the shed which she'd used to reach the farm.

She looked across at her stepfather, concern on her face. Maybe it would help him having Sophie around. Make him feel needed again. Sophie had always been able to work him round her little finger, knowing how to play the helpless little girl. Not that that bothered Pippa, for Derek always had enough love and time for all three of them.

"What d'you think, Dad?"

"Can't refuse, can I?" he answered, smiling. "How do you feel about it?"

Pippa lay back and closed her eyes, considering this turn of events. Maybe this was as good a time as any to tell him of her fledgling plans, but she didn't want to hurt him.

"Fine with me. The hours that I work, I don't suppose I'll see that much of her." It wasn't that she didn't like her sister. She loved her dearly. It was just that they had so little in common. She recalled her mother's words, 'wouldn't do if we were all alike – it's good to have one practical daughter,' and she'd ruffle her short cropped brown hair affectionately. She opened her eyes.

"There's something I want to tell you, Dad." She paused, searching for the right words. "I've seen a job that I think would suit me, only... I... it would mean me moving out." He looked up and smiled, allaying her fears. There had always been a close bond between them. He spoke in that quiet familiar way he had, the way he'd used when his little girls had come home with problems or worries. Pippa couldn't recall him ever raising his voice to them.

"I didn't expect that I could keep you here forever. Girls grow up and get married – well, most do. How will I ever get any grand-children if you stay here with me?" Had she not known how embarrassed it would have made him, Pippa would have jumped up and hugged him for that response. Instead she gave him the benefit of her widest smile, wrinkling her slightly upturned nose.

"Thanks for that, Dad. No matter where I go, I know you'll always be here for me." Derek drained his glass and stood up, giving Pippa's shoulder an affectionate squeeze as he passed her chair. That was as demonstrative as he would get.

"Think I'll turn in now." He paused at the door, glancing back at Pippa. "I'll write to Sophie tomorrow then."

"You do that. 'Night, Dad." Pippa closed her eyes once more and stretched her long legs out towards the fire. She thought about another letter – the one her mother had left her when she died. Perhaps it was time for a change.

She recalled a conversation she'd had with her mother just after she'd left school. She remembered well her mother's words.

"It's turned out very well for me. Derek's a wonderful husband and father but I've been lucky. Don't make the same mistake that I made."

"What do you mean, Mum?" Pippa asked.

"I fell for the wrong sort. Thought it was the real thing and ended up having to get married – something you did then if you got pregnant. It never worked though, right from the start. As soon as Sophie was born he was back to his old ways – drinking, robbing, breaking and entering. I didn't know about any of this when we married. It wasn't long before he was up at court. We'd only been married a year when Jack was sent down the first time. Each time he came home things were always going to be different, especially as he got to know Sophie, but they never were for long. It was a real struggle."

"Why didn't you divorce him?"

"It wasn't as easy as that. I had nowhere to go. Anyway, he was a catholic and wouldn't hear of it. Not a very good example, was he? We'd been married about five years when the accident happened. He'd only been out of jail a few months. I was twelve weeks pregnant with you at the time. He'd gone out drinking as usual with some of his no-good friends. I was asleep in bed when I was awakened by a banging on the door. It was about one in the morning. I ran downstairs in my nightie thinking he'd forgotten his key. When I opened the door there was a policeman and woman in uniform standing on the doorstep. Asked if they could come in. Had some bad news. Apparently, Jack and one of his mates had been disturbed breaking into an electrical warehouse. They'd had to high tail it in a hurry. The car skidded on some black ice and went straight over a bridge, landing on its roof. Jack was killed outright. Twenty-seven years old. What a waste of a young life. The other bloke survived but suffered severe head injuries."

It must have been tough for her mother, being pregnant and having a four year old to look after on her own. It was two years later that Derek had come into their lives. Kind, gentle, unassuming Derek. He'd fallen for her mother straight away and she couldn't believe it, his taking on two little girls as well.

As time passed and it was discovered that he couldn't father children, he'd grown to love them as his own. He'd always been there for them. He'd helped with homework and mended punctures on their bikes. They'd gone on picnics at the seaside, trips to the zoo and holidays at Butlins. They were a normal, happy family. When Sophie had gone through the dancing phase, Derek paid for her ballet and tap lessons. Pippa was having none of that. She pleaded to have riding lessons at the local riding school instead. Her mother had soon discovered that she was a natural rider when it came to horses.

Yes, she would miss her mother for a long time; miss the feeling of belonging and being loved, no matter what. But she had to move on and felt this was the time to do that. Opening her eyes, she finished her now lukewarm drink and stood up, stretching her tall athletic frame. She crossed to the small dining table by the window and opened the local newspaper lying there at the job vacancies page. Running her finger down the second column she soon found what she was looking for –

'Stable manager required for new livery stable. Must be good rider and able to work on own initiative. Start soon. Dowerdale area. Ring for details and arrange interview.'

There was no name but she knew roughly where Dowerdale was. She'd heard Mrs. Davidson, a local hunt follower, speak of it.

"It's good to have a day on the moors once or twice a season," she would say after one of her hunting days there. There were no moors in the country hunted by their local pack. Next day off, Pippa decided, she'd have a ride over that way in her car and take a look round Dowerdale. She didn't know if she was doing the right thing or not; only time would tell. Besides, she might not get the job. For despite her experience, they might think twenty-two too young or they might want a man for the job. Tomorrow she would ring and see what happened.

Chapter 16

Pippa decided to go over to Dowerdale before ringing up to see about an interview. She wanted to make sure that she liked the area and would be able to settle there before committing herself to a new job. She set off to work early on the Monday morning, two days after she'd seen the advert in the paper. After she'd fed the horses, she rugged them up and turned them out into the field. She cleaned out the boxes and laid the beds ready for evening before putting the soaked sugar beet in their feed bowls and filling up the hay racks. Pippa had already agreed with her boss to have most of the day off. One day without being ridden would do the horses no harm, as they'd all been exercised or worked over the weekend.

With a road map on the seat bedside her and Gyp sitting on a rug on the back seat, she was soon travelling north, heading for the moors. She knew from her road map that it would be best to go by Millford and then, hopefully, she would find her way to Dowerbridge. There she would have to make some discreet enquiries. She had never really travelled this way before and was strangely excited as, after several miles, she left the fields behind and found herself out on the open moors. They seemed so vast and forbidding, even on a sunny morning like today. The thought of riding across places like this filled her with a feeling she'd not experienced before. Soon she was travelling down another valley and then along a busy road towards Millford. She parked in a lay-by to consult her map, to make sure she took the right road to Dowerbridge.

It was barely ten o'clock when she pulled up in the tidy little village outside the village shop and Post Office. She looked around, taking in her surroundings, noticing the pub, The Red Lion, a tall church spire behind some oak trees, a neat row of cottages and a school sign pointing up the road. There was a farmstead with large sheds towards the end of the village and more picturesque houses with long gardens on the opposite side of the road.

Just then an attractive young girl came out of the Post Office. She was pretty, with short dark hair and a happy face. She must be local – it was too early in the day for visitors. Pippa got out of the car and approached the girl. She was friendly and helpful, and without giving too much away, Pippa found out what she wanted to know. She'd got back in her car when she suddenly realized she hadn't found out the name of the people with the stables. She called out to the girl, who was walking away.

"Nickerson," was the reply. Nickerson. Pippa repeated the name to herself. She sat a while, taking in this piece of news. Well – she'd come this far, she might as well continue. She followed the instructions given to her by the attractive young girl. Pippa guessed she'd not be much older than herself. Just as described, she found the large iron gates at the entrance to the long drive but drove straight past. She went a little farther on, then seeing a footpath sign, pulled her mini in at a passing place just beyond it.

'Why not?' she thought. 'After all, it is a public footpath.' She took a dog-lead from the door pocket and got out.

"Come on, Gyp. You must be ready for a run out." Gyp was only too happy to go along with his mistress and bounded out of the car. After attaching the lead to Gyp's collar and locking the car, Pippa stood a while, surveying the scene around her. She took in the patch-work of fields, adorning either side of the wide valley. Her eyes followed the course of the stream in the bottom and noticed copses and thick hedgerows which gave way to dry-stone walls running up to the open moors beyond. Red-tiled farmhouses were dotted intermittently along the reaches of the dale, linked with a series of roads. A large forestry plantation nestled high up in the dale head, with smaller ones situated on the bank sides further down the valley. Tinges of copper and orange showed up in the morning sunlight as some of the trees were just beginning to change colour. She couldn't remember ever seeing any place so beautiful.

Yes, she could settle here. It felt strange, almost like a home-coming. And even if she didn't get the job, it had been worth the journey today. She breathed a big sigh and smiled to herself. She was going to make the most of it. Looking back towards The Grange she could see a new building which she presumed was the stables about which the girl in the village had spoken. What a lovely setting in which to work. Seeing all this definitely influenced Pippa in to making a decision to ring up about the job when she returned home. She set off down the path with Gyp and, once over the style, let him off the lead. It was difficult to guess who enjoyed that walk the more.

Heading back towards Dowerbridge, she decided to call in at the Red Lion for a bite to eat. It was fairly quiet and after giving her order for a round of sandwiches and a coffee, she took a seat by the fire. Sitting opposite was an old gentleman, lean and wiry looking, wearing a flat cap and an ancient pair of corduroy knee breeches. A pipe was resting in the ashtray. He lowered his paper, the Sporting Gazette, and squinted across at Pippa, taking in every aspect of the young girl.

"Not from round here, are you?" he wheezed. Pippa looked up, surprised at his comment.

"No," she replied.

His wrinkled weather-beaten face broke into a smile. "Ride horses then, do you?"

"Oh, I see." She smiled at the old man, realizing he'd noticed the jodhpur boots that she was wearing. "Yes, I do." Thinking he welcomed the company she added, "Have you picked a winner?"

"Not yet. I need a bit more time, then I might."

"There's a good bet running at Wetherby today – 3.15pm," Pippa volunteered. A young girl brought a plate of food and coffee over and Pippa started to eat. "Will you join me for a drink?" she asked.

"That's very kind of you. Pull me another half, Rachel, would you." He held out a gnarled hand to Pippa. "Jack's the name. Jack Watson." Pippa shook his hand firmly, taking a liking to this old man. He looked back at the paper. "Wetherby, you say."

"Yes. Fillies' race. Everon Thyme."

"You could be right there. I used to ride her grandmother."

Pippa's face lit up. "Really – Party Thyme? She produced some lovely horses. Were you a jockey, then?" Pippa asked.

"Aye, till I had one fall too many. Where have you heard about this filly, then?"

"I used to work at the stables where she's trained. Very promising as a two year old, she was. Came third last time out but the track was a bit hard. She prefers a soft going. Has a good chance today." Pippa continued tucking into her sandwiches. She would love to have chatted longer but she needed to get back home. Jack continued to study his paper, letting Pippa get on with her lunch but he laid it down when Pippa stood up to go.

"Glad to have met you, young lady, and thanks for the drink."

"It's been a pleasure, Jack. I must dash now. Maybe we'll meet again," she smiled at him. She went out, turning at the door, but the old fellow was once more engrossed in his paper. Pippa smiled to herself as she drove home, thinking about her chance encounter with Jack Watson. Surely it was another sign that it was meant to be.

Derek was out when she returned home, so she grabbed her overalls and left for her work-place. She had an extra spring in her step as she brought in the horses. She soon had them groomed and content, then hurried home to get tea ready. First, she rang the number from the paper. A well-spoken female answered. Pippa gave her name, stated that she would like to be interviewed for the post advertised in the Herald and then answered a few brief questions. The female at the other end then asked,

"Will Friday be convenient? Neil's not here at the moment but he's seeing two other applicants then, so I'm sure that will be okay."

"Yes, fine. What time?"

"One thirty, if that's all right." Pippa agreed and rang off, trembling with excitement. She was singing along to a well known song on the radio when Derek entered the kitchen.

"You sound happy. Had a good day?"

"Yes Dad, I've had a lovely day. I'll tell you all about it over dinner," she beamed at him.

Friday couldn't come quickly enough for Pippa, but in the Nickerson household it was a different story. It was lunchtime, and Neil was discussing the morning's interviews with his mother and looking extremely fraught.

"We have horses arriving tomorrow and nobody remotely suitable for this job."

"Not even at a pinch?"

"Mother, all the riding that man I saw this morning had done was helping out at a trekking centre. He probably is good with animals but we need someone with more experience than that. He probably didn't know the difference between a snaffle and a pelham!"

His mother laughed. "I think you're being a bit harsh there, Neil. And the girl, or woman, rather?"

"I don't know what kind of place she'd worked in with those fingernails but when I mentioned weekend work she backed off straight away. I got the feeling she just needed to get away – anywhere would do. I can see I'll have to get you out there. Things are getting desperate."

"Thanks very much," Grace replied, laughing. "Seriously, though, it's not that bad, Neil. The two horses arriving tomorrow are both self-livery."

"Thank goodness for that."

"There's still this girl from York this afternoon."

"I can hardly think that she'll have the necessary experience at just twenty-two years of age."

"Well, she sounded very sensible on the 'phone. Anyway, you'll soon find out – she'll be here in half an hour."

Exactly thirty minutes later a red mini pulled up in front of The Grange and Pippa Johnson, dressed in a smart but casual brown trouser suit, knocked on the imposing front door. It was opened by Neil.

"Hello. You must be Pippa." He held out his hand. "I'm Neil." Pippa looked up at the handsome young man, standing in the doorway, and shook his outstretched hand.

"Yes. I spoke to your wife on the 'phone." Neil grinned, making his face altogether younger looking.

"Wife? No, no, that was my mother. Come in, please."

"Oh. She sounded very young." Pippa smiled back at this pleasant young man. He led her through the hallway and down the passage.

"This is my study." He opened a door and ushered her in. "It's not very big but serves its purpose." Pippa followed him into the long narrow room. It was lined with filing cabinets and bookshelves down one side, a window at the end and a work station and bureau on the other side. Neil sat down by the work station.

"Please, take a seat." Pippa sat down on the only other chair.

"Sorry there's not much room. It was the old pantry. I realize you haven't much time today so where shall we start?"

"Can you tell me something about the stables and what my duties would be?" she asked. Neil explained as best he could but as he had little idea of how successful this venture was going to be it wasn't very easy. Pippa listened attentively and asked a few questions as they went along.

"Tell me," Neil said, "why do you want this job?"

Pippa pondered a moment then began. "I'm ready for a new challenge and I think I now have the experience and knowledge to do this job."

"What about your family? You will have to live here, obviously."

"That will be fine."

"Will your parents approve? Your mother?"

"She died a year ago."

Neil looked tenderly at the young girl sitting before him. "I'm so sorry. You must miss her a lot." Pippa looked down at her hands, trying to control her emotions. It was always harder when she knew that the concern shown was genuine. She swallowed hard before replying.

"Yes, I do, but life goes on and this job will be good for me."

Neil smiled, admiring her optimism. "And your father?"

"Oh, he's dead too."

Neil looked appalled. "Pippa, I'm really sorry."

"It's okay. I never knew him. I've had a step-father since I was two." Her face had lightened again.

"Do you get on with him?"

"Oh yes. He's a wonderful father. I love him very much."

"I'm glad." It was Neil's turn to stare at the floor. "I lost my father last year and I know how tough it can be."

"Yes I... " She didn't finish what she'd been going to say. There was a short silence as each was deep in thought. It was broken by a knock on the door and Grace came in with two mugs of coffee on a tray and some buttered scones which she placed between them.

"I thought you both might like a drink."

"Mmm, thanks." Neil stood up. "Mother, this is Pippa Johnson." Grace Nickerson wasn't at all as Pippa had imagined her to be. She took in the slim figure, dressed in navy slacks and pale blue sweater. Her light brown hair was swept back and secured with a banana comb. Pippa rose and took the older woman's hand.

"Hello. Pleased to meet you."

"And you, dear," Grace replied, accepting the firm handshake of the young girl. "Well, I mustn't keep you." She smiled and left the room.

Neil picked up a mug of coffee and took a drink. "Tell me, what experience have you had with horses?" he asked, helping himself to a scone. Pippa went on to tell him how she'd had riding lessons as a child, then about the time she'd spent on the farm during holidays and weekends, not only riding but helping with many other jobs.

"What about machinery?"

"I only drove the tractor a couple of times but I was quite happy on the quad bike. During busy times, like silaging, I was more use in the milking parlour or calf house. They could always use an extra pair of hands in the spring during lambing and I came in very useful when there were pet lambs to feed. My first job when I left school was as a vet's assistant in York but that was mainly small animals and I really wanted to work with horses. Then I got a job in a racing stable. I learned loads there. I left last year, when Mum died, to be nearer

Dad. Since then I've been working for a young couple who live just a mile away, looking after their three event horses. I can clip, too. I've also done quite a bit of hunting."

Neil's delight was evident. This girl seemed to be everything he'd hoped for and more, despite her years. "What about your present employers?"

"I have an arrangement with them. I only took the job on a temporary basis because it was nearer home, until I knew dad was going to be okay. Anyway, I know another girl back at the racing stable who'll be dead keen to take my job if I leave."

Neil couldn't believe his good fortune. He explained about the flat, wages and other necessary details.

"Oh, I just remembered these." Pippa pulled an envelope from her pocket. "My references." She handed them over to Neil. "I've put my details, 'phone number etc. on a sheet in there, too."

"Thank you." He smiled at the young girl. "I'll try and give you a decision as soon as possible," he said, showing Pippa out, "and thank you for coming at such short notice."

Driving back over the moors Pippa was unable to take in how well it had all gone. She felt sure she would be offered this job and had decided that she would certainly accept it. The Grange was such a beautiful old house – not that she would be living there, but it would be wonderful to see the rest of it. She had liked Neil and oddly, it seemed as if she had known him for ages. It was surprising how at ease she had felt in his company. Maybe the fact that he'd had to take on responsibility for the farm when still very young would influence him in his decision about employing her. She hoped so, anyway.

Chapter 17

The next few days went by in a bit of a whirl for Pippa. She had only been in the house ten minutes after returning home from her interview when the 'phone rang. It was Neil, and she could hardly contain her excitement as he invited her over to look round the stables and flat with a view to accepting the position. Her heart was beating just a little bit faster as she hung up, a huge grin on her face. She picked up Gyp in her arms and danced around the room.

"We're going to start a new life on a farm, Gyp, with horses as well. You'll love that, won't you?" He licked her face, which was agreement enough for Pippa. She put him down, realizing she now had calls to make before going to work. She contacted her old workmate at the racing stable and, as expected, she jumped at the chance to take on the job. Pippa's employers were very understanding about her sudden departure and agreed to see the new girl on the Sunday. In the meantime, as this girl would have to work out a week's notice, she contacted another local girl who worked part-time at the local riding school and she agreed to help out.

On Saturday morning she'd had to be up very early to get Rollo and Minstrel ready for her bosses to take cubbing. After mucking out the three boxes and preparing two buckets of bran mash, she'd taken Sceptre out for a two-hour ride. She could have gone cubbing too, but opted for a quiet ride on her own. Her ride was tinged with sadness as she realized that this would probably be the last time she would ride this lovely mare. Still, she would soon be getting to know more, new horses and find different places to ride.

All kinds of thoughts were racing through her head. She kept thinking about Neil, the job and the farm and all the other people that she would be bound to meet. She wondered about the rest of his family. She'd have to look for somewhere to stay until the flat was ready, although Neil had said they would help her find a place.

Back at the stable, she made sure Sceptre was fed and content before cleaning the tack. Pippa then put the prepared mashes into the feed bowls for the other horses and filled their hay racks. Her employers would see to their horses when they returned from hunting. She'd arranged a time the following morning, to meet the local girl who was helping out after Pippa left, to show her around.

Derek's car was out when she got home, which surprised her. He usually shopped on Saturday mornings but was always back by lunchtime and it was now nearly one o'clock. She was upstairs getting changed when she heard the car outside. She crossed to the window in her bedroom and glanced out of the window. Derek was lifting a case from the boot, and standing by the car was a young girl, painfully thin, her long dark hair framing a face drawn and pale.

Pippa's usual happy expression changed to a look of real concern when she saw the new arrival. In all the excitement of her new job she'd forgotten that Sophie was arriving today. Feeling guilty, she rushed downstairs to open the door and welcome her sister home.

Ten minutes later, over a cup of tea, Pippa was explaining to her sister how she had to go out straight away but would be back for dinner. "I've got the rest of the day off and we'll have all evening to catch up."

Sophie was still looking rather forlorn. "Derek told me a bit about your new job coming over but I thought we might at least have had the weekend together."

"We will. I'm not going away till Monday. Look, you unpack and settle in. Perhaps you could help Dad with the dinner later." The look on Sophie's face suggested that that wasn't likely. "Anyway, I must dash now. I'll tell you all about it when I get back." She gave her sister a big hug before leaving. "It's good to have you back, Sophie, isn't it, Dad?" she said, seeking a little support from Derek, who was stirring his tea for the third time.

He glanced up, lost in a world of his own, then smiled apologetically. "Yes, of course. We'll be a family again, won't we? Off you go, Pippa, or you'll be late."

As Pippa was driving north, her thoughts were on her family. She hoped it would help Sophie, and her father, having her sister back home. Maybe it would be better for them both, not having her around and relying on her for support. She hoped so, for she didn't want them to think that she was deserting them through this difficult time. She felt sure this move was the right one for her and through it she would be stronger to help her family.

Her visit to The Grange went very well. Neil took her round the stables, which were now ready for the first horses. The wash-room facility was complete and water bowls were fitted in all the boxes. Feed bins, bags of haylage, straw and hay filled the feed house. Two saddles were on the saddle racks in the tack room, with bridles hanging neatly underneath. Horse blankets were draped over two of the boxes, their owners obviously out in the field.

"Yes, the first two arrived earlier today but they're self-livery," replied Neil to Pippa's enquiry. "One of the owners is coming back later to bring the horses in. They're owned by a couple of friends, working girls, who are going to take turns in coming to see to their horses. Let's go and look at the flat." They climbed the stairs to the new apartment above the tack and feed store, and taking a key from his pocket, Neil unlocked the door.

"This is really nice," exclaimed Pippa, her eyes taking in everything as she wandered through to the small lounge with shower room leading off it.

"Well, it will be, I hope, when we get the kitchen appliances fitted and the carpets down. Hopefully, that will get done this next week." He followed Pippa as she walked across to the window, looking out over the fields and the valley beyond. He smiled at the look of amazement on her face.

"Wow. What a view." She turned to Neil, her face radiant. "I never dreamt that I would ever live somewhere like this. It's beautiful."

"I'm glad you like it and we hope you'll be very happy working here. It does get a bit rough in the winter time but I'm sure you'll manage. C'mon, we'll have a quick look round the farm before we go and see Mother. She's bound to be waiting with the kettle on."

Neil took Pippa outside and showed her the parking area and the fields which would be used for the horses. They could see the two new arrivals on the far side of the five-acre, contentedly grazing.

"Hasn't taken them long to settle in," said Pippa, as they made their way back round to the main yard. Neil explained to his young employee about the shooting on the estate as he showed her the new utility and game larder.

"You might even like to have a go at beating when you get to know a few of the people. I must introduce you to a close friend of mine. Her father's the gamekeeper and she loves to go on the moors when she can. She lives further up the dale." Pippa noticed how his face softened as he spoke about his friend. She would look forward to meeting her. They were now looking round the cattle sheds where all the breeding cows with calves were. Pippa's eyes lit up when she saw these and she asked Neil a string of questions. Her interest and knowledge in the stock was obvious and she finished her enquiries by asking if she could help him when she wasn't busy in the stable.

"I'd be more than happy," beamed Neil. "Especially when it comes to jobs like worming, tagging and hoof treatment. It can be pretty difficult on your own, although, I must add, that mother does come out and help but it's not really work I like her to be doing." They were heading back towards the house and Tess came over towards them, tail wagging as usual, when she saw her master. "Now old girl, here's someone for you to meet," he said, patting his sheep dog. "This is Tess, now retired." Pippa crouched down to be on a level with the dog and let it smell her hand and face before she stroked it.

"I love dogs. Oo, that reminds me. Is it all right for me to have my dog with me in the flat? He's a little Border terrier."

Neil smiled. "Of course. He might catch some of the mice and occasional rats that seem to infest the sheds once the weather grows colder."

"Oh, I'm sure he'd love to oblige," said Pippa, laughing. They'd reached the back door of the house and Neil ushered the young girl into the warm, welcoming kitchen where Grace was waiting to greet them.

"Coffee or tea?"

"Coffee, please," Pippa replied, beaming, unable to disguise how happy she was. Neil pulled a stool out for Pippa and they sat down at the large table. Pippa looked round the big, serviceable room with its beamed ceiling, oak fittings, large window and cooking range. "A real farmhouse kitchen. You have a beautiful house, Mrs. Nickerson."

"Thank you." She smiled at the young girl. "Neil, pass Pippa the biscuit barrel, please. I'm glad you like it because we want to ask you if you'd like a room here until the flat is ready."

Pippa was rather taken aback at this invitation. "I...," she hesitated, unsure of what to say, "I don't want to impose on you. I'd be fine in the village – it's only for a while."

Neil came to her rescue. "You're more than welcome to stay here. There's ample room and it makes sense. It's far better if you're on the job and, as you say, it's not for long. Anyway, Mother's always glad of a little female company, especially someone who appreciates horses." He smiled at Pippa, encouraging her to accept.

"Well, thank you very much."

"Good. That's settled, then. Mother will show you your room before you go and then we'll see you back here on Monday. Did everything go all right with your old employers?"

"Yes. They were a bit disappointed but okay really, and I've been in touch with my replacement, who was over the moon at the opportunity to work for them, so I think it will all work out all right."

After Pippa had left Grace poured herself and Neil another cup of tea.

"I hope you'll relax a bit now," she smiled at her son. "I really like her and I'm sure she'll do fine, despite her age. She's got an old head on her young shoulders."

"Yes, it's strange isn't it, that two days can make such a difference. Sorry if I've been a bit edgy lately." He fell silent, staring into his cup, and without looking up asked, "Did you see Ellen Bentley this morning?"

"Yes, I was talking to her."

"I was wondering when Louise would be back home again."

"Ellen mentioned that there was a wedding at Stavely today, so I don't think Louise will be home at all this weekend." She studied her son, concern on her face. "You could always leave a message for her at work – I know you don't like ringing her there. You won't have any cows calving this week," she added pointedly. "She'll probably have a couple of days off mid-week as usual."

"I would like her to meet Pippa – that's all."

Grace smiled to herself as she piled the mugs into the sink.

Pippa's mind was doing overtime as she travelled back home to York. It was difficult to take everything in – it had all happened so quickly. She couldn't wait to tell dad and Sophie all about the farm and her job, and to think, in two days time she'd be coming back over these moors to start work. She knew Gyp would love it and he would be good company in her flat, once she got moved in.

Sophie seemed a little brighter over dinner and took an interest in all that Pippa had to tell. After the meal, when the girls were washing the dishes, Derek offered to take Gyp for a stroll, leaving the sisters to have a chat on their own.

"Dad needs you now, Sophie, so you will have to try and be cheerful for his sake." They'd finished the pots and were sitting in the comfy lounge, curtains drawn and a blazing fire in the hearth. It had turned decidedly chilly on an evening and the nights were pulling in fast.

"It's easier for you Pippa. You didn't lose your dad as well."

"Yes, I did."

"Well, yes you did but you don't remember him, like I do. You weren't even born when Daddy died and now Mum's gone as well." Her voice was breaking and she turned to Pippa for comfort. Pippa put her arms round the dejected girl as she sobbed uncontrollably. Sophie was right in a way. You couldn't really grieve for someone you'd never known. It would have been nice to have known him though.

"You won't always feel this way. You will get better – I know you will – and Dad and I are here to help you."

"You won't be. You're going away," she managed between sobs.

"It's not far and I'll be home on my days off. When I get settled in and into a routine you'll be able to come and stay a night or two with me in the flat. It's really nice. C'mon, we don't want Dad to see you this upset." Sophie pulled several tissues from the box by her side and blew her nose loudly.

"What would there be for me to do? You know I hate animals." She dried the tears from her face.

"It's beautiful – hills and valleys, woods and streams and just so peaceful. It will probably inspire you to start painting again, the scenery is so lovely."

Sophie cheered up a bit at that. She loved her drawing and painting. "Do you think so?" she asked, a weak smile breaking on her tired face. She sat up straight and tucked her long hair behind her ears. "I do want to get better, Pippa, honestly. It's just some days I don't seem to care whether I live or not, and life seems so futile. I miss Mummy so."

Pippa gave her sister a squeeze. "I do, too, but you know, she wouldn't want to see you so sad like this, would she? And it's really hard for Dad as well. You know how much he loved Mum."

"Yes." She raised her shoulders, letting them drop with a big sigh. "I'm being really selfish, aren't I? I will try, Pippa, honestly, and the doctor did tell me it would take a while for the pills to help. You're always so strong and supportive and I don't help you at all."

Pippa smiled at her sister. "Yes you do. Helping you helps me. Don't you see? We all need each other. C'mon, Dad will be back soon. Go and wash your face and then we'll plan somewhere nice to go tomorrow afternoon. All three of us – well, four with Gyp."

Chapter 18

Louise hadn't time to dwell on her disappointment of missing out on an evening with Neil for long, for back at work the next day things were very busy. One of the waitresses was off sick and Louise had to juggle the rota in order to make sure there would be plenty of staff on duty for the weekend. Friday was pretty hectic, with preparations for the wedding in full swing. When Louise came on duty at nine there was no sign of Pearl. When Eddy appeared he muttered some excuse about a headache, so Louise had to check out the guests who were leaving. Every available room had been booked for wedding guests and two needed baby accommodation, meaning that cots had to be assembled in those rooms. As soon as she could leave reception, she went off to find the chamber maids and instruct them about these arrangements.

At mid-morning, workmen arrived to put up the marquee adjoining the fire doors of the restaurant, and there appeared to be general confusion everywhere. Louise took her morning coffee through to the bar to discuss the wedding with Aiden, who also had come in early. He straightened from his task of restocking the bottles in the cooler and gratefully accepted the mug of coffee she'd brought him.

"You look slightly harassed this morning, Louise. What's the problem?" Louise perched herself on a bar stool and explained to him about Pearl.

"Just when we needed all hands on deck," she finished.

"She'll soon be back. She'll have had a tiff with Eddy but it won't last long. They often have a flare-up when things get a bit hectic, then she retreats into her shell."

"Very funny," Louise grinned at him. "I wish she hadn't chosen today." After five minutes of discussing final arrangements, Louise drained her mug, jumped off the stool and went to see Pièrre in the kitchen.

It was later in the day when she was back in reception, booking in wedding guests, that her thoughts drifted back to The Grange. Today was the day that Neil was giving interviews for the stable job. She would love to have rung him to find out how they had gone but knew she'd have to wait. Maybe she'd call in on Sunday.

Unfortunately for Louise, Sunday seemed almost as busy as the two previous days, with guests leaving and all the clearing up to do after the wedding. She had so little free time that it wasn't worth the trip up to Dowerdale, so she decided instead, to pop round to the nursing home to visit her Gran .

Louise did have a nice surprise later in the evening when she was busy laying breakfast tables in the residents' lounge, after the evening meals had been served, when Emma burst in through the door, her face beaming.

"Louise Bentley, you sly creature."

Louise stopped what she was doing, surprised at this outburst.

"What d'you mean? What have I done?"

"Done? What *haven't* you done! You never told me about that absolutely gorgeous hunk of a man at the restaurant bar who's asking for *you*. 'Tell her I'll be in the main bar for a while, if you would,' he said to me, in a broad Irish accent. Is he your boyfriend?"

Louise couldn't help blushing, knowing it could only possibly be one person. "No, we're just friends. He works with my Dad," Louise added, as if that explained everything.

Emma stood there, hands on hips, grinning at her work-mate. "Well, if I had the chance I'd be happy to be more than 'just friends' with him. Go on then. Off you go and see what he wants." Emma held open the door and waved Louise through. "And don't forget, I would love an introduction."

Louise found Tony by the bar, pint in hand. It wasn't too crowded as she made her way towards him. She spotted Roger with some other lads talking close by. She spoke as casually as she could.

"Hello there. This is a surprise. Didn't think you came into this sort of place."

"Oh. And what sort of place should I go to?" he asked, a twinkle in his smiling blue eyes. Seeing her lost for a reply, he went on to explain. "I've been with the lads playing darts up at the Rugby Club."

"I didn't know you played."

"I play most games," he grinned. "They were one short and it was a cup round. I go with them sometimes so they asked me to play." He took a drink from his glass, then, looking back at Louise, smiled that engaging smile. "I was wondering if you fancied a night out. Roger has four tickets for the Hunt Ball, only something's cropped up and the other couple can't go. He wondered, seeing as we'd all had a good night together at Layton, if you fancied going?" Louise was rather taken by surprise. This was quite unexpected and had caught her unawares. She didn't know what to say.

"I'm… er, not sure what shift I'm on," she managed.

"Well, I'm sure in your position you'll be able to work something out. How about it?" Why not, she thought. After all, Neil hadn't asked her.

"Okay. I'll see what I can do. Are you staying long, because I'll have a word with Emma, now?"

"Would that be the attractive redhead I spoke to?" he grinned at Louise.

"Yes, that's the one." Remembering Emma's parting shot she added, "I must introduce you to her. I'm sure you'll like her."

"Oh, I'm sure I will," he teased.

Later in bed she found sleep difficult as she thought about her decision to go to the Hunt Ball with Tony. Part of her was excited at the prospect but also she wasn't sure if this was the road she wanted to go down. Oh well, one dance wasn't a life threatening move, was it? It meant she'd forfeited a full weekend off, as she'd swapped Friday night with Emma. Still, she'd have Saturday and Sunday off as well as her mid-week break.

Next day, she had a couple of hours off in the afternoon and decided to go into town. She would have to have a new dress. It was ages since she'd worn a long dress and she had nothing in her wardrobe suitable for such an occasion. She was studying the contents in the window of one of the more expensive stores in town when she jumped in fright as a familiar voice spoke behind her.

"Going somewhere special then?"

"Richard, you frightened the life out of me." She laughed as he gave her a big hug. "No, well… yes, but not in one of these. Far too expensive."

"You're going to the Hunt Ball, aren't you? Don't tell me. I can guess. The handsome gamekeeper. You said you weren't going out together," he accused her.

Louise wished she didn't blush so, every time Tony's name cropped up. "We aren't. It's just Roger had two spare tickets and offered them to Tony."

"Lulu, you say anything. By the way, have you heard who Melanie got her tickets for?"

"No. Don't *you* know?"

Richard shook his head. "Tell you what I *do* know though. I was on the 'phone to mother last night and they've started a girl at the stables. Sounds very interesting, so you might have to fight for lover-boy Tony if he takes a fancy to her." He dodged out of the way as Louise threatened to punch him.

"You're incorrigible. Well, I must be getting back to work."

"Me too. See you at the dance, if not before." He gave Louise a hug and kiss on the cheek. "Take care."

"You, too. 'Bye." She watched him dodging the traffic as he crossed the road and disappeared among the shoppers. He seemed so happy with the world. Marriage obviously suited him. She realized, in that moment, something that had just been a vague notion in her head before. She would like to find that kind of happiness, that kind of love that Richard and Sue shared. It rather shocked her, admitting such a thing to herself, but she realized that true fulfilment in life would only come when she could share all the things she loved to do and see with someone else.

When Louise finished work the following night it was too late to call at The Grange so she went straight home.

She had just finished dressing the next morning when the 'phone rang.

"Louise, are you up? 'Phone for you," her mother called up the stairs.

"Coming." She ran down the stairs in her stocking feet and picked up the receiver.

"Hello?"

"Louise, it's Neil. I was wondering if you were coming down to ride today."

"I was hoping to. I was going to ring but you've beaten me to it. What time shall I come?"

"As soon as you like. There's someone I want you to meet and Mother wants a word with you, as well."

"Fine. I'll be there within the hour."

"Great. 'Bye for now."

"'Bye." She hung up just as her mother came through with a pile of freshly ironed clothes to take upstairs.

"You look happy. Take these up if you're going back up, please, love."

"Sure. Oh, thanks Mam for doing my ironing." She took the laundered clothes from her mother. "Yes, I'm going riding again. I understand they've got a stable manager now."

"Yes. Grace seemed quite impressed when I saw her Saturday morning. I believe she was starting last Monday."

"Well, I'm bound to meet her, so I hope she's nice."

True to her word Louise was coming down the long drive to The Grange within the hour. The morning sunlight was sparkling through the leaves on the tall horse chestnut trees lining the road – no longer green but wonderful shades of orange, copper and yellow. She pulled up in the yard and, as she did so, noticed a girl wearing a denim jacket over jeans and sweatshirt, coming across the yard from the direction of the stables. There was something familiar about her. Louise got out of the car and as she got a closer look at the girl, who was heading towards her, she remembered where she'd seen her. It was the girl she'd met in the village a while back. The new-comer must have recognized Louise also because she smiled and came towards her, holding out a hand.

"Hello. We meet again. You must be Louise."

Louise was rather surprised that this girl should know her name. As if reading her thoughts the girl added, "Neil told me you were coming to ride." Louise took the outstretched hand.

"Yes, I'm Louise but you have the advantage over me." Just at that moment Neil came out of the house and came over to the two girls.

"I see you've already met. Hello, Louise." He smiled warmly at his friend. "I want you to meet Pippa, my new stable manager." Turning to Louise he said, "And this, of course, is Louise." Neil continued, "I told Pippa that you were coming to ride and that it might be nice if you could go out together."

Louise looked stunned. Manager? But she looked so young. Louise was still trying to take in this news about the girl. She had got it completely wrong. Trying to recover her composure, she again offered her hand.

"I'm very pleased to meet you. I'd be more than happy to ride out with you when it's convenient." Pippa shook her hand firmly for the second time. If she'd noticed Louise's confused expression she wasn't letting it show.

"Well, actually, we were hoping you might come with me today, as I have a horse to take out and Neil says you know all the tracks and bridleways. It would be a great help if you could show me round a bit." Louise couldn't help but notice the casual use of Christian names. Neil confirmed what Pippa had just said.

"Yes, and it's almost thanks to you Louise. Alistair Colleridge rang at the weekend and brought his new hunter over yesterday. He needs full livery for the horse and wants Pippa to take complete charge of it, so he'll need exercising almost daily." He casually put his arm round Louise's shoulder, a happy, relaxed expression on his face. "I know how you like to get up on the moors and there's no-one better to show Pippa around. It will give you two the chance to get to know one another." He said this as if it was important to him.

"Well, I'd better go and get Star in then," Louise replied, smiling up at him.

"She's already in," Neil told her. "I went and brought her up for you after our 'phone call, so you'll soon be able to go."

Louise turned to Pippa. "Let's get started then," she smiled at the newcomer.

Neil walked over to the old buildings with Louise where Star was stabled. "I hope you didn't mind me dropping you in for it like that but it will be such a help for Pippa. You looked unsure."

"Not at all. I will enjoy showing her the area. I was just surprised that she was your new manager. I don't know why. I expect I was imagining it would be someone older." They had reached the buildings and Louise collected the old wooden tack box to take into the little stable. Neil watched Louise as she started to brush the mud from Star's back and neck. He seemed in no hurry to get back to work.

"Yes, she is young but seems very capable and loves what she's doing. I hope she settles here. Well, I must go. Haven't finished feeding up yet. You will call in to see Mother when you get back, won't you?"

Louise paused in her brushing to turn and smile at Neil. "Yes, of course," she replied.

Neil started to walk away then turned as he reached the doorway. "I do hope you get on well together, and oh, do you think we might have that dinner sometime?" He looked very young and vulnerable, silhouetted against the bright sunlight, his hair slightly ruffled in the breeze. Louise was touched by what she saw. He'd had so much to organize and take on lately that he often looked much older than he was. Perhaps the way he was this morning had something to do with the arrival of his new stable manager. It reminded her of that day in this very building all those years ago when he'd been a self-conscious fourteen year old, unable to express the joy and emotion he'd felt that day. She had a sudden urge to give him a big hug but instead went over to him and laid her hand on his arm.

"Yes. I'd like that."

Chapter 19

It was a glorious morning and the overnight frost was lifting fast. It would be good to have company on her ride and share some of her favourite places with this girl, for despite not knowing her, she couldn't help liking her. The feeling that she'd seen her somewhere before was still there in her head. Maybe after their ride today it would come to her.

Louise was mounted and waiting when Pippa trotted across the yard to join her on a big, dark bay gelding, his black mane and tail glistening in the sunlight. Star's head went up when she saw him and whinnied a loud 'hello' to the newcomer. The bay nickered softly in response. Pippa let the big horse come close to Star so that they could sniff noses, a horse's way of acceptance. Star squealed out in excitement, happy to have a companion. She hadn't been out with another horse for a long time.

"I think they're going to get on fine," laughed Louise. "What's he called?"

"Murphy. Probably because he was bred in Ireland."

Soon the girls were making their way down the track at the edge of the big field to the stream. Star was full of herself, showing off to this new arrival on her territory. Louise was pleased she'd had a few rides before today, as the old horse was prancing about like a five year old. By the time they reached the ford at the bottom she had started to settle down and Louise began to relax more. She watched Pippa, looking very confident, as the big bay splashed his way through the water.

"Have you ridden him before?"

"I did get on him in the yard yesterday when Mr. Colleridge brought him. I couldn't see any point really but he insisted. I think he just wanted to see if I was really as capable as I said I was."

"I can well believe that."

"You've met him, then?" asked Pippa.

"Just the once. Can't say that I was impressed."

"No, me neither but time will tell."

They had climbed up one of the many steep tracks leading on to the open moor. The air was cool even though the sun was shining. Pippa stopped and gazed in wonder at the vast expanse of open moorland stretching out before them.

"It's amazing, isn't it? And can you ride over any of it?" she asked, wide eyed.

Louise laughed, realizing that she was going to have to teach this girl a lot about the moors. "Only when you're hunting and then you have to know your terrain. There are many treacherous peat bogs and you have to learn and recognize where it's safe to ride. When you're out exercising stick to the well-marked bridleways until you become familiar with the area. We'll cut across here."

She led the way down a sheep track, pointing out the sieves where it was wet, the red grasses, which only grow where it's very damp, and onto a patch of burnt ling. Here, the horses sank into the ground up to their fetlocks.

"This is just the edge of a peat bog. Don't go any further Pippa – you'll never get back out. Come on, we'll go back where it's safe. There are vast areas where it's like that and sometimes there's no warning."

They rode back through a bilberry bed and paused on a stretch of heather littered with grey rocky outcrops and stones. Pippa stood looking around, listening to everything that Louise was telling her and trying to remember it all. This was a whole new world to her but one that she felt sure she was going to love.

"It all looks so flat and the same from the roads. I had no idea what it was really like. I love it though and want to get to know it all. It must feel amazing to gallop over places like this where you know it's safe." She paused, gazing round the miles and miles of wild open country.

Louise watched her, thinking how fortunate she herself had been. It was difficult to realize what it must be like to have lived in a world without all of this. It had always been there in her life. Louise studied the young girl, noticing the broad shoulders, sitting straight yet relaxed, totally at home in the saddle. Her short hair was completely hidden beneath her riding hat. She could have been taken for a boy.

Pippa, face radiant, suddenly turned her head and smiled at Louise. "You will come out with me again, won't you? I have so much to learn."

Louise smiled and readily agreed. They crossed to a track that took them back along the edge of the ridge overlooking the dale and Louise pointed out certain landmarks and roads, helping Pippa to get a picture in her mind of the valleys and moors. They took a track leading down to a small stream in the bottom and Louise found the place where they used to cross over when they were children. It was stony in the bottom and not very deep. The horse's shoes clattered on the stones, ringing out clear in the still air.

"You must have ridden a lot to know it all so well," Pippa remarked.

"Well, you learn to look out for different things, like these mountain ash trees. I know the crossing is where those three grow close together. You can pick them out from up on the ridge. And see that stunted pine up there on its own? Well, we climb out just to the left of it." They started to make their way up the side of the little valley on a narrow track. Some of the bracken in the bottom was still green but most was now a golden brown. They reached the top where the track widened and rode along side by side. As they rode, Pippa asked Louise about her background and family.

"I have one brother but he's much older than me and works away so it's been more like being an only child. I suppose that's why I spent so much time down at The Grange."

"You're very close to Neil, I can see that. Were there other children?"

"Yes, he has a sister, Kathy, the eldest. I suppose she was like a big sister to me. I missed not having a sister. She's married to a doctor and they have two children. And there's Richard." She smiled as she thought of him. "He's one of my best friends."

"Do you go out with him?" Pippa asked curiously.

Louise laughed. "No. He's just got married!"

Pippa laughed then. "Serves me right for asking too many questions." She paused awhile, then had another question for Louise. "You would know Mr. Nickerson then. I understand from Neil that he died just last year."

"Yes, it was very sudden." Louise's face grew sad.

Pippa pondered a moment before continuing. "What was he like?"

"I didn't see much of him after I went away to college, as I usually took a summer job in the holidays but he was hard working, a good business man and well respected in the area. He loved his family. He often played cricket with the boys when he had time and went to watch their matches when he could."

"Did he ride?"

"Yes. He used to hunt a bit, years ago, when the hounds were in this area, but it was Grace who taught them all to ride."

They were each deep in their own thoughts as they rode along. Presently Louise spoke. "I don't know how they all coped with it. I've been so lucky in my life. Do you have family?"

Pippa avoided Louise's questioning look. "I have one sister. Come on. Can we canter on this bit?"

"Okay, as far as the shooting butts, then we have to turn off."

"Shooting butts? What are they?"

"I'll explain when we get there," shouted Louise over her shoulder as she squeezed Star into a canter.

There was no more talk of families during the rest of the ride but Pippa did tell Louise about the other places where she'd worked and how happy she was to be at The Grange. A pair of startled grouse flew out from the heather close by and winged their way low across the moor.

"Were they grouse?" asked Pippa.

"Yes. They're nearly always in pairs, apart from a short time in the winter when they form packs." As they trotted along Louise pointed out more farms and where there were bridleways. "Can you see that pinewood over there?" She was pointing right across the valley. "And that house a field below? That's where my parents live. Dad's the head 'keeper on the Estate. It's owned by Colonel Barrington and includes several farms as well as lots of these moors. He doesn't own The Grange but has the shooting rights on the farm and the Nickersons' other farms. You might see the shooting party on Saturday because they'll be going to the utility for lunch. Neil's mother sees to them."

"Will you be there? Neil said you go on the moor."

"That's the grouse shooting on the moor. It's finished for this year. No, this is pheasant shooting and partridges – in the woods and fields. Alistair is the Colonel's nephew and was out with them last time. That's how I met him, when they all came back to Stavely Manor, where I'm working, for dinner."

"He's going cubbing on Saturday but they'll be finished by ten, so he must be joining the shooting later."

"I don't think he's a full member of the shoot – I think he just goes as his uncle's guest sometimes."

The girls were almost back at The Grange and Pippa was saying how much she'd enjoyed herself. "I've never had the chance to ride anywhere like this. There are two more horses coming at the weekend and sometimes they'll be to take out, so another time maybe you can ride one of those and we can go on a longer ride."

"If my riding's up to it. I know this has been about far enough for Star. She does very well for her age. I'm off at the weekend so maybe we could ride out again on Sunday."

"That would be great. Thanks very much for riding with me."

They were back in the yard and Louise was dismounting. Pippa watched, thinking how lucky she'd been to meet Louise. She was glad Louise was a friend of Neil's. The way Louise talked it seemed as though she was almost one of the family. Pippa smiled to herself as she made her way back to the stables.

An hour later Louise pulled into the yard at home. She picked up some bags from her car and went in to find her mother, for once sitting down with a cup of tea.

"You've had a long ride. I've had my lunch. You must be starving."

"Yes, I am." She put the bags onto a chair and went to switch the kettle on.

"What have you got there?"

"It's some riding clothes that were Kathy's. Grace gave them to me. She found them when she was sorting the jumble out last week. She thought I might as well have the use of them as they were too good to throw out. We had a lovely ride today."

"We?"

"Yes. I met the new manageress, Mam, and we rode together. I got quite a shock – she's ever so young."

"How young?"

"Well, younger than me, I should think."

"You're a manageress." She smiled at her daughter.

"True. Anyway, she's really nice and a very good rider. We got on really well and she wants me to go out with her again – to show her round the moors and bridleways."

"You haven't got that much free time, dear."

"No, I know I haven't but I'm off this weekend so we're hoping to go on Sunday." She made herself a sandwich while she chatted with her mother. "Dad's not burning today, then?"

"No, he's picking up over at Barnwell. I think Tony's gone as well. You must be a good teacher 'cause your Dad was very pleased with the charts of last year's burning that he's done."

Louise brought her sandwich and coffee and sat at the table. She considered telling her Mam about the Hunt Ball but decided against it. Instead, she just smiled saying, "Well, he was a good pupil."

"What time are you back at work tomorrow?"

"Not until six. Why?"

"We're decorating the church for the Harvest Thanksgiving Service in the afternoon, if you'd like to help. I'm picking Grace up after lunch."

"Yes, I'd like to help. It's years since I did that. I used to love it when we children went from school and did our window – pulling all those flower heads off and sticking them in the moss."

Next morning Louise helped her mother to clean all the vegetables that her father had brought in from the garden for the church. There were beetroots, leeks, carrots and parsnips. They packed them all in the boot of the car and after lunch set off down the dale.

When they arrived at The Grange, Ellen asked Louise to go in and help Grace to carry all her flowers out. The back door was open, and when Louise knocked before going in she could hear laughter and voices coming from the kitchen. It was Neil's voice that called "Come in," and much to Louise's surprise as she walked in, she found Pippa and Neil sitting at the kitchen table, obviously having just eaten lunch. Neil jumped up when Louise entered the kitchen.

"Louise, hello. I thought it was your mother – coming to pick Mother up." Louise was still trying to take in this situation, wondering why Pippa was eating lunch with Neil. He must have read her thoughts, for he went on to explain. "Pippa is living with us temporarily, until her flat's ready. Hopefully, by the weekend. I thought you knew. They've promised to have the kitchen completed by tomorrow and they're fitting the carpets on Saturday morning."

Louise didn't know what to say. "I... er... didn't know. That was very kind of your mother." She managed a smile. "Is she ready? I've come with Mam to pick her up."

"I'll go tell her. She's probably picking a few more flowers." He disappeared, leaving Louise alone with Pippa who looked very much at home in the large kitchen. She smiled at Louise.

"Neil was telling me stories about what you used to get up to when you were young. You must have had a wonderful childhood.

"Yes, we did."

"I'd better get back to work. Are we still okay for Sunday?"

"Yes, I hope so."

"Good. I'll see you then." She stood up, took her jacket from the back of her chair and went out, giving Louise a broad smile as she did so. Just then Neil came back down the hallway, finding Louise alone.

"She's coming." He paused a moment before going on. "Pippa says you're off work at the weekend. Do you fancy going to the service and then going out for dinner on Saturday night?"

Chapter 20

It took the ladies longer than anticipated to decorate the church and Louise had a bit of a rush to get to work on time. She only saw Eddy briefly that evening, when he asked her to come to his office the following morning. Next day, after helping to serve residents' breakfasts, Louise made two mugs of coffee and went along to Eddy's office, wondering what this was about. They usually had their meetings on a Monday.

"Come in, come in, Louise." He took a pen from the holder and watched it as he twisted it round and round in his fingers.

"Good morning, Eddy. I've brought you a coffee."

"Thank you, thank you. Sit down, please." Louise sat down at the desk and eventually Eddy stopped fiddling with things and sat down opposite. He picked up his coffee and took a sip, then put the mug back down and started rubbing his chubby hands, nervously. Without looking directly at Louise, he started to speak.

"I'm afraid I have some bad news for you. I had a letter from your predecessor yesterday and her mother has made a very good recovery. The operation went well and things were not as serious as at first thought."

"Oh well, that's good news," said Louise cheerfully.

"Yes, yes, it is… but she has asked if she can come back to work as soon as possible." He looked up then, apologetically. "I really can't keep you both on, you see."

"No, of course. I realize that. After all, I knew it was only a temporary job when I agreed to work for you."

"I'm so sorry it's happened so soon but am glad you see it this way. You really have done a splendid job for us here and for that we're very grateful."

"When would you like me to finish?"

"Next weekend, I'm afraid. I will, of course, pay you any holiday money that you have due."

Louise left the office feeling a little shocked. She'd known it was only a short term job but it had ended a bit suddenly. Oh well, she'd enjoyed it while it had lasted. She hoped her father would be right about one door closing and another opening. There was one bright side to it – she would have more time to ride and help out at the stables. It was late when she finished work that night and as she'd had a drink in the bar with some of the staff when everything was done, she stayed at the hotel for the night.

Next morning, on the way home, she decided to call at The Grange and tell Neil her news. It was a miserable morning, damp and drizzly, as she drove up the valley. There was a black saloon in the yard, which she recognized as Colin's. Louise wondered if that meant Melanie was back from London. Before she had time to get out of her car everything seemed to start happening at once. The quad bike, with the trailer on behind, arrived in the yard bearing Neil and Pippa, looking very damp and bedraggled in working clothes but they looked happy enough, laughing and talking as they jumped off. Just then a Land Rover came screeching to a halt close to it and a rather muddy, irate Alistair in riding clothes jumped out, slammed the door and marched up to Pippa.

"My horse is in his box and needs seeing to," he barked. His face, crimson with rage, was streaked with mud and his breeches looked wet and very dirty. It was obvious that he'd taken a fall. Pippa, regaining her composure, answered him before turning and heading for the stables.

"I'll see to him straight away, Mr. Colleridge."

"Wait a minute, girl," he shouted at her retreating figure.

Pippa turned in her tracks. "Yes, Mr. Colleridge?"

"I need that stupid animal clipping for the opening meet next week."

At this point Neil intervened. "I'm afraid that clipping is not included in your charges, Alistair, but I'm sure that if you are happy to pay Pippa the going rate she'll be able to oblige you."

Alistair looked as if he was about to explode but managed to calm himself and agree to this in a most ungracious tone. Pippa then left to go, just as Melanie appeared from the house looking completely out of place in white trousers and a blue velvet jacket. When Alistair saw her, his whole expression changed. Melanie, however, was heading for Neil and met him as he walked towards the house.

"Neil, darling, I thought you were never coming back. What have you been doing? You're filthy. Your mother said you'd only be a few minutes."

"Sorry. It took longer than I thought." By this point Alistair had joined them, his foul mood forgotten, and demanded to be introduced to this delightful creature. Neil obliged and made his excuses, heading for the back door. Suddenly he stopped and called back to the unfortunate rider, who was now turning all his attention on Melanie. "You can use the utility if you want to clean up before you join the shoot. And your uncle says you'll find them over in Ing's Dell."

Louise decided now was the time to get out of the car and she followed Neil into the house. "That was a very interesting scene," she grinned at Neil.

"I didn't realize that you were still in your car. I thought you were in the house when I saw the car parked there."

"I'd only just arrived before you and Pippa."

"She would have been at the stable waiting but Alistair wasn't due back just yet and I had a problem over in the far pasture and Pippa offered to help." He was filling the kettle and getting two mugs ready for coffee as he told Louise his story.

"Nothing serious, I hope?"

"Yes and no. One of the cows that was supposed to be three months in calf has come over and was a-bulling, causing havoc. She'd smashed through a hedge and got mixed up with the heifers."

"Will you get her served again?"

"No. She'll have to go. It was going to be her last calf anyway. She's getting on a bit and was light in a quarter so it's not serious."

"What about the hedge?"

"Well, we patched it up temporarily. It's like a lot of other jobs that I never got done this year. The whole lot wants seeing to. I seem to have more work than I can manage at times."

Louise suddenly had a thought. "Can I help at all?"

Neil smiled with affection at her. "No, but thanks. I'll get caught up eventually. Anyway, you've got a job."

"Not anymore I haven't." She went on to tell Neil her news about work.

He was disappointed for her but seemed happy that she wanted to ride more. "Pippa will be pleased and it will mean she might have a bit of time to help me. She's real keen on the farming side." They finished their drink and as Louise was about to go, a thought struck her.

"Where's your Mam?"

"It was a bit chaotic here this morning. As the Colonel pulled up to tell her what time they would want lunch, the fitters arrived to put the carpets down in the flat, so she had to go down there. She was going to the village after that to pick up the bread buns for the shoot lunch.

Colin said he'd go with her. I thought Melanie would have gone with them but she preferred to stay here. Says she wants to help outside. I think I might have to lend her some overalls and wellies."

Louise couldn't really see that lasting for long. Time would tell. "Are we still okay for tonight?" she asked.

"Yes. Why?"

"I just thought, with Melanie being back..." she faltered.

Neil gave her a puzzled look. "Come to church in your dad and mam's car and I'll run you home later on. I've booked us a table over at Langton Hall."

Louise could see he was keen to get on so she made for the door. "See you tonight, then?"

"Yes, barring any more mishaps."

Melanie was still talking to the unfortunate rider as Louise drove away from the house. As she went past the entrance to the stables she noticed another Land Rover and trailer in the large car park. It must, she supposed, be the other horses arriving that Pippa had mentioned. When she arrived home her mother told her there were two letters for her. Louise picked them up off the sideboard and recognizing the hand-writing of Kate, her friend in Keswick, went upstairs to read it. The other was printed and didn't look important.

She curled up in her cozy chair by the window and opened Kate's letter. It was full of news about her old workplace. The alterations were going really well and were on schedule. The hotel would be re-opening fully in early December and everyone was looking forward to that. She wanted to know what Louise was up to and how life back in the dale had gone. Louise smiled to herself as Kate brought her up to date with all the bits of gossip concerning some of the other staff members. Kate finished off wanting to know if Louise had had any offers of work abroad and if not, had Louise time for a visit to Keswick? She replaced the letter in the envelope, resolving to write back as soon as possible. Now that her job was ending she might just find time to have a drive back over to the Lakes to visit Kate.

Louise was still thinking about Kate and the others at the King's Head as she picked up the official looking envelope and opened it. Her eyes widened in astonishment when she read through the short letter. It was from the agency in London offering her a supply position in Italy for a period of six weeks. The location was in a hotel on the outskirts of Rome, and as she would be covering leave for other staff it meant not coming back until after Christmas.

Louise stared out of the window at the dull, grey, damp morning and tried to picture what it would be like in Rome at this time of year. Her mind was in turmoil. Part of her was very excited at the thought of being in a beautiful bustling city like Rome, yet she felt something inside tugging at her to stay. There were so many things to consider and only a few days in which to come to a decision. The agency had asked for a reply within the week. Louise was glad she was going out with Neil that night and would be able to discuss it all with him. She went downstairs to tell her mother about the sudden changes in her circumstances.

Later that evening, after the service, she settled herself in Neil's car for the ride over to Langton Hall. She was looking forward to her evening out. Langton Hall was one of those beautiful aristocratic houses that had opened up to the public to pay for the expensive upkeep of such an old building. Louise had never been before but had heard that it had an excellent reputation. She'd decided to wait until they were settled with their meal before telling Neil about her two letters. Instead, she asked him how his day had gone.

"Melanie didn't stay around long. Colin decided they'd better be getting back. He hadn't realized that mother had the lunches to do and felt they would just be in the way. Pippa came over and had lunch with me after she'd sorted out Alistair's horse and the new arrivals."

"Are they full livery, too?"

"No, just part. Then I had a call this evening from another customer and they're bringing their horse over tomorrow."

"Is Pippa going to manage all this on her own? When does she get any time off?"

"I've been thinking about that. She's been with us a while now and doesn't seem to have had any time off yet." He laughed before continuing. "She says most of it's not really like working – she's enjoying it all so much."

"I know someone who would love to come and help out part time."

"Someone local?"

"Yes. Mam was telling me. It's Joan Horton's daughter, Rachael. Joan had mentioned it to Mam at the WI meeting last week. Rachael left school this year and has been doing part time work at the Red Lion with her mam. From what Mam gathers from Joan, she's horse mad. Can't ride but would love to learn."

"Might be worth asking Pippa what she thinks. I feel she ought to have some time off but when I spoke to her about it she just said she'd come and help me instead."

They pulled up in the car park and Neil ushered Louise through the large wooden doors where an attendant greeted them warmly.

"Good evening, Mr. Nickerson. Lovely to see you."

Louise hadn't realized that Neil was known here. They went through to a cozy lounge with a small cocktail bar in one corner. When Louise was seated Neil went to get them both a drink and the waiter brought the menu to them.

"This is very nice. I hadn't realized you'd been before," said Louise, as Neil seated himself next to her on the settee.

"I brought Mother after Dad died. We've been back a few times."

Soon their order was taken and it wasn't long before they were shown to their table in the dimly lit dining room. Their meal was excellent, as expected, and it wasn't until their coffee arrived that Louise began her story.

"I'm still rather in shock over it all and can't decide what to do. I knew my job at Stavely was only temporary but I'd given up on the trip abroad."

"But you still want to go, don't you?"

"I don't know. Sometimes I think I do and then I'm not sure. After yesterday I was looking forward to riding more and... oh, I don't know. What do you think I should do?" She looked up and faced him but he was concentrating on stirring his coffee and she couldn't read his expression. After what seemed like ages he looked up and smiled at her.

"I can't advise you, Louise. It wouldn't be fair. After all, if you decide not to go it might be something you'll regret later. I'm sure that whatever you decide to do, things will turn out right." He reached across the table and squeezed her hand. "After all, six weeks isn't that long, is it?"

Chapter 21

Next morning Louise awoke early and lay thinking about the previous evening. She was still no nearer coming to a decision. Neil hadn't mentioned the Hunt Ball so she hadn't either. He had asked that, if she decided to go to Rome, could they go out again together before she went. When he'd dropped her off at home he'd hugged her warmly and kissed her lightly on the cheek, thanking her for a lovely evening. She jumped out of bed. Maybe a good ride up on the moors would help her make up her mind.

When she arrived at The Grange, Pippa was waiting in the yard.

"I recognized your car coming down the drive. I've got Star down at the stables. Neil thinks she ought to be in at nights now, so I said I'd see to her. One job less for him to do. We've plenty of boxes and it's no trouble to me to clean out an extra one. I brought her in last night." She had a big grin on her face as she told Louise all this. "Get your riding stuff and then come down. I want to show you the new horses."

Louise collected her boots and hat from the house and went down to the stables. After viewing the new arrivals the girls soon tacked up the horses they were riding and were ready to go. Although it was not as damp as the previous day it was still very blustery. Louise led them on a different route up the opposite side of the dale. She wanted to show Pippa as much as she could, especially if she was going away. It was difficult holding much of a conversation when they were up on the moor tops because of the wind. It wasn't until they dropped down into the forestry plantation that they could have a chat.

"You must have a coffee with me when we get back."

"Have you moved in?"

"Yes, yesterday afternoon. I love it. I'm going home this afternoon for an hour and bringing my dog back."

"What sort is it?"

"Border terrier, male."

"He'll be good company for you. We have lots of dogs at home, mostly Labradors that are trained gun dogs. I take one when I go on the moors beating."

"I'd like to have a go at that. Do you have to have a gun-dog to go?"

"Oh no. Lots of the beaters don't have a dog at all."

Louise thought she ought to tell Pippa about her work. She'd only got as far as telling her about finishing at Stavely when Pippa interrupted her.

"But that's marvellous. You'll be able to ride more with me."

"Only until I get another job." She went on to tell her about the job in Italy. "I can't decide what to do."

"What an opportunity. You *must* go." She looked across at Louise smiling. "It would be selfish of me to say I didn't want you to. Still, we can do a lot of riding in a fortnight, can't we?" she laughed.

Louise loved her enthusiasm. Although they'd only just met Louise already felt affection for this open, friendly girl. It was true what she'd said. It *was* an opportunity and Neil was right too. Something she might regret it if she didn't go. Leaving home this time would be much different from the other times. She knew that she would be counting the weeks till she came home again. Her mind was made up. She would go home and write the letter accepting that afternoon and she'd ring Neil in the evening and tell him of her decision.

Louise's last week at Stavely went quickly and, as she was finishing on the Friday, she didn't take a day off mid-week. She did manage to get a couple of hours in town one day, when she visited the hair-dressers for a trim and found a dress for the Hunt Ball. She would have to tell Tony about her impending departure and wondered what his reaction would be. When Friday came she said her farewells and as Emma was the only one she'd become real friends with, she promised to keep in touch with her.

Louise took one last look in the mirror and was pleased with what she saw. The pale blue dress fitted perfectly. It was sleeveless with a v-neck, fitted at her neat waist, flowing gently from the hips. Her hair was swept back at the sides, emphasizing her high cheekbones. The amethyst pendant ear-rings and matching necklace picked out the blue in her eyes. Picking up her jacket and bag she went downstairs. She had volunteered to drive this evening and was picking the others up on the way. Filled with excitement about the coming evening, she drove over to Crag Cottage. It was ages since she'd been to a 'posh frock' do.

The night was clear and fine, with a half-moon dipping in and out of the clouds. She pulled up at the cottage and knocked on the door. She was not prepared for the sight Tony presented when he opened it, making her heart skip a beat. He looked very dashing and even more handsome than usual, dressed in a dark evening suit, bow-tie and white shirt.

"Gosh, what a transformation. You look very elegant," she beamed at him.

"Thank you kindly, ma'am. You don't look too bad yourself! Right, let's go to the Ball."

Several people were already there at the Town Hall when they arrived. Some were standing around talking on the dancing area. Others were at the bar, which had been erected at the farthest end. Several were already seated at their allotted tables between the bar and dance floor. On the left hand side was a stage where musical instruments were set up and also a disco. It all looked very grand and once seated the girls were soon admiring the many beautiful dresses on show.

It was impossible to see everyone as they arrived but Louise did notice Richard and Sue as they made their way towards the tables. She couldn't see Neil anywhere but thought she spotted Alistair at the far side of the room. Eventually order was called and all were requested to take their seats. When everyone was settled grace was said and the waitresses began serving the first course. The meal was provided by an outside catering firm and consisted of a cold starter, ham and beef salad, a choice of sweets and coffee. Towards the end of the meal the musicians arrived on the stage and were fine-tuning their instruments, adding to the excitement and anticipation of the evening. When the tables had been cleared the lights were dimmed and the dancing began.

When several couples were on the dance floor, Tony got up and invited Louise to dance. It was a slow fox-trot and Louise was pleasantly surprised at how well Tony danced.

"It's the Irish in me," he grinned. "My grandparents were great dancers. I don't know a lot of the proper dances but I'm sure you'll teach me. And may I say how beautiful you look in that dress?"

"Why thank you, kind sir. I seem to be making a habit of teaching you," she replied. "I love to dance and was in a ballroom dancing club at college, so I learnt most of the old dances."

"I think Roger will be waiting for the disco session. Do you know many of the people here?"

"Some. I haven't seen everyone here yet. I saw Richard, Neil's brother, and Sue arriving. I will have to give you an official introduction to them." Just then she noticed someone she knew. "That's Grace over there, dancing with Colin. She never told me she was coming."

"You maybe never told her *you* were coming." He raised a quizzical eyebrow at Louise. She glanced away, knowing she hadn't mentioned it on purpose.

"Well?" When he didn't get a reply, he continued. "You were expecting Neil to ask you, weren't you?"

She blushed, unsure of what to say. She didn't want to hurt his feelings. "I didn't expect it. I was just a bit surprised he hadn't mentioned it. Anyway, I'm here with you," she smiled.

"And very happy I am about it. He doesn't know what he's missing," he said, with a twinkle in his eye.

The dance had finished and they made their way back to their table. The next dance was a St. Bernard Waltz and Liz managed to coax Roger in to having a go. While the floor was filling with people, Louise suddenly spotted Melanie on the other side of the room. She looked absolutely fantastic in a tight fitting gold coloured dress with a plunge neck line and a slit up to her thigh at one side. So. She must have got Neil to come after all.

"You look as if you've seen a ghost."

"Mm? Oh, sorry. No, just someone I know." She paused a moment and took a drink from her fruit juice, then smiling, continued. "I've got some news for you."

"Good or bad?"

"I don't know. I'll let you decide that." She told him about her new work in Italy. "I hope I've made the right decision. I was looking forward to riding more with Pippa. Have you met her yet?"

"Yes. One day this last week. I was with your dad when we called at The Grange. Neil introduced us all. They'd been moving some stock ready for the suckler sale. I thought she was a stable manageress?"

"She is but she loves helping Neil on the farm as well."

"Maybe it's Neil she likes. She seems a fine girl." He had a wicked grin on his face. "Come on. Let's have another dance." It was a slow one. He made a point of holding Louise very close and she found herself succumbing to his roguish charms.

Later in the evening Louise took Tony over to Richard and Sue, who had just arrived back at their table after some very energetic disco dancing. Louise made the necessary introductions.

"Good crowd here isn't there," said Richard.

Just at that moment Melanie arrived to speak with her cousin and on seeing Tony, with barely a glance in Louise's direction, begged to be introduced. "Would you like to dance?" she asked in her most persuasive voice, placing her hand on his arm.

Not wanting to appear rude, Tony held out his hand. "Why not? Never could refuse a lady. If you'll excuse me, Louise?" he said smiling.

They had barely stepped onto the dance floor when Alistair appeared, a drink in his hand.

"Louise, isn't it? From the Manor? I seem to have lost my partner." He put his glass on the table and held out his arm. "Would you do me the honour of dancing with me?" He was swaying slightly and his speech was slurred but Louise couldn't think of an excuse not to dance with him.

"Yes, of course." Glancing at Richard she added, "Don't forget the next one's ours."

Throughout the dance Alistair held her very close and tried to smooch with Louise. He kept telling her she was wasted behind a bar and that he was sure she would be very good at other things. Louise tried to hold herself away from him and pretended she couldn't hear what he was saying above the noise. As they passed Tony and Melanie, he suddenly raised his voice.

"There's my partner, dancing with that gamekeeper. Quite a corker, isn't she?"

Louise was totally confused and was glad when the dance ended. Alistair came and claimed Melanie, who smiled coyly at Tony.

"Thanks for the dance. Maybe we'll meet again," she added, fluttering her long lashes, as Alistair led her away.

"*She* doesn't waste much time," said Richard, after they'd left. "She only met Alistair last Saturday."

"So, who *were* the tickets for that she'd ordered," asked Louise, curiously.

"She got them for her dad. It was a surprise for his birthday so that he could bring mother," replied Richard. He looked across at Tony who had been chatting to Sue. "Mind if I have a dance with Lulu?" he asked.

Tony grinned broadly. "Lulu? Oh, you mean Louise! No, off you go. I've got the rest of the night with her." And he winked knowingly at Richard.

The rest of the evening passed quickly and Louise enjoyed herself immensely. As she was returning from the ladies cloakroom, she bumped into Grace, looking very relaxed and happy.

"So good to see you out enjoying yourself," said Louise.

"Yes, it was a complete surprise. I only found out on Wednesday that I was coming. I did wonder what people might say – thinking it was too soon after Philip – but everyone's been lovely."

"Life has to go on, hasn't it? And Colin seems very kind."

"Yes. It's good just to have a friend around sometimes. I told Neil he should have been coming but he said it was too late. We've all been so busy lately and had forgotten all about it until Colin rang. Anyway, he said the girl he would have asked was already spoken for." Louise didn't ask who that might have been.

Tony danced and flirted with her at every opportunity. He asked Louise if she would call round at Crag Cottage one evening before she went off to Rome. She only half believed his story that the computer was playing up but happily agreed to go.

She had several dances with Richard and told him about her trip to Rome. He was delighted for her.

"Tony's a nice guy. I can see why you fell for him. He'll miss you"

"I keep telling you – we're just good friends."

"Well, you've got plenty of competition, what with Melanie around and the new stable manageress." He grinned cheekily at Louise. "But I'm sure he knows a good thing when he sees it."

It was almost two in the morning when Louise drew up outside Crag Cottage. Tony put his arm round her shoulders.

"I'll not ask you in. It's a bit late and we're going picking up again tomorrow at Barnwell but thanks for a delightful evening."

"Thank you. I've really enjoyed myself."

"Good. So, I'll see you one night next week, then?"

"Yes. I'll give you a ring."

"You're a beautiful girl, Miss Bentley." Putting his arm round her he leaned over and kissed her – a long lingering kiss. On releasing her, he tilted her chin with his fingers, and lightly brushed the tip of her nose with his lips before getting out of the car. "Good night, Louise," and shut the door.

As she drove home, Louise tried to analyze her feelings for Tony. It was very difficult. She liked him a lot and found herself responding to his kisses. He certainly knew how to treat a girl but did

138

she want to take their friendship further? Sometimes she thought she did but there always seemed to be something holding her back and she didn't know what. She felt sure that Tony was leaving her to make that decision. Perhaps it was as well that she was going away for a while. Maybe when she returned home she would be able to answer her own questions.

Chapter 22

The following week Louise went down to the stables most days. On the Monday Pippa let her ride a hunting pony called Turpin, whose owners only came over at weekends and holidays. He was 14.3 hands high, very dependable and he jumped well.

"Don't they mind a stranger riding their horse?" Louise was tacking up the stocky bay pony.

"No. It's getting him fit for them. They hunt him every Saturday. Anyway, I told them you were a good rider. I'm taking him hunting tomorrow. Alistair is giving me a lift in his trailer. I think he just wants me there to see to his horse for him at the end of the day. He came back shattered after the opening meet on Saturday."

"He was at the Hunt Ball the night before, rather the worse for wear."

"I thought he looked a bit under the weather when he arrived in the morning. At least he was in a better mood than the previous Saturday. He actually told me I'd made a good job of clipping Murphy."

"He does look smart. I wouldn't know where to start."

They were soon mounted and starting their ride. Louise felt quite at ease on her new mount.

"Did you enjoy the Hunt Ball?" Pippa asked. Louise looked a little surprised at Pippa's knowing she'd been there. "Neil told me," Pippa explained. They were making their way down the fields to the crossing over the stream.

"Yes. It was a good night. You get on well with Neil, don't you?"

"Yes. It feels like we've known each other for years. He told me you'd been with Tony. You didn't tell me you had a boyfriend," Pippa grinned at Louise. "And a good looking one. I met him last week with your dad."

"We're just friends. That's all," replied Louise. Pippa just smiled, not pursuing the subject.

They were climbing out up a steep rocky track and Louise was impressed by how sure footed the pony was. When they cantered he wasn't as smooth as Star but was still quite comfortable. Wherever they rode, Louise tried to show Pippa the different tracks, how to recognize the dangerous boggy places and the best crossings over the little moorland streams. Pippa was gradually getting to know her way around and loved riding up on the moors, especially when Louise was with her. In the short time they'd known each other, the two girls were fast becoming close friends.

After they returned from their ride on the Friday, Pippa said she had a favour to ask.

"The hunt is meeting at the Red Lion next Tuesday. Will you come with me for an hour or two? Alistair wants Murphy taking, as he'll be back in London."

"I don't think I'm ready for that yet."

"You'll be fine and Turpin will look after you. He was brilliant on Tuesday when I took him. We can hack there in half an hour."

"I'll think about it and let you know on Monday."

It rained most of the weekend and Louise stayed at home making lists, sorting clothes and studying her Italian. She also wrote a long letter to Kate. In five days she would be leaving. She rang Tony and said she'd go over on Tuesday evening. The next day, against her better judgement, she told Pippa she would go hunting with her the following morning.

Louise was full of trepidation as she rode with Pippa into the pub car park. There were several other mounted followers and many more people on foot: men, women and children of all ages, standing around talking. There were two gentlemen wearing hunting pink on fine looking horses, and hounds milling around everywhere.

"That's Monty Morrison, the huntsman," said Pippa, indicating one of the men in a red coat. "The other is Jed, his whipper-in." Louise tried to relax on Turpin, who was standing perfectly quietly and wished she felt as calm. She looked around at all the jovial faces, recognizing one or two of the lads who went beating and a few local farmers. She saw the bow-legged form of Jack Watson making his way over to have a word with the huntsman. Pippa looked so relaxed and confident and Louise wished some of it would rub off on to her.

"Why, hello, Pippa. Not seen you for a while. How are you?" A rather heftily built lady on a large black cob had trotted over towards them. Not waiting for a reply, she continued. "So sorry to hear about your mother, dear, but it's good to see you out hunting again. Are you still at the stables?"

"No, I'm working here in Dowerdale and took advantage of the opportunity to get out with the hounds," Pippa replied.

"Well, it's good to see you again," and, smiling, she turned her horse and went to greet another new arrival on horseback.

"Mrs. Fothergill, one of the joint-masters from the hunt back home," explained Pippa.

Louise was curious about what the lady had said concerning Pippa's mother but decided this wasn't the time or place to start asking questions. Just then the landlord appeared with a tray of drinks, the traditional 'stirrup cup,' and offered one to each of the mounted followers. Two of the girls who worked at the pub handed round trays of sandwiches and sausage rolls. Louise accepted a drink but refused the food. She found it difficult enough hanging on to her reins and riding crop and glass, without coping with a sandwich as well. Besides, the butterflies in her stomach might not have coped too well with food but she hoped the hot punch might give her a bit of Dutch courage to face what lay ahead.

Everyone seemed in high spirits, laughing and talking. Some of the braver children stroked the hounds that wandered around, hoping for tit-bits. There was an air of excitement and anticipation which increased when Monty took out his horn and pressed it to his lips. After sounding a short blast on it he set off, with most of the hounds eagerly following him. The whipper-in cracked his whip and encouraged the stragglers that were still sniffing around in the car park, to do likewise.

"Git on to him!" he shouted, as he trotted behind them, followed by the rest of the riders at the meet.

"Don't look so worried, Louise," Pippa smiled at her charge as they trotted up the road. The huntsman took a track on their right up onto the common leading to their first draw, followed by the rest of the field. They entered a rough, wooded area where he left the track and urged his hounds to seek out their quarry. The riders stayed a good distance behind the huntsman, on a ride through the middle of the wood.

"C'mon Louise, we'll go down to the other ride at the bottom of the wood," suggested Pippa, when they came to where the ride divided into two tracks. Jed was quite a way in front of them, trotting on fairly briskly.

"Where's he going?" asked Louise, looking puzzled.

"Out to the far end of the wood to stand point, just in case a fox slips away," Pippa explained.

Monty was encouraging the hounds to search through the dense undergrowth of bracken and briars and the overgrown branches of fallen trees. "Loo' in there!" His voice could be heard above the wind in the trees, as the girls walked quietly along the ride. Some of the hounds came down to where the girls were riding, bustling about, noses to the ground, searching for any scent left where a fox might have passed through in the night. Suddenly the high-pitched voice of a hound rang out excitedly, only to be followed by a stern command from Monty.

"Come away, leave it!"

"Must have been a rabbit," explained Pippa. "Probably a young hound. It takes some of them a season or so to learn not to run them."

"I suppose it's a bit like training a gun-dog," replied Louise.

Just then a pheasant squawked out in alarm as it was disturbed by a hound. Louise was still very tense and jumped in fright as it flew past, narrowly missing her face. Turpin didn't even seem to notice it. His ears were up as if listening for something as he carefully picked his way over a fallen tree and jumped over a little gully of water that crossed their path.

"Been a fox through there at some time," said Pippa, pointing to a dark coloured hound, its stern lashing. Another hound joined it as, noses to the ground, they pushed ahead following the bit of line they'd found. Occasional glimpses of Monty's red coat could be seen through the trees to their right, ahead of the girls. They could hear him continually encouraging the hounds.

"Try on, loo' in there." There was a sense of urgency now, in the voices of the hounds, forcing their way through the bracken, as they picked up bits of drag here and there. Odd ones even spoke on it every now and then.

Suddenly a loud holler was heard from way ahead. Pippa halted her horse, listening. A series of sharp repetitive notes on the horn echoed through the trees, followed by an encouraging command.

"Git away forrard, git on to him!" shouted Monty.

Louise could feel the tension in Turpin, as if poised for flight. She realized that he knew exactly what that sound meant. Her own heart started beating madly, unsure of what would happen next. Hounds rushed past the girls, in pursuit of the ones ahead that were speaking. Pippa gathered up her reins and, with an excited urgency in her voice, explained to Louise what had happened.

"Jed's seen him. Come on Louise." With that, she squeezed Murphy into a canter and, with some trepidation, Louise followed. Her heart was in her mouth as, clinging on as best she could, she rode Turpin along the ride after Pippa.

Suddenly the wood rang out with the cry of the hounds as they hit the spot where the fox had been disturbed from its slumbers. Louise clung on. It was too late now to be thinking that this wasn't such a good idea after all, as Turpin jumped a fallen branch and then dodged a huge rock, almost sending her out of the side door. She regained her seat just as a warning came from Pippa.

"Watch out," she yelled. Louise only just ducked in time, as the leaves of an overhanging branch brushed the top of her hat.

As they emerged from the wood they could still hear the hounds tonguing way ahead of them. They galloped along the grassy ride and out from the trees where dead bracken beds flanked them on either side. Louise hardly dared take her eyes off where she was going but managed a quick glance to the right and saw the other riders, high up the hillside, heading for the moor.

Ahead was a small hand-gate and Pippa was off her horse in a flash, holding the gate open for Louise. "Keep going up that sheep track, – go on," she urged, as Louise hesitated. "I'll catch you up."

Louise turned Turpin's head up the hillside and with only a slight squeeze of her legs he set off at great speed up the track. Louise didn't know how she stayed on as he bounced his way up the steep bank side. 'Keep your heels down, keep your heels down,' kept ringing in her ears, as memories of those lessons with Kathy many years ago came flooding back. She could feel her heart thumping inside her.

"Keep your heels down!" That wasn't Kathy – it was Pippa as she came flying up the hill after Louise. "You're doing fine. Come on," and she surged past, heading off up a track through the heather and rocks. By the time they'd climbed to the top, the hounds had gone quiet and Monty was standing ahead of the rest of the field, who were a short distance from the girls. He was watching his hounds as they cast around, trying to find the line. To the left of the group of riders lay the sunken hollows of some old disused quarry workings.

Monty suddenly turned his horse around and started trotting back towards where the field were standing. "Try back," he called to the hounds.

Jed cracked his whip as he rode round beyond the ranging hounds. "Git on to him, git on." The hounds lifted their heads and hurried back to where Monty was encouraging them down a narrow path into the old quarry.

"Must have overshot it," Pippa remarked to Louise, who was still panting to get her breath back, as they joined the other riders. Almost instantly a hound spoke from among the gorse bushes that were growing up the side of the quarry. "Crafty so-and-so's tried to gain a bit of time."

More of the hounds were now speaking as they worked the line through the hollows and grassy knolls and ponds of stagnant water. Monty carefully guided his horse down to the bottom between the gorse bushes, keeping as close as he could to the hounds. The other riders watched from above while trotting along the rim of the quarry.

Suddenly there was more urgency in the voices of the hounds and all the pack seemed to be speaking. Louise viewed them streaming out through the far end of the quarry. She watched as they crossed over a large area of bracken and took off in full cry across the open moor once more. As the hounds picked up speed the riders had to canter to keep them in view. Through the heather, dodging rocks and water holes, the horses and riders were strung out across the moor. Still the hounds forged ahead, taking the line up the side of the valley, their voices ringing out loud and clear. The riders had to circle round a large green mossy bog, losing them precious time, before heading down into a deep ravine with a steep-sided stream in the bottom. Hounds were disappearing over the next hill as Pippa and Louise made their way down the hillside to the ditch below. Pippa approached the ditch at a canter and, with a loud 'giddup' to her horse, cleared it with ease. Louise panicked – she daren't do that – and pulled up two or three yards before the edge. Pippa was trotting up the far side of the ditch.

"Come on, try it here, it's not so wide," she called back to Louise, who was making her way up her side of the stream, between the rocks and tall heather clumps. Eventually she found a sheep track leading right down to the edge of the stream where Turpin could actually stand in the edge of the water. The opposite bank was a good two feet higher than the take-off side.

"Go on, kick him on, he'll jump out up this side," encouraged Pippa. Not wanting to be left behind, Louise swallowed hard, closed her eyes and squeezed. She felt herself fly through the air and didn't realize she'd parted company with her saddle till she found herself dumped in a heap in the heather out on the other side. She sat up, feeling slightly winded, and winced, as she moved her arm. Hugely embarrassed, she struggled to her feet. Pippa was holding Turpin's reins, as he stood patiently waiting to be re-united with his rider.

"You okay?" enquired Pippa, grinning down at Louise, who was brushing the peaty black soil and heather seeds from her sleeve.

"I think so, thanks."

"Come on, then, we're getting behind."

Louise took the reins and scrambled back into the saddle. She glanced sheepishly at Pippa. "Sorry about that."

"Don't worry, even the best riders can come a cropper out hunting. Let's kick on," and she pushed her horse into a canter up the steep side of the ravine and Louise followed. When they reached the top they could see the other riders quite a distance away to the left. Pippa was standing still, listening and staring straight ahead, out across the moor.

"We're going to be okay, they're swinging back right-handed. Charlie must have slipped back through that plantation. Look, there they are," she added, pointing across the distant moor. Louise followed her gaze and could just make out the moving specks of white, the light coloured hounds showing up against the dark moorland background. The other riders, following Monty and Jed, were cutting across the moor, having spotted the hounds as they emerged from the plantation.

"Is it sound over here?" asked Pippa.

"Yes, it's wet but not peaty."

"Come on, then, we can catch up again across here." She set off at a canter, with Louise close behind. Louise didn't know whether it was fear or excitement she felt but it was certainly an exhilarating feeling that she had never before experienced, as she tried to keep up with Pippa. She hung on, letting Turpin pick his own way through the heather and bracken beds, bilberry patches and clumps of sieves. She was quite pleased with herself as she stayed with him when he flew over rather a wide open water ditch. Pippa had been right; he certainly knew how to look after himself over this rugged terrain. The hounds sounded much clearer now, pursuing their quarry, as they stretched out in a line across the horizon.

By being able to cut across the moor when the fox had swung round, the girls had now caught up with the rest of the field. The hounds had disappeared from view but could still be heard.

"He's heading for Taylor's slack," shouted Monty. "He knows where he'll be safe."

The riders cantered on until they drew rein at the top of a knoll and, looking down, could see, three hundred yards away below them, all the hounds close together, baying loudly at the entrance of what was obviously the fox's den.

"He's gone to ground," Pippa informed Louise.

"Aye an' 'e'll not come out in a 'urry. Big sandy spot," came from one of the other riders. Monty started to blow his horn, calling the hounds to come away and Jed was making his way down towards the baying pack. Pippa went and thanked the huntsman and the girls made their farewells.

"I think that will have exercised these two by the time we get back home," Pippa told a flushed and still breathless Louise.

Chapter 23

Louise lay soaking in a hot bath, reliving the events of the day. She had a feeling that she was going to be quite stiff in the morning. Already her arm was very sore where she'd landed on it when she'd fallen off Turpin. Still, nothing was broken and stiffness would wear off eventually. It had taken her and Pippa over an hour to hack back home and she'd helped un-tack and see to their mounts before leaving. Both horses had been fine, no cuts or bumps and were soon tucking into their bran mashes. Tomorrow would be her last ride with Pippa.

Louise told her parents about her day's hunting while they had dinner and later that evening she set off down the valley. She'd decided to call at The Grange on her way to Crag Cottage, to confirm with Neil their dinner-date arrangements. Grace opened the door and welcomed her in.

"Come on through, Louise, where it's warm. It's freezing out there tonight. Neil's in his study, trying to catch up on the paper work. Go and sit in the lounge. I'll tell him you're here."

Neil soon appeared, a smile replacing his harassed expression. "Hi. You're looking rather radiant. How did the hunting go?"

"Fine. I think I might be rather stiff in the morning though," she smiled at him.

"Managed to stay on, then?"

"Well, actually no," she grinned, "but fortunately I had a soft landing." She told him all about her escapades, much to his amusement.

"Are you staying for a drink?"

"Er... no thanks. I'm on my way round to Tony's, to sort out his computer before I go off to Rome. I said I'd be there for seven."

He turned away and bent to pick up a log for the fire. "Well I need one. That paperwork is never-ending. I'm glad Mother and Pippa are going to do the livery accounts."

Just then Grace returned to the room. "Did I hear my name mentioned?" she asked, smiling.

Louise soon left, after arranging a time to come down to The Grange the following night. Neil said they would go over to Layton for their meal.

Tony was unusually quiet as Louise worked on his computer.

There was nothing seriously wrong with it and Louise soon had it behaving itself once more. Tony had gone into the kitchen and as she was closing down the computer he returned with two mugs of coffee.

"This will warm you up before you go. There's going to be a frost, I think."

"Mm, it's really chilly outside."

"Mind the road isn't icy down by the ford."

"I will. They're talking of snow at the weekend."

"It won't worry you, will it?" he smiled. "You'll be enjoying the attentions of all the Latin Romeos under a Mediterranean sun. I hope you'll drop me a line now and then. We're all going to miss you."

"All?"

"Pippa, Neil, your parents and I will certainly miss you." He took the empty cup from her and pulled her to her feet. "I'll say my goodbyes tonight." He took her in his arms and kissed her longingly before holding her at arm's length. "Don't let them change you, Miss Bentley." Then rather abruptly added, "Now, off you go." He held her coat for her before opening the door, letting her out into the cold night air.

Her face was burning as she walked to her car, the frosty atmosphere biting into her flushed cheeks. Strange emotions raged through her, filling her with desires she'd never felt before, and she knew that Tony was aware of the feelings he evoked in her.

She drove carefully home, watching for the icy patches of frozen water on the road, as jumbled thoughts raced through her head. Perhaps it was good that she was going away for a while. She was glad when she was safely back in her parents' cottage and the warmth and security of her own bed.

Louise groaned as she awoke the next morning. Every muscle in her body seemed to ache, especially the arm on which she had fallen. Never mind, nothing another ride wouldn't cure, she thought to herself. The sun was shining as she looked out of the window but frost glistened everywhere.

"You'll have to be careful today, won't you?" her mother greeted her as she entered the kitchen. "Dad says it's been a keen frost and the ground is quite hard."

"Well, I'll still go, as it will be my last ride with Pippa." Her mother poured her a cup of tea as Louise popped some bread into the toaster. "Thanks, Mam. We'll probably stick to the roads."

"Make sure you wrap up well, then. You don't want to be catching a cold to take to Italy."

"Did I tell you I won't be here for dinner this evening? I'm going out with Neil," she said, sipping her hot tea. Ellen smiled affectionately at her daughter.

"He's going to miss you when you go away."

Louise was buttering her toast and didn't turn round. "Oh, I don't know. Anyway, he's got Pippa around now."

"Well, I'm sure he'll be very pleased to see you when you come back," her mother insisted.

It took Louise quite a while to get the frost off the window on her car and she had to drive carefully down the dale, eventually arriving safely in the stable yard at The Grange. Pippa was tacking up Murphy and greeted Louise warmly.

"Hi, not too stiff I hope, this morning?" she said with a grin. "Can you saddle up Turpin? I've groomed him ready."

"I ache all over," Louise laughed, "but I'm sure I'll survive." She went to the saddle rack and lifted down Turpin's saddle, wincing as she did so at the pain in her arm.

"We'll just stick to the roads today, as the ground's pretty rocky," said Pippa.

Louise was glad she'd taken her mother's advice and wrapped up well. Even with gloves on, she couldn't keep her fingers warm and kept tucking each hand in turn under the edge of the saddle where the heat from Turpin's body soon warmed them through. The horses snorted and blew, their warm breath forming clouds in the cold frosty air. They walked the horses where there were icy patches on the road and trotted where it was safe to do so. They rode a loop round the valley, taking an old green lane across the dale head and down to a pack-horse bridge over which they crossed with care. The water in the stream was crystal clear and looked very cold as it danced and bubbled over the stones. Frozen daggers of ice had formed on the bank sides below the frosted grass.

"It looks really beautiful, doesn't it?" said Pippa, as they paused for a moment.

"Mmm, it's like some of those Christmas cards you see."

"Will you miss not being at home for Christmas?" asked Pippa as they continued their ride.

"Yes," replied Louise. She paused a moment. "Yes, I will." She looked across at the young girl and realized just how fond she'd become of her. She had lots of friends – she made friends easily, with her cheerful, caring manner – but this girl was different and Louise knew she would miss her very much. "But it will be nice to come home again and see you all. Will you go home for Christmas?"

"Yes, just for the day, I expect." They trotted on, the cold wind in their faces now, as they rode back down the valley. It stung their noses and made their eyes water. The horses didn't need any encouraging, knowing they were not far from a warm stable and food. When they arrived back at the stables, Pippa left Louise to un-tack the horses, while she went to sheet up Star and the other ponies, ready to turn them into the field for an hour. The girls soon had the horses they'd ridden settled in their boxes and munching away on their hay.

"Come on up and have a coffee with me before you go home," Pippa invited. It was nice and warm in the little flat and Gyp greeted them excitedly. Soon the girls were settled with a warm mug of steaming coffee.

"I hope you don't mind me asking you this but what did that lady mean at the Hunt meet yesterday about your mother?" Louise asked.

Pippa stared into her hot coffee a moment before looking up. "I don't mind now, now that I know you. My mum died a year ago."

Louise was horrified. She moved over to Pippa instantly and put an arm round her shoulders. "I'm so sorry Pippa. I'd no idea. I can't imagine what it must be like."

Pippa looked up and smiled. "It's okay, most of the time. I'm learning to carry on with my life, so don't be sad for me."

Louise felt overcome with emotion. She stood up and went across to the window, staring out across the valley – a view that was all too familiar to her. She was unaware that the other girl had come and stood next to her until Pippa's voice broke into her thoughts.

"It's beautiful, isn't it, even when it's cold and bare? It must be beautiful in the summer, too. It's things like this that help me to cope." It was her turn to put an arm around Louise. "And meeting friends like you. You will write to me, won't you?" she asked.

Louise brushed a tear from her face and turning, smiled at Pippa. "Yes, of course I will, and you'll write and tell me everything that happens here, because I shall be thinking about you all." For a long moment they held each other close, both aware of the strong bond that had grown between them.

The sun had disappeared and dark clouds were racing across the skies, mirroring Louise's mood, as she drove back up the dale on that frosty day. A smell of home cooking greeted her as she entered the kitchen and she found her mother baking. After tugging off her gloves and jacket, she went across and gave her mother a big hug.

"Now what have I done?" she asked, smiling at her daughter.

"Nothing," Louise replied, "I just want to tell you how much I love you."

Later that evening it was again very frosty as Louise drove back down the valley to The Grange. She was just getting out of the car when Neil came out to greet her.

"Lock yours up Louise; we'll take the Land Rover. The forecast isn't too good."

Soon they were travelling over the moor to Layton and Louise tucked the blanket Neil had given her round her knees.

"Takes a while for this old machine to warm up," he grinned at her. "They're saying it's going to snow but I think it's too cold tonight."

There were several other customers in the small dining room, even though it was a cold November's night, such was the reputation of the small village inn. Their food was excellent, as usual, and they decided to take their coffee in the bar, where a welcoming log fire was blazing up the chimney. Conversation had been pretty general while they'd been eating and it wasn't until they were seated with their coffee that Neil asked Louise about her ride.

"It was freezing cold and we daren't go up on the moors but we enjoyed being out and the horses did too. I stayed and had a coffee with Pippa, as it was our last ride together. I asked her about her mother, not knowing that she had died."

"I should have told you but we've all been so busy lately and it must have slipped my mind," said Neil.

"Does she have other family?"

"Yes, a stepfather and one sister."

"A stepfather? When did she lose her father?"

"She never knew him. He's dead too. Her mother remarried when Pippa was just two."

Louise remained silent, trying to take in all that Neil had told her. It seemed impossible that Pippa could be as she was. "But how can she be so brave, so practical, so, so happy so soon?"

"She's a strong girl – her life has made her so. I'm really glad that she has found somewhere where she can be happy, working with us."

"Why have I been so lucky? I don't think I could cope with that. There's Tony who never knew his father and had to search for his family. Then you, you lost your father, and now Pippa. My life has been so perfect. How will I ever learn to face sadness?"

"Everyone has to find that inner strength. You will, too, if the time ever comes." He smiled and reached across the table, and squeezed her hand. "When you find happiness, you must take it with both hands and treasure it – like Pippa has."

The frown left Louise's face and she returned the smile, comforted by the strong reassuring hand of Neil, his thumb gently caressing the back of her fingers. "I can understand why you like her so much. She has so many qualities to admire and you two have such a lot in common."

"Yes, I think it has helped me a lot, too – not just having a helping hand but knowing someone else understands how I feel." He removed his hand to take a drink from his cup and went on to ask her about her departure plans. The rest of the evening passed pleasantly enough and when they arrived at The Grange Neil invited her inside to have a few words with his mother. Grace was anxious to see Louise before she went off on her trip to Italy. Louise jumped from the Land Rover and ran to the back door, anxious to get in from the cold. Grace had heard the vehicle arrive and met her in the back kitchen. She ushered Louise into the lounge, where the warmth of the fire, its blue tinged flames leaping and dancing, greeted them.

"I probably won't see you again before you go, so I just wanted to give you this small gift." She crossed to the sideboard, picked up a parcel and handed it to her young friend. "Think of it as an early Christmas present. We shall all look forward to your return, and hearing about your experiences in Italy."

Louise took the gift, thanking Grace by giving her a warm embrace. She was putting it in her handbag, as Neil came in.

"Do I have to wait till Christmas to open it?" she asked, smiling.

Neil had walked over to the fire and was rubbing his hands in front of the welcoming heat. "You won't be able to wait till then," he teased.

Grace chided her son, good humouredly. "That's why I'm giving it to her now." She turned to the young woman. "Open it once you've started your journey, Louise."

"Well, you won't be getting my present until after you come home. Come on, it's getting late and time you were making back up the dale before it snows. I'll see you to your car." Neil didn't linger long out in the cold, but as Louise wound down her window to say goodnight, he replied by saying he would try and see her on Friday morning.

Chapter 24

Through the window of the train, as it sped swiftly through towns and countryside on its way to London, Louise watched the snow gently falling. She felt strangely alone, more like a schoolgirl on her way back to boarding school than a young woman embarking on an exciting six-week period of work in a European capital city.

She had awoken to find the world outside covered in a white blanket of snow. Two or three inches had fallen during the night and it clung to everything. Once the sun had risen it had soon melted the snow from the trees and hedgerows but not from the ground. Neil had rung around ten o'clock and offered to take Louise to the station at York, knowing his Land Rover would fare much better than her mother's car over the moor. George, unfortunately, was away on another shoot, so Ellen had been more than happy to let Neil make the journey to the station.

When Neil had arrived at the cottage to pick Louise up, she had been surprised to see Pippa already seated in the Land Rover. Once on their journey Neil had explained their plan to Louise. He was going to drop Pippa off at her home for a visit, while he took Louise on to the station. It was a good opportunity for Pippa to see her family in case the snow stayed and made it difficult for her to travel over in her mini. Louise could still see Pippa's smiling face, waving by her front door, as the Land Rover pulled away and headed for the city centre.

Louise shivered involuntarily, remembering the icy wind blowing through the draughty station at York as they'd crossed the footbridge to the platform on the other side of the tracks. Neil had bought Louise a newspaper to read and a packet of boiled sweets in case she felt sick on the plane. They'd had a coffee together to help pass the time before the train arrived in the station. She could still feel his strong arms wrapped round her as they'd said goodbye on the platform. She had felt his breath, warm on her cheek, before he'd kissed her gently on the mouth.

"You look after yourself and that tender heart of yours. Don't let anyone go breaking it." One day those words would come back to haunt her. Then he'd held her at arm's length and smiled. "I'm off now – don't forget to send me a card." And with that he'd turned and was gone, soon lost among the many people hurrying up and down the platform, struggling with their luggage as they searched for their places on the train.

Half an hour into the journey the snow turned to rain. Louise took out the newspaper from her bag and tried not to dwell on what she was leaving behind.

Kings Cross was the usual heaving mass of people hurrying in every direction. Why was everyone always in such a rush? The inevitable din of chattering people, clanging doors, undistinguishable messages coming over the loud speakers and noisy engines, was constant. She made her way through the bustling crowds to purchase her ticket for the tube train to Paddington and only had a short time to wait before it came clattering down the line. She was fortunate to get a seat and was pleased when her stop came, as she never felt at ease on the underground. Then she caught a ride on the Heathrow Express to the airport.

After checking in, Louise went for something to eat for she had almost two hours to wait before takeoff. Later, having endured all the queues of passport and security, she eventually found herself in the departure lounge. The plane had a smooth take-off and Louise quite enjoyed the flight, watching the lights of London grow farther and farther away.

It was only when they were airborne that she remembered the present from Grace. Hunting in her hand luggage she found the small packet and carefully unwrapped it. Opening the gift box inside, Louise found a gold chain bearing an exquisite medallion of St. Christopher. She touched it lovingly and with a smile placed it round her neck. Somehow, she didn't feel quite so lonely after that and began to look forward to her new experience.

On emerging from the airport building Louise was surprised by the almost warm, balmy air that met her. Although nine o'clock in the evening, the temperature was very different from the cold wintry conditions she'd left behind in Yorkshire. She managed to hail a taxi, as instructed, which took her to what would be her home for the next six weeks. She gave the swarthy looking driver the name of the hotel as he loaded her cases and climbed in. He was pleasant enough but soon gave up talking as Louise's Italian wasn't brilliant and he spoke no English. He frightened the life out of her, zigzagging through the traffic on what appeared to be the wrong side of the road. She would get used to that, no doubt. Eventually they turned off down a short drive with palm trees on either side and pulled up in front of the La

Casa Grande. Stone statues stood guard on either side of the double glass doors at the entrance to the hotel. Having paid the taxi driver, Louise picked up her cases and went inside.

The large reception area was light and airy, with a long bar on the side opposite the entrance. Several guests were standing around talking and others were seated on the comfortable looking settees and chairs around the small tables. Louise put her cases down and made her way towards the bar, where a slim young man was serving. While waiting to gain his attention, she was approached by a rather stout middle-aged lady, wearing a navy skirt and blouse with a white frilly apron tied round her ample waist. Her extravagant blue eye-shadow matched the tints in her once jet-black hair, which was coiled round on top of her head.

"Mees Bentley? Welcome to Roma." She held out her hand. "I am Signora Francesca." Louise took the hand, smiled and greeted the lady, who she knew was the proprietor, in her best Italian. Signora then motioned to a bespectacled young man who was collecting glasses from the tables and, from what Louise could understand, she instructed him to take Louise's cases and show her to her room. Turning back to Louise, Signora Francesca told her that Simona, who would be waiting upstairs, would look after Louise and show her where she could get something to eat.

The young man smiled timidly at Louise, picked up her cases and made his way through the guests. Louise followed him down a corridor and into the lift. They got off on the fourth floor and proceeded to the end of another long corridor, where her companion knocked on a door. It was opened by a young dark-haired girl in her late teens with a rather sallow complexion and shoulder length dark hair. Her blouse revealed the cleavage of her ample bosom. When she smiled her wide mouth showed a set of beautiful white teeth.

"'Ello, please come in." Louise followed the young man into the spacious room. He set the cases down and as he turned to go the young girl called after him, "Grazie, Marco." The shy young man smiled and left. Then the young girl offered her hand to Louise, saying in her broken English, "I am Simona. I 'ope you weel be very 'appy 'ere."

Louise shook her hand warmly. "Thank you. I hope so too." She looked around the room. There were twin beds, a television in the corner, two comfy chairs and a large fitted cupboard all along one wall. A door opposite the beds presumably led to a bathroom.

Curtains were drawn across a wide window at the far end of the room.

"First, you 'ave food then I tell you about 'ere while you unpack"

"Sí. First, the bathroom?" asked Louise.

"Altro ché!" exclaimed Simona, putting her hand to her mouth, "I show you," and she opened the door into the small but serviceable bathroom.

"Grazie."

Ten minutes later the two girls made their way down to the large kitchens, which was still a hive of activity. Simona left Louise at a table in the staff dining area and returned with some tomatoes, cold meat and a croissant. Then she went to bring two mugs of coffee for them both. Later, she introduced Louise to some other staff members before they returned to their room. There, Louise managed a short call on her mobile to her mother, just to let her know that she'd arrived safe and sound.

The following day Louise awoke early after her first night in Rome. She'd slept well and heard Simona already up and in the shower. During the morning Simona showed Louise round the hotel and took her into the grounds. These consisted of a huge garden, with lots of trees and shrubs and many seats for the guests to sit on, where they could enjoy the peace and quiet away from the bustle of life in the city. There was a water fountain in the centre of which was a statue of Flora, the goddess of flowers, with water nymphs seated at her feet.

Later she'd had a meeting with Signora Francesco, who had outlined the duties Louise would be undertaking and explained the house rules for the staff to her. In the afternoon she'd done her first shift under the guidance of an older member of staff. On Sunday morning she'd gone to church with Simona – she wanted to see as many as possible of the beautiful churches in and around Rome. On her return, with two hours to spare, she'd written her first letters home. She wrote to her parents, then, curled up in one of the chairs, wrote to Pippa.

> Dear Pippa,
>
> Well, here I am in Rome! I can't believe how different it is from England. Almost like summer! I arrived late on Friday evening, and met Simona, a fellow employee. She is a young Italian girl, 18 years old, and I share a room with her in the staff quarters on the fourth floor. We do three early shifts and three late shifts, with

one day off each week. Yesterday I did my first shift alongside Simona, from three until 11pm. yesterday evening. The morning shift is from 7am until 3pm. The restaurant seats two hundred and fifty – the largest that I've worked in.

Simona seems very pleasant and does speak some English. One of my tasks is to help her improve her English, so I have devised a plan. One day, we only speak English to each other, then the next day we only speak Italian – I wish I had studied harder before I left!

This morning I went to Mass with Simona in one of the many churches that are quite near. It seemed enormous and a service was being held at three of the several altars there. I'm afraid my Italian wasn't up to understanding the sermon! Simona is a Catholic, as are many of the staff here, including the owners, Signora Francesca, who runs the place, and her husband. He doesn't work here but two of their sons do.

We have an excellent view from our window looking across to the hills of Rome. We can see tall spires and steeples and architectural domes dotted among the rest of the many colourful buildings. It still looks quite green, as most of the trees are still bearing their leaves. On Wednesday, when it is our day off, Simona has promised to take me to St Peter's Square. I am making a list of all the places I want to visit during my six weeks. Simona tells me that there is a riding establishment about 3 miles away but I don't know if I will be able to go. Anyway, it won't be the same as riding up on our moors, will it?

Louise continued telling her about the hotel and her surroundings, the kind of people who stayed there and what her duties would be.

I must get ready for work now. Give my regards to Neil and tell him I'll write soon. I look forward to hearing from you with news about everyone.

Fondest love, Louise.

It was several days before Louise got a reply from Pippa. She was working the front shift and at her mid-morning break went to find a quiet seat by the fountain to read her letter in private.

Dearest Louise,

It was so lovely to hear from you and to know that

you are happy. I gave Neil your message and he was pleased to hear that you have settled in. It has been pretty busy here since you left – because of the snow we had to bring all the heifers in and the rest of the stock. The snow went after about three days but has left everywhere very wet and muddy. It takes much longer to groom the horses when they come in from the fields, as you can imagine. We have a Welsh pony arriving next week and it will be in full livery until Christmas. It is to be a surprise Christmas present for a little girl in the village.

Young Rachel has started working for us, which means I have more time to help Neil with the feeding up. Rachel is a good worker and is learning fast. She is desperately keen to learn to ride, so I have started giving her lessons on Star. So far all has gone well. She seems to enjoy spending most of her spare time here. From what I can gather things are not too happy at home for her.

Mrs. Nickerson took Star for a ride the other day – I'd no idea that she was such an expert rider. Neil was telling me all about her past accomplishments when he called and had a coffee with me.

I bumped into Tony the other day when I was riding Murphy up on the moor. He was setting stoat traps up behind Wheelers Wood. I've never seen a trap before, so he showed me how they are set up. He asked if I'd heard from you.

The rest of her letter was about the horses and where she'd been riding before she ended it.

Write soon! Love from Pippa.

Louise put the letter back in its envelope and slipped it into her pocket. It was funny how little she'd thought of Tony since arriving in Rome. It was mid-December when she replied to Pippa's letter.

Dearest, Pippa,

It was so good to hear from you. When I read your letter, I wished I was back there in Dowerdale with you all but most of the time I'm too busy to be homesick. The first half of my time here has passed very quickly. I am enjoying the work and Simona and I are getting on very well. Her English has improved no end – If only I could say the same about my Italian! I have learnt to travel on the buses and have done lots of exploring during the mornings when I'm off. Simona accompanied me to St Peter's Square, which was just amazing. I couldn't get over how huge everything was – the columns, the statues, the enormous granite obelisk in the centre of the square standing on the backs of four bronze lions and the great bronze doors, one of which has 16 carved panels depicting scenes from the Bible. Inside was even more impressive, with its marble floors, columns, paintings, sculptures and statues and the bronze canopy over St Peter's tomb, which is permanently lit by 99 lamps! It was overwhelming and I only managed to visit about half of the 44 altars. I would need to write a book to describe it all to you.

Another morning I got up early and took a bus into the city to visit the Colosseum, on a day when the public could go inside. It was awesome – nothing like what you imagine it would be when you see it on documentaries. It's just overwhelming. And to think that it was built all those hundreds of years ago. I have taken lots of photographs, but they will not be able to convey the atmosphere of how it feels to be here among these ancient ruins.

One afternoon, Simona and I returned to the city, where we dined at one of the many pavement cafés, then explored some of the side-streets and piazzas. There are market stalls set up all over, selling everything imaginable. I managed to find some lovely presents for Christmas. Everywhere there are flowers, in window boxes, tubs and on the balconies of houses, all still giving a colourful display. Every time you try to cross the street you take your life in your hands! The traffic is terrible, and they seem to beep their horns at everything. There are hundreds of scooters, which nip in and out around the cars all the time. It is so noisy! I try to shut out the noise and imagine I am up on the moors. The only animals that I have seen are a few dogs and the occasional cat. Of course, we had to visit the Trevi Fountain, where I threw in some coins and made a wish.

In case another letter doesn't reach you in time I hope you have a wonderful Christmas.
Lots of love, Louise.

Chapter 25

Three weeks later and Louise found herself on a plane bound for England. The latter part of her stay in Rome had gone very quickly with the excitement of Christmas and the New Year. Christmas had been special but it wasn't like being at home with friends and family. Many of the guests had been pilgrims from all over the world, who wanted to be in St Peter's Square on Christmas Day to receive the papal blessing. All the staff had been given time off to attend a service and Louise had gone with Simona to a Mass early in the morning. Christmas dinner had been served mid-afternoon and then all the staff who were unable to go home had sat down to their own dinner with Signora Francesca, her husband and sons.

Two weeks before Louise had sent off her Christmas cards, including one for Neil, in which she'd written a short note, ending with how much she was looking forward to coming home. Lately she had done a lot of soul-searching and decided that, much as she was attracted to Tony, it was not the kind of love that would endure. It was only fair that she should try and explain the situation to him if the right opportunity should arise. She didn't know how deep his feelings for her were but wouldn't like him to think that she'd been leading him on and hoped that they could still remain good friends.

As the earth below grew ever closer her thoughts turned to home. She'd spoken briefly with her mother yesterday, once she'd known what her connections would be, to let her know what time she'd be arriving in York. Louise was very happy to know that she would be seeing her brother, although only briefly, as he would be setting off again on his travels in two days time. Her thoughts turned to Pippa, and Louise hunted in her bag for the last letter that she had received from her friend. She turned to the last page.

Last Saturday evening I spent with Neil. I had gone to work out the feed order with him when he asked me to stay for supper. Mrs. Nickerson had been invited over to Scarborough by Colin for a visit to the theatre and was staying the night. Neil seems very happy that she is starting to go out and enjoy herself again. On the Sunday I met Kathy and the children – they are quite lovely, aren't they? I invited them down to the stable where I introduced them to Toby, the Welsh Mountain pony. Rebecca was very excited and wanted to sit on him straight away. After seeing her sister have a little ride (just inside the stable yard) Sam decided she would try it. As I held the pony, Kathy lifted Sam on, keeping a firm hold of her, and let Sam hold the reins. The look on Sam's face was incredulous – I wish you'd been there, Louise. Kathy was almost in tears.

On Christmas Eve Mrs. Nickerson asked if I would like to go along with them to the Christmas service in the village. It felt rather strange, as I hadn't been to church since Mum's funeral but overall I think it helped a little. Back home at The Grange, I was invited in to have a Christmas drink and Neil made a toast to absent parents – it was quite special. Later, Neil walked me back to my flat.

The next morning, the people who bought Toby brought their little girl Alison to see her new pony. She was was over the moon and jumped up and down in excitement. I had a word with her parents about Kathy's girls, and they were more than happy for us to use Toby now and then. After seeing to all the horses, I went home for the day and didn't come back till late. Neil said Rachel would manage the horses in the evening and he would keep an eye on things. Of course, I had to be up early the next morning to get those horses ready that were going hunting. Afterwards I helped Neil finish off the doing-up as he was taking his mum over to Richard's for lunch. Alistair was in excellent spirits, and brought me a bottle of wine! Maybe he's not so bad after all!

By the time you read this I expect you'll be packing ready for your return home. Have a safe journey and I'll see you on our next ride in the New Year!

Love Pippa

Louise put the letter in her bag and, leaning back in her seat, closed her eyes. She could picture it all so vividly – the little church in Dowerbridge, Kathy's girls experiencing their first ride and the warm farmhouse kitchen on Christmas Eve. Despite her exploits in Rome she felt a little envious of all that she'd missed. It sounded as if Neil and Pippa were getting on very well together. She was pleased she would soon be home.

"Fasten your seatbelts." The voice startled Louise. Gosh, she must have dozed off. Sitting up, she looked out of the window to see London spread out far below and she could make out the twisting course of the Thames. It didn't seem too long before she was hurtling along in the underground train, heading for King's Cross. The journey north seemed to pass quickly and soon the train was pulling into the station at York.

As she stepped out of the carriage she again felt the cold wind blowing through the station, reminding her of those last moments with Neil. She set down her cases to fasten up her jacket and looked about, hoping to see her mother among the scurrying people. Then a well-dressed young man, sporting a short dark beard and rimless glasses, came striding towards her, smiling.

"Louise! Hello, it's me."

Louise stared, open-mouthed, for a minute, then realization hit her. Beaming, she held out her arms. "Nick, I didn't recognize you!"

He took her in his arms, giving her a big hug then held her at arms length. "You haven't changed at all," he grinned. "Happy New Year."

"And you. It's so good to see you. I was afraid you might have had to go again before I got back." Nick picked up the cases and they made their way out of the station.

"Mother is busy making a special meal for your return," he told his sister. "I think it's probably another Christmas dinner!" Louise laughed.

"That sounds like Mam. So tell me all that you've been up to since last I saw you, apart from growing your beard."

The conversation was non-stop as they journeyed back to Dowerdale. The united family spent a very happy evening together after enjoying one of Ellen's special dinners. Louise handed out her late presents and told them all about her time in Rome. Nick amused them with stories of distant lands and scrapes he'd got into when filming in remote locations. George added his bit to the conversation with some of his humorous quips but most of the time he was content to sit and listen, watching his wife and family enjoying their time together.

Louise found that her brother's last day at home went all too quickly. They'd gone for a walk together up on the moor with the dogs in the afternoon and he'd told her all about his next assignment. He'd been given a contract with one of the leading publishing houses to do the photography for a travel book, covering the game reserves on the east side of South Africa. When they'd returned home her mother had a message for her. Neil had rung saying he was disappointed that Louise hadn't been down to see them yet.

The next morning she drove Nick to the airport near Teesside to catch a flight to London. After one night in his flat in the city he would be taking a plane to Johannesburg before flying on to Port Edward on the east coast. Louise was surprised how well they had got on considering that she'd hardly seen anything of him during the past seven years. Although a little sad at saying goodbye to Nick, her mood was buoyant as she drove back down to the dales.

It was only two o'clock when Louise arrived back in Dowerbridge so she decided to call in at The Grange and surprise Neil. She hadn't realized how much she was looking forward to seeing him. And Pippa, too. Louise had a present for her friend in the car and was excited at the thought of going riding with her again. She drove down into the stable entrance and parked her car. As she entered the stable block the lovely smell of horses and hay met her and her face was radiant. It felt so good to be back.

She was about to call out when she heard voices and went towards the feed-store from where the sounds were coming. She recognized Neil's voice and was just about to go in when she stopped abruptly, frozen in her tracks by Pippa was saying.

"I want to stay here with you, Neil."

"And I want you to stay. Come here."

Unable to stop herself, Louise took one more step and through the half-open door she saw Neil embracing Pippa – one hand stroking her hair, the other holding her close. Pippa's arms were wrapped round Neil's neck. Numb with shock Louise tried to move away but not before hearing Pippa speak again.

"I've wanted to tell you for so long. I haven't been so happy for ages."

Then she heard Neil reply. "I'm very glad you came here because I love you very much, too."

Stepping back swiftly, Louise turned and fled from the stable. She couldn't believe what she'd just seen and heard. Blindly she got in her car and drove away as fast as she could. Her mind was in turmoil. Neil and Pippa? Why was it such a shock to her? It didn't make sense. She knew that they'd been getting on well together but it had never entered her head that there was anything else between them.

She couldn't understand why it had upset her so, seeing them together like that. Why hadn't they told her? They were her best friends. She kept brushing the hot tears from her face as a raging pain swept through her body. She was blinded by her tears and shaking uncontrollably. Unable to concentrate on what she was doing she pulled in at the next passing place and laid her head on her arms over the steering wheel, sobbing as if her heart would break.

Suddenly she heard a vehicle and, looking up, saw that a blue pick-up had pulled up in front of her. Tony was marching towards her car, concern showing on his face. He pulled open the car door.

"Are you all right? I thought... Louise, what's the matter?"

She buried her face in her arms again. "I'm okay. Please leave me alone," she sobbed.

"I will not leave you alone." Closing the car door, he strode straight round to the other side and climbed into the car beside the stricken Louise.

"Well, what is it? Are you hurt?"

"No, I'm fine. It's nothing," she gulped, pulling a handkerchief from her pocket.

"You don't cry for nothing. What's wrong?" he persisted. His concern touched her.

"Oh, I don't know. I don't know why I'm so upset." Her sobs were subsiding.

"Well, tell *me* about it and maybe I'll be able to tell *you*," he coaxed, smiling.

"It's nothing, really," she said, drying her tears. "It was such a shock, that's all."

"What was? What's happened?"

She hesitated, wondering what he would think. It was silly really. Neil could do as he liked so why was she so shaken and upset? She began to tell him what she'd witnessed in the stables. When she'd finished her story, he took hold of her hand, a serious expression for once on his face.

"I would have thought it was obvious – it is to me."

"What is?"

"Louise, you're in love with the man. You have been for ages."

She stared at him in disbelief, numb, trying to take in what Tony had just said. He was right. It had been staring her in the face and she hadn't realized. And now it was too late. The tears welled up once more as the implications of the situation hit her. Tony put a comforting arm about her shoulders. She wondered why she hadn't recognized what was happening to her. She'd just presumed that Neil would always be there for her, always her friend- but now she knew her feelings went far deeper. Seeing Neil with Pippa today had awakened emotions in her she'd never felt before – shock, anger, jealousy, love, hate. It frightened her. How could they possibly remain friends now? Life without Neil would be unbearable. Suddenly, she thought about Tony. What were his feelings in all this? She looked up at him to find him smiling down at her.

"What about you? Have I hurt *you*?" she asked.

"No, of course not. I've always known you would realize one day what Neil meant to you but I wish it hadn't happened like this. I don't like to see you hurting so. Mind, it would have been easy to fall in love with you," he teased.

"So we can stay friends, then?" she asked, a smile returning to her tear-stained face. He gave her shoulders an extra squeeze.

"I hope so." They sat in silence for a while. Eventually Tony removed his arm and said he'd better get going, as he had a load of grouse grit in the back to get unloaded that evening.

"How would you like to go somewhere tonight for a quiet drink? I'll come and pick you up."

"Thanks. I'd like that. I'll only get upset at home, and I don't know how I can explain it to Mam."

Later that evening they were settled in the snug bar in the Red Lion when Tony issued Louise with an invitation.

"How do you fancy a few days in Ireland? Get away for a while?"

"Are you propositioning me?" she asked, wryly.

"No, strictly platonic." He flashed his brilliant smile, a twinkle in his eye. "I'm going back to see my grandparents in a few days. The shooting season's almost over – there are mostly just beaters' days left and I'll be back for our last day here. Grandpa will be eighty and I haven't seen them for a while. I thought it would be a good time to go. I've no doubt my aunt will be arranging some sort of celebration for him."

Louise thought about it. It was going to be very awkward staying around Dowerdale now, under the circumstances. Every time she thought about Neil or Pippa she was close to tears. Tony's invitation would help her over a bad time. Still she hesitated.

"But I've never met your folks. I'd be intruding."

"No you wouldn't. The Irish love parties and meeting new friends

– the more the merrier. Anyway, I'd be really glad of your company."

Louise thought about it. Why not? It would get her away from the dale for a while until she decided what she could do.

"Okay, I'll come."

Over the next few days, Louise tried to keep herself occupied. She sorted lots of clothes that she'd used in Rome, washed and ironed them. She went for long walks up on the moor, trying to come to terms with what had happened. Her mother kept giving Louise strange looks but it wasn't until the day before she was due to fly that Louise told her about the trip to Ireland. They were having lunch in the kitchen. Her mother had asked her if she'd been to The Grange, adding that Neil had rung again for her while she'd been up the moor.

"Yes, I called in." (That wasn't exactly a lie.)

"I thought you would have been going riding?"

"Turpin's owner is still on holiday, so she's riding him most days." (She made that one up but thought it would be true.)

Ellen studied her daughter. Louise had looked so happy and well when she'd returned from Italy. Now she looked pale, her cheeks drawn and shadows under her eyes. "Are you all right, dear? Not sickening for something, are you?"

"No, I'm fine." Louise avoided her mother's questioning look. "I think I just need a break, so I'm going off to Ireland for a few days."

"Ireland?" Her mother's eyes opened wide.

"Yes, I'm going with Tony. He's invited me to go with him to visit his grandparents."

"Well, I hope you know what you're doing."

Louise stood up and went and put an arm around her Mam's shoulders, trying to look happy.

"Yes, of course I do. I shall be fine, don't worry Mam," she said, hoping she sounded convincing.

Chapter 26

Tony had booked their flights and arranged for them to stay in the village pub. The flight had gone smoothly and they'd taken a taxi from the airport out to where they were staying. They pulled up outside Flanagan's, the rambling whitewashed inn that also served as the local store in the small sleepy village. The landlord's wife handed them their keys, eyeing them curiously.

"Top of the stairs and turn left. The rooms are next door to each other," she added pointedly. Louise dropped her hold-all on the floor of the small but adequate room and crossed to the window. Rolling meadows and hedgerows stretched away to gentle hills in the distance. A couple of farmsteads were visible, their red tiled roofs showing up clearly above their whitewashed walls. Suddenly Louise was aware of Tony standing close behind her.

"Your door was open – beautiful, isn't it?" he added, following her gaze.

"So peaceful and gentle."

"See that farm over there, to the right? That's my grandpa's."

"It must bring back lots of memories."

"Mm, mostly good ones. Well, come on, there are folks to meet."

"Have you let them know we're coming?"

"No, I want to surprise them."

They walked down the narrow little road leading from the village and turned right up a farm track. As they rounded the corner of the farmhouse into the yard, a black Labrador came to meet them, wagging its tale.

"Not much of a guard dog, are you?" Tony said, stroking its head. At the sound of his voice another dog started barking inside one of the buildings and the back door of the house opened. A tall, grey-haired woman stood in the doorway. A long dark skirt and jumper covered her slender but erect frame and she wore a woollen shawl around her shoulders. Louise could see straight away from where Tony had inherited his tall angular build. The woman's face, lined with age, was a mixture of astonishment and joy when she saw her visitors.

"Praised be to Jesus!" She hurried towards the approaching couple, arms outstretched. "Well I'm blessed, if it isn't young Anthony Maguire," she cried, clasping Tony in her arms, tears of joy in her eyes. Then, she stood back and looked at him. "My, but it's good to see you. And who is this fine young lady?" she asked, smiling at Louise.

Tony put his arm around his friend. "This is Louise, Gran, a good friend who needed to get away for a few days."

"Well, my dear, you've come to the right place. You're more than welcome here." She linked her arm through Tony's and led them into the house. "Your grandpa will be over the moon. He's away at Billy Reilly's with your uncle Callum but he'll be back soon." She busied herself making a pot of fresh tea and buttered chunks of homemade bread, spreading them with strawberry jam, for her guests, chattering away all the while.

As they talked, Tony looked around the all too familiar room. An open fire blazed in the old range, with a wooden armchair close by on one side and a rocker on the other. The black Labrador was now lying on the huge homemade clippy mat that covered the floor in front of the fire, and on the hearth, enjoying the warmth, was a sleepy tortoiseshell cat. The faded brown leather on the single-ended sofa by the window looked even more worn than he remembered. Clothes hung folded on the bars of the pulley drier suspended from the beamed ceiling, and the wooden crucifix that had often held his gaze when a toddler still hung on the wall above the sideboard.

The guests were on their second cup of tea when Michael Maguire appeared in the doorway. Slightly bent and leaning heavily on his stick, he paused and surveyed the scene before him. Little of his wispy white hair remained and his face showed the effects of time and a life of working outdoors but his bright blue eyes had not lost their sparkle.

"Well, well, 'tis a sight for sore eyes, to be sure it is." Tony had stood up to greet his grandfather – the man who had been like a father to him for the first ten years of his life. The look on the old man's face said it all. Louise felt like an intruder, made an excuse to go back to Flanagan's and left the family to enjoy their re-union.

When Tony returned from his grandparents' house, he found Louise looking a little better. She'd had a leisurely soak in the bath and was feeling quite hungry. Tony suggested they walk to the next village, where he knew there was a small fish restaurant specializing in local produce. Later, they returned to Flanagan's, where they had a drink in the bar before retiring to bed.

The next morning Tony informed Louise that his grandfather had offered to lend them his old car for the day.

"I thought we'd have a ride over to the coast," said Tony. "Get some bracing sea air and visit one of my favourite coves. Gran wants us to go back and have dinner with them this evening. She's been telling me about the plans for the party tomorrow."

Louise wasn't sure that she was in the party mood. She'd had a restless night, thinking over what had taken place back home. She couldn't get that picture of Pippa in Neil's arms out of her head.

It took them just over an hour to reach the coast. Tony parked the car near a farm and they took a track leading down towards the shoreline. He'd brought the black Labrador with them and was going to take him for a walk.

"I think I'd rather be on my own for a while," said Louise, "if you don't mind? I'll just go down to the beach."

"Are you sure? Will you be okay?" Tony asked.

"Yes, I'll be fine. I've got my 'phone. I'll head back for the vehicle about one o'clock." She smiled and waved him off, with the dog trotting along beside him.

Louise made her way across the tightly cropped grass, towards the open sea. A few sheep were grazing some distance away. Shallow hollows in the ground were filled with almost white sand, blown in by past strong onshore winds. She could smell the salty air on the gentle breeze, coming in off the sea, as she made her way down the slope towards the sand and rocks below. There were many small, delicate shells scattered over the sand-covered grass and wondered if they'd been deposited by an exceptionally high tide or dropped by passing birds. She walked along the stretch of beach, where several sand-pipers were frantically searching among the seaweed and flotsam in the damp sand, left by the ebbing tide, always keeping a safe distance ahead of her. Seagulls soared and swooped overhead, calling noisily to each other. She reached the rocky outcrop that stretched out into the sea and climbed up onto it. The black and grey granite shapes, washed smooth by the incessant pounding of the waves, were adorned with stranded lengths of tentacled seaweed that had been left behind by the receding waters. When she reached a high vantage point she sat down on a large flat rock, cupping her chin in her hands, elbows resting on her knees. She listened to the rippling of the water, lapping against the rocks in the pools behind her. This was interrupted by the systematic crashing of every wave as it rose and broke against the rocky barrier, before receding to meet the next oncoming swell. The continuous pounding of the breakers was like the turmoil in her heart; there was no way of calming it.

Tears ran down her face, mingling with the spray thrown up by surging ocean waves. The words that Neil had spoken to her on the platform in York echoed in her mind. How ironic that he should be the one to break her heart. She knew now that no man but Neil would ever fulfil her completely. The physical attraction that she felt for Tony was not the deep lasting love she knew now that she felt for Neil. It was Neil's face she wanted to see and touch, his arms she needed to feel holding her and his closeness she wanted to know. Hot tears burned her cheeks as she thought of what now could never be.

She'd been so blind. How could she not have seen what was happening between Pippa and Neil? It should have been obvious to her. They'd hit it off right from the beginning. She'd been blinded by the attractions of Tony and blinded to what she really wanted. She couldn't bear the thought of staying around and risk seeing Neil with Pippa. That would be too painful. And knowing it was Pippa, to whom she'd grown so close, made it even more hurtful. She would have to go away but to where? She could go back to Keswick. Harry had told her there would always be a job for her there. Kate had written a long letter at Christmas and said prospects looked good and they'd been very busy since reopening. She'd also added that Martin had moved away and taken a job down in Morecambe. Kate wasn't sure but had heard that someone else had been the focus of his unwanted attentions and had told Harry. Anyway, he'd gone before Christmas.

Louise gazed out to the ever churning sea and the inevitable rise and fall of every foaming wave. The ocean was never still and neither would time stand still, nor could she turn back time. She stood up and blew her nose and dried her eyes. She clambered over the rocks, jumping over the cracks and fissures, wishing the tide could wash away her pain and sorrow. Life wasn't going to stop, so she'd have to find some way of carrying on. She'd ring Kate as soon as they got back to Yorkshire.

Somehow Louise managed to get through the weekend by putting on a brave face. At the dinner on the Saturday evening she met Tony's Uncle Callum and Aunt Brid. Callum worked the farm for his father-in-law and Brid took in visitors in their own home a mile away. They were all very kind to Louise and no questions were asked about her circumstances, for which Louise was very grateful.

The next day many more friends and relations of all ages arrived for Grandpa's eightieth birthday, all bringing either food or liquor or both. Louise was persuaded to try some of the kegged Irish stout which all the others seemed to be enjoying. By evening everyone was in fine fettle and the singing started. One of the neighbours had brought a fiddle and another one an accordion. After a few more drinks, Louise managed to relax a little and join in the celebrations. Grandpa Michael gave a rousing rendition of the Irish Rover and a couple of the younger relations performed an excellent display of an Irish dance routine. Tony got his Gran up to dance and it was obvious she'd been quite an expert in her younger days. The singing and merrymaking went on until way after midnight.

When it was finally time to leave, Louise was feeling rather heady. She presumed it was the mix of the stout and red wine, not to mention the champagne that Aunt Brid had produced for her father. The cold night air that hit them as they left the farm made Louise feel even worse and she was more than glad of Tony's supporting arm as they made their way down the narrow lane to Flanagan's. The place was in darkness and Tony let them in with his key provided by the landlady. He guided Louise up the stairs to her room. He found the room key for her in her bag and walked her to the bed.

"Can you manage?" he asked.

Louise wasn't too sure of how she felt and was rather unsteady on her feet. She sat on the edge of her bed, head in hands.

"I'll try."

"Go to the bathroom and get into bed. I'll come back in ten minutes to make sure you're okay." He left the room, closing the door behind him.

Louise felt very tearful and sorry for herself. She realized that she'd had far too much to drink. She did manage to get herself into bed eventually and was sobbing into her pillow when Tony returned.

"Hey, come on," he said and he took her in his arms to comfort her. "You did fine tonight. You'll get through this, you know."

"I don't know how," she sobbed.

"Yes, you will. You'll find a way. The drink's making you feel worse." He laid her gently back on to her pillow. "Shall I make us a coffee?"

Louise shook her head. "No thanks." She pulled a tissue from the box by her bed. "I'm sorry. I didn't mean to spoil your evening."

"You haven't. It's been a great evening. Don't worry about it."

He stood up as if to go but Louise clung to his hand. "Please don't go just yet. I feel so lonely. Stay with me a bit longer."

He sat down again, near her on the bed. She looked so lost and forlorn. "Okay, I'll stay a while, 'til you fall asleep." He lay next to her on top of the covers, hands linked behind his head.

"You've been so good to me, Tony. Goodnight." She turned on her side and put her arms round his neck and kissed him. A kiss full of passion, a kiss full of wanting, knowing what she'd lost. Tony found it impossible not to respond.

Chapter 27

It was dark when Tony dropped Louise off at home after they returned from Ireland on the Monday evening. She went in, not realizing that the Land Rover in the yard was not her father's. Her mother greeted her with a smile.

"Hello, good to see you home safe. Everything all right?"

"Yes, thanks Mam. A bit tired, that's all." She followed her mother through into the kitchen. Her dad was seated at the table, reading the paper but looked up and smiled at his daughter.

"Now, mi lass, good flight back?"

"Fine, thanks, Dad," she replied.

Her mother was hovering close by. "Louise, there's someone here to see you," she said.

"Me? But..." was all she managed to say before her mother interrupted her.

"It's Neil. He's waiting in the lounge. He wouldn't leave once I told him that you'd be returning home this evening." Louise stared at her mother, unable to speak. "Go on through, Louise. You can't *not* see him, can you?"

"Mam, I don't want... I mean..." What was the use of trying to explain? She wasn't ready for this. She'd no idea how she was going to face Neil.

Her mother put an arm around her daughter's shoulders, seeing the distress on her face. "Come on love, it's only Neil. Go and have a word with him; he's waited nearly an hour." She guided Louise through the hallway and opened the door into the lounge. When Louise entered the room, Neil had his back to her, staring into the fire. He turned as the door closed and took a step towards Louise, a tentative smile on his face.

"Hello, Louise. I hope you'll excuse this intrusion into your home but I had to see you. May I sit down?"

"Sorry, yes, of course." Louise felt the pain all over again as she looked into his face. His eyes seemed to mirror her sorrow and she couldn't work out why. She moved across to the settee and sat down. Neil sat down too, leaving a safe distance between them. Louise could smell the fragrance of his aftershave, reminding her of their last evening out together.

"I had to see you to find out why you haven't been down to The

Grange. I know you were spending time with Nick while he was here, but we were all looking forward to seeing you and hearing about Rome. Mother wanted you to come down for dinner one evening, seeing as you missed Christmas. I thought that no matter what went on in our lives we'd be friends forever." He paused, waiting for some comment, hoping for some kind of explanation.

Louise stared at the floor, conscious of his nearness to her, yet the distance between them seemed immense. She couldn't find the right words to say; in fact, she struggled to think of anything to say. It would be mortifying to tell him the truth, knowing he'd declared his love for Pippa, but she'd have to offer some explanation.

"Tony invited me to go to Ireland with him," she managed at last, looking up at him. She could feel the colour rising in her cheeks as she recalled the events of the previous evening.

Neil had a strange expression on his face but he smiled before replying. "Yes, I know. Mother told me. She'd spoken to your Mam the day you left for Ireland. Surely, though, you can still come down and see us, and Pippa. She's been desperately unhappy about things. She was so looking forward to your homecoming so that you could ride out again together."

Louise's lip trembled as she tried to hold back the tears. "I would've thought that she would be very happy now," she managed.

Neil stared at Louise, totally dumbfounded. "Louise, what do you mean? Pippa has grown so fond of you, as we all are. She loved your letters from Rome. I don't understand."

Louise turned away, unable to face him and brushed a tear from her face with her hand. Neil was waiting for a reply. Eventually, Louise blurted out the truth.

"I know about you and Pippa."

His face paled visibly. "What about me and Pippa?"

"About your relationship." Her statement fell into an empty silence. Neil gazed at her for a moment, as if unable to comprehend what she was saying. He stood up and paced around the room before returning and, standing in front of the fire, he looked at Louise. All semblance of a smile had left his face. Eventually he spoke and his tone was cold and distant.

"I don't know how you found out but I didn't think that you, of all people, would let that come between our friendship and the friendship that you have formed with Pippa. I wasn't going to let your relationship with Tony come between you and me. I thought our friendship was worth more to you than that. That it was forever. I'm sorry I've misunderstood you." He strode to the door and opened it but before leaving, turned and looked back at Louise once more. "Goodnight Louise. I hope you'll be very happy." There was something very final about the way he closed the door.

Louise sat, holding her head in her hands, unable even to cry. The shock of it all had struck her motionless. Her mouth felt dry. He hadn't denied any of it, so it must all be true. Somehow, there'd always been a glimmer of hope in the bottom of her heart that she'd made a mistake; that she'd misheard or misconstrued what she'd seen that day in the stable. It had been pointless telling him the truth about her and Tony. He might as well believe what he wanted to because it didn't really matter now. Slowly the tears began to trickle down her cheeks as the reality of it all struck her once again.

Next morning Louise got up with a new determination. She'd tossed and turned most of the night thinking long and hard about all that Neil had said. He was right, of course, as usual. He knew her so well. As she recalled his words to her she realized that now was the time that she would have to find that inner strength of which Neil had spoken. She knew that, despite all the heartache, she did want to remain his friend. To begin with it would be very painful but if she was really honest with herself, if she couldn't have him, then there was no one else but Pippa with whom she would rather see him.

She understood now why Neil and Pippa had always got on so well together. It was as if they'd known each other for ages. She knew they would be happy together. She would have to get used to it and, despite all of this, she really did like Pippa. Who could blame Pippa for falling in love with Neil? – they were so alike in lots of ways.

Louise made up her mind. First, she would ring Kate in Keswick and see what the chances were of her returning to work there. She would go over for a visit. Next, she would go to The Grange, see Grace and hopefully see Neil to apologize for her attitude in all of this.

Her mother was pleased to see a more cheerful girl at breakfast the next morning and was delighted to hear that her daughter had sorted things out.

"We had a disagreement, Mam, but I've churned it all over in the night and I'm going to go down today and put it right. I'll take their Christmas presents with me." She brought her toast and marmalade and sat at the table with her mother.

"I'm very glad, dear. Neil was most concerned when he came last night and looked most unhappy when he left – he's such a lovely lad, you know. Will you tell Grace I'll pick her up tonight for the WI, it will save me ringing."

"Okay. Has dad gone to work?"

"Yes, it's the last day of the pheasant shoot today and he'd promised Roger he would go and pick up."

"Of course it is. Tony told me. I'd forgotten." She stood up and took her plate and mug over to the sink.

"I have a 'phone call to make and I think I'll go for a walk up the moor before I go to The Grange."

Louise felt in a more positive mood when she returned from her walk. She had arranged earlier to leave for the Lakes later in the day.

For the first time in her life Louise felt nervous as she drew up in The Grange yard. She knew Grace would be at home because she'd be getting lunch ready for the guns. She went around to the back entrance and went inside, knocking on the kitchen door. When it opened she could tell from the look on Grace's face that she wasn't expecting to see Louise standing there.

"Louise, what a lovely surprise. Come in." Louise followed Grace into the warm kitchen. The kettle was boiling on the range. "I was just about to have a coffee before I go over to the utility. Will you join me?"

"Please, that would be nice." She perched herself on a stool at the table, thinking about what to say. Grace had her back to Louise, making their coffee.

"Grace, I'm sorry I didn't come down to see you before I went off to Ireland."

"Well, you're here now." Grace turned and smiled at the young girl, sensing her unease. "And how did you like Ireland? I've often fancied going but you know how it is in farming – holidays are almost impossible."

Louise slowly began to relax as she told Grace about Tony's family. She pulled a large envelope from her bag. "I brought your Christmas present and my photos of Rome to show you. I loved your pendant. I wore it all the time I was away – it reminded me of home." She took out a wrapped parcel from her bag and gave it to Grace. "Is Neil home?"

"No, dear. He had to go to the mart today; there was someone he needed to see about a bull." She was opening her present as she

177

chatted. "Oh, Louise, this is beautiful." She held up the blue silk scarf that matched her eyes perfectly. "Thank you so much."

"As soon as I saw it I thought of you. I'm glad you like it. I'll leave Neil's present with you." She laid the gift-wrapped parcel on the table, unsure of what to say next. Grace took the scarf with its wrapping and walked over and laid it on the dresser. Louise knew she was expecting a reason for her not visiting sooner but didn't want to say anything about Neil and Pippa. After the way Neil had reacted, she guessed that they hadn't told anyone about their relationship. Eventually Louise raised her head and managed a smile. "I hear you've been getting out a bit more?"

"Yes, Colin and I see quite a bit of each other. No, nothing serious, Louise," as Louise's eyes lit up. "I know that look on your face. I'm pleased to see you looking a little happier. I thought you looked rather sad when you arrived."

Louise picked up her mug, examining the contents. "Yes, I was a little but I'm hoping it won't last. Neil and I had words."

"Do you want to talk about it?"

Louise shook her head. "No, not really. I'm hoping that we can put it right."

"Oh, I'm sure you will." Grace paused, studying the young girl. "Tell me about Rome, Louise. Did you enjoy it?"

After Louise had given a brief account of her time in Italy she went on to say how much she'd missed Christmas at home. "I hear the girls had their first ride?"

"Yes, they were so excited by it. We're going to let them have another go sometime. Pippa was so good with them. I'm so glad she came here – Neil's been like a different person since she's been around." She paused, waiting for some comment from Louise, noticing the pained look on her face. When nothing was spoken, she continued. "I'm hoping to see more of the girls in the future. As you know, Rebecca is at school now and Kathy is hoping to return to work soon, so I'm thinking of getting a flat in Scarborough. It will be useful for Kathy having me around to baby-sit and take Sam to physiotherapy and things like that."

"You mean you'll move?" Louise asked, looking up at last, her eyes opening wide.

"No, not altogether. I'll still be here a lot but I expect the day will come when there'll be a new Mrs. Nickerson here," she replied.

The smile left Louise's face and she wondered if Grace *did* know about Neil and Pippa. She tried to sound normal. "I'm sure the girls will love having you so near."

"Yes, and I'll be able to bring them over to ride."

When Louise left later she was no happier but felt better about herself. At least she'd made things right with Grace. She'd left a message for Neil, saying she would be in touch. She knew she ought to go and see Pippa but couldn't bring herself to face her just yet. She'd write to her when she got to Keswick.

Chapter 28

Louise had risen early and had gone for a walk down by the lake side. She had been back in Keswick for three days now and was slowly coming to terms with what had happened to her. Her friend Kate had been wonderful, letting Louise stay with her in the hotel. When she returned from her walk, she found Kate in the kitchen after serving breakfasts.

"Hi, Lou, fancy something to eat? I see you've got a bit wet."

"Yes, it's just started raining," Louise replied, as she took off her damp jacket.

"There's some bacon left if you fancy a sandwich? Oh, by the way, there was a letter for you. I took it upstairs."

"Thanks Kate." She made herself a coffee to have with the sandwich. "I'll take these upstairs and see who's been writing to me."

She sat by the window in Kate's room to eat her breakfast. The view today was very different from the day when she'd left Dowerdale less than six months ago. No sunny skies or clear mountain tops this morning. Such a lot had happened to her in that time. She reached for the blue envelope and opened it, without really looking at the hand-writing. Inside she found two sheets of paper and picking up the smaller, blue one, she unfolded it, and began to read.

> *Dear Louise,*
>
> *I had to write this letter when I couldn't see you. I went to your home as soon as Tony explained to me why you have avoided coming to The Grange. I was devastated to find out that you'd left for the Lake District. Your mother was happy to give me your address when I explained that I could sort things out between you and Neil. I always knew how fond you were of Neil but I hadn't realized that you were in love with him and this is why it's so important that you read this letter. Only then will you believe the truth about me and Neil. I cannot bear to think of the pain and heartache you must have been going through.*
>
> *Please, please read it, Louise, for it is the only way we can remain friends. When you saw Neil and me in the feed store, I had just finished explaining to him the contents of*

this letter. I'm so sorry that you left without seeing me – I could have explained everything to you. I really hope that when you've read this you will get in touch, as I do so want us to remain friends.

With all my love, Pippa.

With trembling hands Louise picked up the other sheet of paper and slowly opened the single folded page. A flicker of hope was rising in her heart. The enclosed letter was obviously a photocopy of an original.

My dearest Pippa,

> *When you read this letter I will no longer be with you. Please don't grieve too much for me, for I'm sure that you will have a great life ahead of you. I had a wonderful life with dear Derek and my two wonderful girls. Girls so very different, and now I can tell you why. I only ask this of you, Pippa – please don't be angry with me for not telling you this until now. Your father is dead, but that wasn't Sophie's dad, Jack. I'm telling you this now, because I will no longer be there to tell you, should life so work out that you meet people who are related to you.*

> *I met your father when Jack was in prison. He was a good, decent man, and I was lonely. It was never planned but accidents do happen. He'd been perfectly honest with me, telling me about his beautiful wife and their three lovely little children. He'd also explained to me that their marriage wasn't a marriage in every sense of the word and that I fulfilled a need in him. I had just conceived when Jack was released but I still hadn't told Jack that I was pregnant when the accident happened. Later, when I'd got Jack's affairs sorted, I moved with Sophie to York, where you were born.*

> *I feel that you have a right to know who your father is. I'm just sorry that you were never able to know him. He was Philip Nickerson, a farmer from Dowerdale, and I named you Philippa after him. He never knew of your existence. I moved away to avoid any gossip that might arise, and also because I didn't want to embarrass Philip or put a burden on him. We had agreed that our relationship was never going to be permanent and after I*

left he never tried to contact me.

After you were born I never felt the need for anyone else. It was different, of course, when I met Derek. I was so blessed. We shared a wonderful love. Look after Derek – he's been a worthy father to my little girls, and please watch over Sophie. She hasn't got your common sense and strength of character. Don't forget that I'll be with you in spirit, dearest Pippa. No mother could have loved you more than I loved you.

Your loving Mum.

Louise stared at the letter in disbelief as silent tears trickled down her face. This very personal letter had moved her beyond words, knowing what it must have meant to Pippa. The tears she shed were not only for Pippa but also for herself. She felt wretched about the way that she had ignored Pippa. Pippa, who had never meant to hurt her and was no threat to her happiness – she was Neil's half-sister. Just how wrong could she have been? No wonder Neil had been so angry and hurt at her behaviour, and hadn't been able to understand why she was so upset at Pippa being his sister.

She sat up straight and brushed the tears away from her face, determined at least to try and put things right. But how? Without knowing what Neil's true feelings were for her, it was not going to be easy. She could at least attempt to mend their wounded friendship but had no idea how he would respond. The way he'd said goodbye that night at home had sounded very final. They had always been so close but that was before all this. How could she possibly explain her actions without letting him know her true feelings for him? She would have to swallow her pride and apologize to him and somehow hope that she could win his heart. Would he even want to see her?

Now she understood why it had been so easy to befriend Pippa. Poor Pippa – how terrible to lose your mother and straightaway be told the father you'd never known was also dead. She knew now why she'd thought she'd seen Pippa somewhere before – it wasn't that she had, it was just the likeness to Neil. She thought back to that morning in the village when she'd first met Pippa. No wonder she had looked surprised when Louise had given her the Nickersons' name. Tony would understand what it must have been like for Pippa, searching for a family she'd never met. A family she'd only known about for such a short time.

Louise sat staring out of the window at the dull grey skies and mountain tops shrouded in mist, with the rain now sweeping across the lower fell sides and the choppy waters of the lake. She couldn't stay here now. She would return once again to Dowerdale, for that was the only place she would find happiness. And the first person she would contact would be Pippa. Their friendship must mean a great deal to Pippa for her to have shown Louise such a personal possession as the letter from her mother. Again she marvelled at the other girl's resilience and determination. It must have taken a great deal of courage to do what she had done and even more finally to admit to Neil her true identity. She pondered on how the rest of the family would accept the news. Neil had obviously taken the news well but what about the others?

Louise jumped up and, gathering her plate and mug, rushed downstairs to find Kate to tell her that she was leaving.

Kate was delighted to see a smile back on her friend's face. "I'm glad your letter was good news. I didn't like seeing you so down but it was grand seeing you again. I'll always be around for you." She gave Louise a big hug.

"Oh, Kate, you're a true friend. Thank you so much. I promise I'll come back soon to see you."

When Louise had left the mountains and lakes behind and was high on the Pennines, she pulled in at a lay-by and searched in her bag for her pocket diary. She soon found the number she was looking for and picked up her mobile 'phone.

"Hello?"

"Pippa, is that you?"

"Louise? Thank goodness you've rung. Are you okay? Did you get my letter?"

"Yes. I'm better now than I was – well, I will be when I see you. We have a lot to talk about. Is it too late to ride with you today?"

"No, of course not. I'll wait till you get here."

"I'm on my way now. I can be with you by eleven."

"Great. I'll tell Neil you're coming home."

"No, don't do that. I need to see him but I want to surprise him."

"If you're sure?"

"Yes. I'll be with you soon. 'Bye."

"I'll have the horses ready. 'Bye."

Louise had left the rain behind and the sun kept breaking through the cloudy skies as she drove the last forty miles to Dowerdale. Ellen Bentley was pleasantly surprised at her daughter's speedy return and delighted that she looked more like her old self. She was equally surprised when, just as Louise was about to leave to go to the stables, she turned and rushed back to Ellen and gave her a huge hug.

"I love you, Mam. See you later." With that, her daughter, looking very slim in her cream jodhpurs and long riding boots, beamed widely and rushed off. Ellen smiled to herself. Thank goodness all appeared well again with her daughter.

As Louise entered the stables, she could hear Pippa singing in one of the boxes. After she'd left her jacket and riding hat in the tack room, Louise approached quietly and, looking over the door, watched as Pippa methodically went on brushing Star's mane. The old mare looked well and turned her head and stopped munching on her food, aware of Louise's presence. As Pippa turned to see what had caught the mare's attention, Louise opened the door and entered the box.

"Louise!" Pippa threw down her brushes and rushed to Louise, flinging her arms round her. "I'm so sorry," Pippa whispered, hoarsely.

Louise held her close, near to tears once more. "No, it wasn't your fault. I'm the one who's behaved badly." Louise stepped back to face her friend, an anxious look on her face. "Please forgive me" she begged.

"There's nothing to forgive. I'm just glad everything's okay between us." Pippa picked up her grooming brushes and the girls left the box and went across to the tack room. "I knew you were close to Neil but I thought it was Tony you loved, especially after you went to Ireland with him, but Tony explained everything to me."

Louise turned to pick up her hat as her cheeks flushed and hoped that Pippa didn't notice. She wondered just how much Tony had told Pippa. "Yes, Tony's been very good to me." She was fastening up her jacket. "I'm sure we'll remain good friends."

Once they'd set off on their ride Pippa began to explain how she'd found out why Louise had gone away.

"Tony was working in the game larder the evening before you left. I went in, hoping he might be able to tell me why you were avoiding The Grange. There were several drawers containing dead pheasants stacked on the table in the centre of the room. Tony had his back to me, hanging birds on the rows of hooks on the far wall. I said something about him working late but he didn't answer, just gave me a funny look, then went to pick more birds up from the table. When he turned again, he asked me if I wanted something. I said some information, hopefully, about why you hadn't been down to see us all since you'd got back from Rome. He then stood his full height, folded his arms and looked straight at me, saying he'd thought that you and I were good friends. I told him we were and that's why I couldn't understand. Didn't we tell each other everything? I grinned and said not quite everything but *he* wasn't smiling – in fact he looked quite angry. He wanted to know why neither I nor Neil had said anything to you about our relationship. Well, I was a bit taken aback at that, 'cause Neil was the only person I'd told. Puzzled, I asked him how you'd found out. Even after he'd told me, I still couldn't understand why you should have minded. When I said that, he was furious, telling me I didn't know you at all and that if I did I would have known that you were in love with Neil. Well, I was stunned." She looked across at Louise as they rode along. "I'm sorry, Louise, I'd never realized. Then it hit me what you must have thought when you saw us that day. I was horrified and it was all my fault."

"No, it wasn't. I shouldn't have jumped to conclusions. If only I'd stayed a bit longer I would have found out the truth."

"Well, you know it now." She grinned at Louise as she finished her story. "Suddenly I realized that I could put everything right and I told Tony how marvellous it was. He thought I'd gone completely mad. I rushed round the table to him and gave him a big hug, thanking him for the information."

They'd arrived at a hand-gate leading to the track up the bank side and Louise got off to open it, as it was tied with string. When she remounted she brought up the subject of the letter that Pippa had sent to Louise.

"I don't know why I didn't see it – you're so like Neil. It must have been a tremendous shock to you finding out about your real father, especially having just lost your mother," said Louise.

Pippa's face clouded over. "Yes. It took me a while to get my head round it. I still haven't told my sister Sophie or Dad. I wanted to find my new family first. But now it's out in the open with Neil, I'll probably have to tell them. I'd been wanting to tell Neil for a while. I'm so happy here and didn't want him to think that I'd been deceiving him. Once I got to know him and things were working out so well, I wanted to tell him but couldn't find the courage. I needn't have worried, for as you saw to your cost, he was wonderful about it. I'm afraid about how Mrs. Nickerson will take it. I don't want to hurt her as she's been so good to me. I would hate to have to leave here."

"If I can talk to Neil first, I might be able to help you." A frown came over Louise's face. "Trouble is I don't know how he's going to be with me."

"I'm sure he'll understand why you acted like you did, once you've explained. I know how concerned he's been about you." She glanced across at her friend's worried face as they climbed up the last few yards of the steep bank side. "It'll work out fine, you'll see." They'd reached the top of the track and Pippa jumped off to open the gate on to the moor. A cool wind was blowing across the open moor and Turpin tossed his head impatiently as they waited for Pippa to remount. "Come on, let's canter along here," suggested Pippa, as she gathered up her reins. She set off along the rough old cart track on Murphy and soon both riders were galloping side by side, the wind in their faces, enjoying the freedom of the moors in a world all of their own.

Much later Louise guided Turpin down a very steep rocky track in the dale head. On one side was quite a drop into a small ravine, and the horses hooves loosened small stones and pebbles that echoed clearly, as they rattled down the sheer rocky face to the bottom. Louise was glad when the track veered away from near the edge and levelled out on to a grassy pathway which wound its way between bunches of sieves and large rocks and boulders. Slowly they made their way down into the valley below. Pippa glanced at her watch, aware that they'd been out longer than intended.

"If we go back through the farm up ahead and follow the road back, it will save us an extra half hour instead of taking the bridleway across the ford and down the other side," said Louise.

They'd gone through the farm yard and were passing an old stone building behind the wall in the field when it happened. Turpin suddenly froze in his tracks, snorted loudly and, whipping round on the spot, fled back towards the farm. Louise had no chance of staying in the saddle and was flung onto the narrow muddy grass verge by the road, banging her head against the wall. She lay there motionless as Pippa leapt from the saddle and, while hanging on to Murphy's reins, rushed across to her friend. She grabbed hold of Louise's hand and, relieved to feel her pulse, called her name several times. There was no response. Louise lay limp and lifeless. Pippa searched for her mobile and, slipping her arm through the Murphy's reins, managed to dial The Grange number. Luckily, Mrs. Nickerson was home and answered almost immediately. Pippa tried to explain where they were and asked if Neil could come as soon as possible. Next, she removed her jacket and wrapped it round Louise as best she could. Louise opened her eyes for a fleeting moment but, without uttering a word, closed them again. While hanging on to the reins of her horse, Pippa remained kneeling down on the wet grass next to Louise, held her hand and kept talking. She guessed they were a couple of miles from The Grange and, as Mrs. Nickerson had said Neil was knocking about in the sheds, he should soon be with them. It seemed a very long ten minutes for Pippa.

Chapter 29

Louise awoke to find herself in a strange bed, in a room she'd never seen before. She moved to sit up and winced out loud as pain rushed through her head.

"Hello Louise. I'm glad you've woken up."

Turning her head with care, Louise wondered why Grace was standing by her bed. It was a double bed with sweet smelling sheets and a green and pink flowered duvet. "Where am I? Why am I in bed?" asked a bewildered Louise.

"You've had a bit of a fall and the Doctor is coming to check you over. Don't look so worried, dear, I'm sure you'll be fine," Grace told her. "No, don't try and get up. Just rest until the doctor's been."

"But I feel fine, just a bit of a headache. What happened?"

"You took a fall from a horse, dear. Pippa will tell you all about it. I'll go and get her for she's been very worried about you. You just rest until the doctor comes." She smiled at Louise and left the room.

Louise lay trying to remember what had happened. It all seemed a bit vague. She remembered setting out for a ride with Pippa and galloping along the track over Highfield Moor but nothing more. Suddenly Pippa burst into the room, a big grin on her face.

"Thank goodness, Louise. I thought you were never going to wake up." She came to Louise and kissed her on the cheek and sat on the edge of the bed. "How do you feel?"

"Okay, I think. A bit stiff and my head hurts. Grace wouldn't let me get out of bed. I presume I'm at The Grange. I don't know how I got here. Grace says I fell off. Is that right?"

"Sort of." Pippa smiled at her friend. "You didn't have much of a choice, really. Turpin spun round and bolted."

"Bolted! But why? He's never done anything like that before."

"No, it was the pigs!"

"Pigs?"

"Yes, apparently there were a couple of them in a stone building in the field that we passed and he smelt them. Most horses are terrified of pigs unless they've lived near to some and got used to them."

"I never knew that. Is Turpin all right?"

"Yes, he's fine. He landed back at the farm and someone there managed to get hold of him and calm him down and put him in a building. I went back later and led him home – the long way round."

Just then Grace reappeared to let Louise know the doctor had pulled up in the yard. Pippa stood up to go. "I'll come back later when I've finished the horses. Good luck!" She left with Grace.

Louise lay trying to remember about the fall but couldn't. She must have slept, for she'd been dreaming. Dreaming about Neil. It must have been because she was in his house. She smiled to herself as the dream came back to her. He'd been carrying her across the threshold of The Grange so she thought they must be married. She recalled the words he'd whispered as she'd nestled against his chest. 'My darling Louise' – she couldn't remember any more. She must have woken up then.

She turned her head as the door opened once more. This time Grace ushered in the Doctor. "I'm just going to ring your mother, Louise. I tried not to worry her too much before but she'll be pleased to know you're going to be alright." She turned and left, closing the door behind her.

Doctor Ferguson had been the family doctor since Louise was a little girl. His tall, bespectacled frame smiled down at his patient.

"And what have you been up to this time, young lady?" he asked, in his deep, gravelly voice. "They tell me you parted company with your horse and fell out with a stone wall."

"I don't know what happened," laughed Louise. "I hope I didn't knock the wall down. Dad won't be too chuffed if he has it to rebuild."

"Well, let's have a look at you." He began his examination, all the while asking Louise questions. Had she any pain? Did she feel sick at all? He let her get up and walk round the room. Having convinced himself that she wasn't going to die just yet, he prepared to leave after making Louise promise to ring him should she start to feel sick. "Your hard hat obviously saved you from any serious injury to your head. Stay here tonight and rest and then you can go home tomorrow. If the headache doesn't ease by tomorrow, call me. I'll tell Grace you can have a cup of tea now. Good day, Louise."

"Thank you, Doctor." Louise got back into bed and closed her eyes. She'd actually felt a little giddy when walking round the room but hadn't want to tell the doctor or he might have sent her to hospital for an x-ray and she didn't want that. She wondered how she'd got back here and who'd put her to bed. There hadn't been time to ask Pippa all the things that she wanted to know. She must have dozed, for she woke with a start when there was a knock on the door.

"Come in." She was surprised to see Neil enter the room, carrying a tray with tea and sandwiches. Quickly she sat up and reached for the wrap that was lying on the bed and pulled it round her shoulders, avoiding looking at Neil. She presumed the lacy white nightgown that she was wearing was one of his mother's. He walked over to her and set the tray down on the bedside cupboard.

"Doctor said you could have a bite to eat if you wanted, as long as you feel all right." He paused, waiting for a reply. "How do you feel?"

Louise had to look up then for a moment. She smiled and then turning away, began nervously to straighten the bed covers. "I'm fine thanks. Just a little shaken."

"You had us all worried."

"I'm sorry. I've caused you all a lot of trouble."

At that he sat on the edge of her bed and picked up her hand. "It was no trouble. We're relieved to know you're okay." He stood up to go and Louise took a deep breath.

"Neil?" He turned as he reached the door. "I... I'm sorry about the way I behaved – I misunderstood the situation. I should never have reacted the way I did."

He smiled at her before replying. "I know. Pippa told me the whole story. Don't worry about it. We'll talk tomorrow. Drink your tea and I'll send Pippa up. She felt awful about what happened. She feels responsible for your fall."

"But it wasn't Pippa's fault."

"I know. I think she needs you to tell her that. Goodnight Louise." When he'd gone she reached for her tray and was surprised how hungry she felt. She felt much better after seeing Neil; the first hurdle was over.

She was drinking the last of her tea when Pippa came in the room. "You look better already," she beamed. "Shall I move that for you?" She picked up the tray and placed it on the dressing table. Moving a wicker chair closer to the bed, she sat down facing Louise.

"So, tell me what happened," said Louise. "The last thing I remember is galloping along the track across Highfield Moor."

"Well, we came back through a small wooded area, crossed a little slack, then rode over a wettish piece of moor and descended down a steep track, with a nasty drop on one side, into the dale head."

"Right, I know where you mean now. So we must have come down Oak Ghyll and on through Hamill's place, Rock Head Farm."

"You said it would be much quicker than taking the bridleway over the ford."

"Yes, well it would. So then what happened?"

"We'd come through the farm yard and were trotting down the lane near where there's a stone building in the field. We were nearly opposite the building when, suddenly Turpin stopped dead in his tracks, snorted loudly, his head shot up in the air and he whipped round like lightning, sending you flying out the side door."

"What did you do? Was I knocked out?"

"Yes, like a light. Fortunately there was a signal and I managed to ring The Grange for Neil to came. We lifted you into the car and Neil brought you back here. He didn't want to worry your mum. I arrived later on Murphy with Turpin but by then Neil had carried you up here."

Louise look appalled. "He didn't put me to bed, did he?"

Pippa grinned. "No, silly. Mrs. Nickerson did. Neil came and sat with you while Mrs. Nickerson 'phoned the doctor and your mum. Any more questions before I leave you in peace? The doctor said you had to rest."

Louise smiled at Pippa. "Thanks for looking after me. You mustn't blame yourself for what happened Pippa. I shall still want to ride with you but not near the pigs!"

Pippa stood up and replaced the chair. She came back and leant down to give Louise a hug. "I'm so glad you're okay. So is Neil. He was worried sick, you know." Pippa saw the hopeful look in Louise's eyes. "It's true, he was; but you'll have to meet him half way," she added, a cheeky grin on her face.

Next morning Grace brought her an early cup of tea and a pair of navy trousers. "Just get up when you're ready, Louise. There's plenty of hot water if you'd like a bath. It may help to soak away a little stiffness. You can borrow these trousers of mine – they might be a little too long but your jodhpurs were rather muddy. How do you feel this morning?"

"Much better thanks. I slept really well. This bed is so comfy."

"Yes, Pippa said that. This was the room she used."

"Thank you for all you've done for me, Grace."

"Don't mention it. We're happy that we could look after you." She smiled down at Louise. "I have to go out this morning but Neil will run you home when he's finished doing up. Help yourself in the kitchen, won't you?" She left Louise to drink her tea.

As she sipped the hot tea Louise thought about Pippa and Grace. If she got the chance she'd talk to Neil about them. She wondered how he'd accepted the news about his father's past affair. After her bath she felt almost as good as new and, wearing the trousers turned over at the waist, went downstairs. She found some cereal and after eating it made herself a mug of coffee and took it through to the lounge.

Later, while absently leafing through a magazine, she heard Neil come into the kitchen. She padded back through in her stocking feet and rather surprised him.

"I didn't realize that you were up. Feeling better?"

"Yes, much better, thanks. Shall I make you a coffee?"

He turned and smiled at her. "Yes please. I'll just go and have a wash. Bring it through to the lounge." Louise wondered why he needed to bother to wash just to take her back home. When he came back to join her in the lounge he'd changed as well, into a clean shirt and a pair of jeans.

"Are you going out, too?" Louise asked.

"That depends on you." He came and sat next to her on the settee. She could smell the aftershave that she liked so much. "I haven't thanked you yet for my Christmas present, so I'm thanking you now." He smiled at her and pulled a gift-wrapped parcel from his pocket. "I think it's time you had your present. I thought about this when you were in Rome. I had hoped to give you it before now but things didn't work out."

Louise remembered what Pippa had said to her and decided to take a chance. She smiled as she took the present. "I had an odd dream yesterday. I dreamt we were married and you were carrying me over the threshold and calling me 'darling'. A bit weird, that, wasn't it?"

"Why? Why is that so weird?"

"Well....," she started, averting her eyes.

"Would I have any chance at all if I asked you to marry me?" His voice was barely above a whisper.

Louise's heart skipped a beat. She looked at him, her face expectant. "But... do you love me?"

"Oh, Louise, if you only knew just how much I love you."

"But all this time I thought you just wanted to be friends."

"I thought you'd fallen in love with Tony. I didn't want to stand in the way of your happiness. Tony's a good enough bloke. Then, when you were in Rome, Pippa led me to believe that you and he were just good friends, so I wrapped this present for you." He was watching Louise intently as she turned the present over in her hands. Neil continued. "When you went off to Ireland I thought I'd lost you for good." He dropped his gaze.

Louise couldn't bear it – she laid aside the present, slipped off the settee and knelt on the floor facing him, and took hold of his hands. "Neil, I'm so sorry. I would never have gone to Ireland if I'd known how you felt or if I'd known the truth about you and Pippa."

He pulled his hands from hers and held her face, looking into her eyes. "So many times I've wanted to tell you and was frightened I'd get the wrong answer. Are you really sure? I thought I'd lost you yesterday – I couldn't bear to lose you now."

Louise put her arms round his neck and pulled his face close. Neil put his arms round her and held her tight, pressing his lips to hers. It was several moments before they managed to tear themselves apart.

"When did you know?" she asked.

He smiled then, that engaging boyish smile she loved so much. "I think it was that first day you came to tea when you returned from the Lakes. You'd grown into such a beautiful young woman. We'd always been friends but after that I wanted us to be much more." He kissed the tip of her nose. "Open your present."

Louise picked up the small parcel and began to unwrap it. Inside she found a small velvet covered box holding the most beautiful emerald ring. Neil took it out and, as he lifted Louise's left hand, told her its history. "It was Mother's but when she guessed how I felt she wanted you to have it. Will you marry me, Louise Bentley?" Gently he slipped the ring onto her finger.

"Yes, please," she replied, sealing it with another long and passionate kiss.

"I did carry you through the doorway but next time I do you won't be dreaming." Louise got back onto the settee and snuggled up to him while they drank their now lukewarm coffee. "Mother will be so pleased," Neil continued. "I think this was another reason why she's getting the flat. She guessed a long time ago how I feel."

"Neil, what about Pippa? How are you going to tell your mother about her? She'll have to know."

"Will she? Would it be so awful if she didn't?"

"Maybe it wouldn't but I don't think it would be a big surprise to her and she does like Pippa."

"Let's leave it for a while. Ring your mum and tell her you'll be home later. This is the best day of my life and the work can wait."

He pulled Louise to her feet and swung her off the ground. "You have made me a very happy man, but tell me," he asked, setting her on her feet, his hands clasped behind her waist, "when did you discover that it wasn't Tony you wanted?"

"When I was in Rome. I hardly thought of him – only you. I was so looking forward to seeing you and couldn't wait to get back home." Her face clouded over. "And then my world fell apart when I saw you with Pippa."

Neil wrapped his arms around her and held her tight. "Louise, darling, I thought I'd lost you for good when you went off with Tony."

"Neil, when I went to Ireland…"

"It's all right Louise. I don't want to know. You're here with me now."

"I want to stay with you forever. When I saw you with Pippa it made me realize how much I loved you. I think I've always loved you and now I can show you just how much." She pulled his face to hers and kissed him with a total commitment from her soul and body that filled her with an emotion she'd never felt before. She was lost completely in the love that Neil shared with her in the hour that followed. It was a love born from a childhood friendship, culminating in a deep and passionate love that would withstand all the tests of time. They would now be more than friends, forever.

The End

GLOSSARY

The Guns . . . . The men (and women) who pay to shoot

The Shoot . . . . All those who are part of the shooting party

Sieves. . . . . Rushes (plants) that grow in damp places on heathland

Bag (cow's). . . . . .Udder

Baling ⎫
Bawling . ⎭ . . . . Loud noise made by cattle

Fothering. . . . . Local word for foddering (as in feeding animals)

A–bulling . . . . A cow that is ready for mating

To come over . . . . (cow) One that hasn't held in calf when mated

Light in a quarter . . . . To have a teat that produces less milk than the others

Hand Food. . . . . Concentrated food fed in troughs to animals

Clipping . . . . As in horses' shoes, meaning one is loose

Pelham, snaffle . . . . . Bits – the metal part of a bridle that goes in the horse's mouth

<u>Hunting terms</u>

Hunting Pink. . . . .The scarlet coat and white breeches as worn by the Master and other staff (not the colour of the jacket)

Charlie. . . . . .The name for any fox being hunted

Cubbing . . . . Pre–season hunting, to teach young hounds to hunt with the rest of the pack

Cast. . . . . .The spreading of the pack when searching for the line of the fox

Field. . . . . Mounted followers other than the Master and other hunt staff

Whipper–in . . . . Member of hunt staff who assists the huntsman with the hounds

Scent. . . . . .The distinctive musky odour left on the ground, foliage or in the air by a fox, secreted by a gland

Pack. . . . . .All the hounds taken out on a given day

Speak, Tongue, ...Sound made by hounds when following a line

Line. . . . . .The scent trail left by a fox

Stern. . . . . The tail of a hound

Meet. . . . . The assembling of a hunt and followers on a given day

To stand point. . . . . To ride ahead of the hounds and watch for a fox breaking cover

Hack . . . . To ride on horseback to or from a day's hunting

Side–door . . . . .As in falling from a horse – to be thrown off either side

Full Cry . . . . Sound of many hounds when hunting as a pack

Drag . . . . Cold line of a fox

Run. (1) . . . . To chase or follow a scent

Run (2) . . . . The time when hounds are actually following a line

Lashing . . . .Sweeping movement of a hound's tail when on the scent